Laurel

Addison James

Addison James

Paperback ISBN: 979-8-9924453-2-9

Book Cover by Nina of Author's Aura

To those about to give up on their dreams—give them time. Everything can bloom.

Contents

Content Notes

Before you begin, I want you to know that this book has a lot of blood in it, and some scenes that verge into body horror. The magic in this world is rooted in blood and pain, and Laurel has experienced some of the darkest parts of it. If you need further warnings, please don't hesitate to reach out via social media or my email, addyjames@addyjameswriter.com.

This book contains:

*Violence, including copious amounts of blood

*Torture, body horror, and dissection (the dissection is not of a main character)

*Death, both on-page and not, of minor characters

*Imprisonment and captivity of major and minor characters

*Non-graphic blood drinking

*Long-term lying to a significant other (not the main couple)

*18+ language

*Sexual content

Chapter One

I t gets more expensive to live as the centuries pass on.

Don't get me wrong, humanity has also gained a lot. Vaccines are great. Literacy is higher than it's ever been, while infant mortality is at an all-time low. TV, libraries, the internet—all good things.

I'm not *unhappy* with the modern world, but when I have to buy a new ID, fake college transcripts, and everything from a birth certificate to a social security card just to get a new job, it gets taxing.

And I need new jobs a lot.

Not because I'm bad at my job. I actually like to think I'm damn good at what I do. But the problem is *time*.

Time is everyone's problem, I guess. Normal people mourn the passage of time and what could have been. Parents mourn their children growing. Children mourn their parents' deaths. And I don't change.

Time ticks on and I don't. I'm exactly the same as I was nine hundred years ago. The same scars I had before then are still there. The too-thin frame, the practically skeletal eyes. Even my hair grows back to the same exact length moments after cutting it. I am a permanent time capsule.

Being a remnant of a particularly awful year at the beginning of the twelfth century isn't all fun and games. It's loneliness, and loss, and constantly needing to move on.

Which means new towns, new jobs, and new IDs. Once upon a time, if you knew a trade, you could show up somewhere and largely be accepted. Today, everything requires paperwork.

The college transcripts might be fake, but the skill behind them isn't. I've been doing library work for far longer than these people have been alive, and as I hand over my new documentation to sign the final paperwork, I sign *Laurel Smith* on the line and think that this place could be good for me.

Temporarily, anyway. But that's all anything ever is.

***

A small town library in the middle of New Hampshire has busy days, and it has quiet days. I much prefer the busy days, because at least time goes by faster when I'm hunting down books and helping people learn to use the copier and assisting the elderly with the computer.

Today has been a quiet day. I've been weeding books, updating the ancient system, and spinning around in my chair until my head spins to keep myself entertained.

"You need to eat lunch." Like she appears out of thin air between one spin and the next, the bubbly, colorful children's librarian is standing in front of my desk, watching me with a slightly tilted head.

"*Fuck*," I mutter, then glance around, but there're no patrons around to hear me. Not for the first time, I wish I got some sort of enhanced senses with everything that happened to me. Sadly, no such luck. I have regular old human senses, which means that women who wear dresses with dinosaurs on them can sneak up on me.

"Lunch?" she prompts again.

"I'm coming." Apparently able to provide a maternal attitude to more than just toddlers, Callie the children's librarian seems to think she's the mom friend of the entire workplace. She caught onto me skipping lunch practically on my first day, and has taken to finding me daily to ensure I eat something.

It's annoying as hell. Sure, my body likes food. It gets incredibly annoying when I don't feed it enough. But not eating can't technically kill me; it won't even hurt me that badly. As a result, I skip a lot of lunches. Packing a lunch is more hassle than it's worth. Or at least, it was before Ms. Fairy Princess Earrings here decided I was her personal project.

Only, it's not annoying. Not really. Packing a lunch the night before feels ridiculous, but Callie ensures I eat it by taking her own break with me every single day, and she's more than pleasant to spend time with.

Friends are hard to come by in my life. Not that I've never had them—of course I have. I have a history of friends littered throughout the centuries, people I've loved and left behind. But it's hard to break through that barrier and connect with someone when I know how it'll end. But Callie did it almost effortlessly, and I look forward to our lunches together.

I stand up to follow her, putting out the little sign that directs patrons to the circulation desk, should they need something before I'm back. Her dinosaur dress swishes as she moves, the full skirt poofing out around her.

I subconsciously tug my cardigan closer around me. We have two very different senses of style, to say the least. Callie looks like a cartoon. I look like the librarian who scolds noisy children.

The break room is really a glorified closet, but there is a fridge on the far wall, so we both pull out our lunches. Callie has what looks like last night's leftovers, and I have yet another peanut butter and jelly sandwich. If it takes me any longer than three minutes to make the lunch, then I probably won't do it, so I've been leaning hard on modern conveniences like peanut butter.

"You would not believe the morning I had," Callie says, stirring her meal with her fork. "The Carson twins projectile vomited during story time. Both of them."

Good lord. I have no idea who the Carson twins are, but I gather they're probably toddlers, and that sounds miserable. I wince, biting into my sandwich.

I've only been here a little less than three months, but no one's puked in my area yet. I can say that, at least.

"Oh, that's only the start," Callie continues. "Billy Michaels stepped in it. And his mom wouldn't stop complaining." It's amazing that so much chaos can be happening on the other side of the building without me hearing any of it at all. "How's your day been?"

I think this woman could make friends with a tree. I'm not trying to be an obstinate brick wall to her, but I know that's how I come off. I can't help it; trying to minimize my connections is part of how I've survived so long. I genuinely like Callie. I think we'd both define ourselves as friends, so I want to act friendlier with her, but it's not easy.

But she's a patient woman, and she never lets me not knowing what to say get in her way. I take another bite of my sandwich, then tell her, "Not bad. Quieter than yours, apparently. I think I helped plan a dinner party earlier, and helped with a family tree project. No one vomited."

"Well, that's a relief."

While I'm sure it's not entirely unheard of to have vomit in other areas of the library, privately I think that avoiding the children's room is probably your best bet if you want to avoid puke.

Then again, everything about Callie *screams* kid friendly. When they toured me through the library on my first day here, she'd had sparkly star earrings to match her sparkly star tiara, a blue fairy princess tutu on, and had been reading a book about a fairy princess, complete with silly voices. She glows when she's around the kids. It would be a crime to not have her in the children's room.

We eat in silence for another minute. I'm almost done with the sandwich when Callie asks, "How long have you been here now? Two months?"

"Almost three," I correct automatically. It's practically a habit at this point to keep track of that type of thing. How long have I stayed somewhere? How long will it be before I have to leave again?

If I'm lucky, in a quiet little town like this, that time will be measured in years, not months. Maybe even a decade. I can pretend I have a truly fantastic skincare routine, and no one has to know that I literally don't age.

I've been lucky before. There have been a lot of places throughout history where I could settle down for a few years. It was even easier before cameras were invented, snapping incontrovertible proof that I don't change. The human mind will fill in so many details on its own, believe just about anything if it's persuaded gently enough, after all.

I cherish those times. They're periods when I can get a glimpse of normalcy, where I can set down roots and learn what it would be to have a normal life, whatever a normal life might look like in that time and place. I get to meet people, and sometimes truly get to know them. There are people out there, long dead by now, who might have remembered my name after I left them, and some part of me always appreciates remembering that.

I glance sideways at Callie. I don't know her that well yet, but I think she might be one of those people.

Like we're on the same wavelength, she follows up her question and says, "So, have you gotten to know anyone yet?" When I don't answer fast enough, she makes a face and clarifies, "Not that I'm calling you anti-social or anything, or saying there's anything wrong with whoever you knew from before, but—"

"It's fine," I interrupt her as gently as I'm capable of being. I don't know anyone—I am anti-social, and I don't have any connections remaining to where I was before. The last time I'd consider someone a friend before Callie was about twenty years ago. People dying while I have to stand by and watch *hurts*, and it takes its toll on me for a long time. "No, I haven't gotten to know anyone outside of work."

She nods slowly, considering something. "Want to get dinner?" she asks. "My husband is out of town tonight; we could go out?"

"With me?" I ask, like an idiot, but I can't help but thinking it. Callie is bubbly and vivacious and anyone can see she's an integral part of this little town. I am the reclusive nobody who rolled into town practically yesterday.

"Yes, with you. If you're okay with it? No pressure if today doesn't work, I—"

"I'd love to," I say before she can work herself up about it.

To tell the truth, *love* is putting it a little strongly. I'm terrified to. She'll ask questions. People have expectations, and I always, inevitably, let them down eventually. And they die. That's the way of things; when I love someone, they die and I don't. I've loved and lost too many times to think that this will be the time that I get a normal life.

But doing this is the only thing in my life that assures me I'm not a complete coward. Yes, I run when things get tough. Yes, I've spent centuries hiding. Yes, I live in fear and have nightmares that are older than most people can imagine. But I can do the regular, every day thing of building friendships, so it's all fine.

"I'm working until close tonight," I tell her. "You?"

5

"Same. We can leave from here and walk over? Marty's isn't far and they have the best pizza in town."

Marty's is the only pizza place in town, but I don't mention it. "Sounds good. I'll see you then."

She beams so bright I'm a little worried I'll be temporarily blinded, then reaches across the rickety old table to squeeze my hand, which is still clutching the last remnants of my sandwich. "Perfect. Alright, I'm going to go back—event organization to do, you know how it is—"

I nod and she flounces off, poofy skirt bounding around her as she vanishes, and my hand still tingling from where she touched it.

***

I spend most of my remaining shift organizing the periodicals, disposing of the newspapers that are older than our cut-off date, then organizing them so they're in the correct order. I frown when I get to today's paper; a local kid was supposed to come home from college for the weekend, but never made it. But when her mom called the school, she wasn't there either. It's like she vanished, and it looks like half the state is out looking for her.

She's probably on some wild, impulsive trip with friends, or else falling head over heels for someone and doing stupid shit that people who are young and in love do. Not that I'd know much about that personally, but I've certainly read about it plenty.

I hope they find the poor kid soon. Her mother seems distraught.

When it's time to close everything down for the night, Callie appears, again as if from thin air. You'd think a woman whose personality is as loud as hers would make some noise when she walks, but she must practice sneaking up on people as a hobby.

"Ready?"

"Mhm." We head out the back door, skipping the parking lot and walking around the side of the building to meet the crumbling old sidewalk. It's getting colder now, but there are still some weeds clinging to life as they push through the cracks.

"You said your husband is out of town?" I ask her as we walk. The lone street lamp flickers on above us, giving the road a slightly eerie glow. I don't know what to talk about with someone like Callie. She's probably in her late twenties, which means she was probably born in the late nineties. What's her life been like? What important things make up who she is? I have no idea. All I know is she dresses like she's going to become a character in her own children's book, she likes her job, and she's apparently married. This seems like as good a place to start as any.

"He goes away for a night every few weeks to visit his sister."

"That's nice." I had sisters once. I'd lost the opportunity to visit them after everything. Her husband sounds like a good guy, making sure to keep those family connections strong even now that they're both adults.

"Yeah. They're all each other have, and there's the twin thing, you know?" She pushes open the door to Marty's, gesturing me inside. "Blaire comes down here sometimes too, and it's kind of freaky watching them together. I swear to god, someone should study the twin thing. I think they share a brain, like before they split apart in the womb, they literally got half of each other's brains."

I open my mouth to tell her that there have been plenty of studies about the so-called *twin thing*, and that I can refer her to a dozen when we get to work tomorrow. But that's not her point with this story, so I shut my mouth and slide into the booth.

Marty's hasn't seen new upholstery this century, if I had to guess. The seat feels like rocks beneath my ass. And the pizza smells amazing.

Most people do takeout from here, but there are four tables along the two side walls, and there's a mother with two kids sitting at the table furthest from us, everyone with half-eaten slices of pizza on their plates. Callie waves at them, smiling, and then turns back to me.

It strikes me then how much Callie *belongs* here. Here, in this town, in this place and time. She knows the mother and kids at this restaurant because she sees them at the library. She's married to a guy she clearly loves, and eats at Marty's and defends the quality of the pizza. She's undeniably, unquestionably *right* for this place.

I have no idea what that feels like. The only place I might have ever belonged is somewhere I never want to be again.

7

I rub the scar across my palm under the table, hunching my shoulders as I look around for the menu.

Callie must notice my roving eyes, because she says, "Marty will kind of make you whatever you want, assuming he has the ingredients. Haven't you eaten here yet?"

No. This is way more effort than I ever put into meals, but explaining that will lead to questions, especially when I look like this. I can't get rid of the sickly, half-starved look, no matter how much I try, so explaining how little I care about food is liable to get me some concerning looks.

"Not yet. Is it really someone named Marty back there?"

"It is, and he's been cooking pizza since 1987," she says. "Best in town."

Only one in town. I heroically resist pointing it out again.

A teenager who I am assuming is *not* Marty makes her way to our table. She's a riot of electric-colored hair, facial piercings, and in-your-face makeup. Callie smiles at her. "Hi, Sammy."

"Hi, Mrs. West." I start doing mental math. Unless Sammy here was an incredibly delayed reader, there's no way she was still in the children's room while Callie's been working there, right? Surely Callie isn't old enough for that.

"What do you like on your pizza, Laurel?" Callie asks me, shaking me out of my musing.

Oh, fuck. I feel momentarily panicked—it's a stupid thing to panic over, but food preferences are on my list of things I don't really have, and something that makes me stand out as different—but I manage to take a deep breath and hold it together. "I'm not picky."

"Are you okay with onion and pepper?"

"Sounds good."

"One medium onion and pepper. And I'll take a Coke. Laurel?"

"One for me too, please."

Sammy nods and goes toward the kitchen. "Do you know everyone in town?" I demand before I can stop myself.

"I went to high school with Sammy's cousins. So... yeah. I know pretty much everyone. It's not a big town." She looks at me curiously, head tilting. "Are you from somewhere bigger? I imagine this must be a hell of an adjustment, then."

That *would* be a good story, wouldn't it? But my employment paperwork says otherwise, and I can't get my stories muddled now, so I shake my head. "I'm from Wyoming." Wyoming, because I had bet on it being boring enough that very few people who live here would have gone, and that being there forty years ago and some hasty research would be enough to answer any questions they have before they get bored.

Callie's eyes light up, though. "Wyoming! That's a hell of a move. What made you come out here?" When I hesitate, she bites her lip. "You don't have to answer that if you don't want, Laurel."

She's sweet and considerate in a way that just makes me like her more. The truth is I don't have a socially acceptable answer. It had been time to move on from my last place, and I'd ended up here. It's a story I've lived hundreds of times before.

"Thank you," I say quietly. I have no idea what conclusions she's drawing, but any of them would be better than the truth.

She nods. "Of course. Well, their loss is our gain. We're lucky to have you."

I don't know about that. Other than having a pretty strong memory for things too old for me to explain, I'm pretty average, actually. I remember thousands of books and useless pieces of information, but I've learned to stop myself from connecting too deeply to any one place. What can I say I contributed to any given community after I'm gone?

But it feels good to hear her say it regardless, and I can feel myself flushing as I turn my head away, studying the ancient parmesan shaker on the table while Sammy brings our drinks over.

Chapter Two

It turns out that Callie is more than a happy-go-lucky sparkly children's librarian. She's also funny, and kind, and talks way more than any one person should, but in an endearing way.

We stay at Marty's until it closes, and then we walk back through the streets to the library parking lot. Callie doesn't even seem to notice that it's long past dark, or that the single streetlight doesn't illuminate nearly enough. I wonder what it's like to be that assured about your safety somewhere.

Then again, I also don't kick up a fuss about it. Not because I inherently trust my surroundings, but because what can someone really do to me? Many people have tried to hurt me, but I always bounce back. That's kind of the problem, actually.

"Will I see you tomorrow?" Callie asks when we reach out cars.

I nod. "After noon, though."

"Good." She impulsively reaches out and squeezes my hand again, and I think for a second that I've been touched more in the last few hours than I have in years. "It was really good spending time with you. We should do this again."

I summon a smile that I think looks real. I want it to look real, I genuinely mean it—but I'm aware that smiles from me often look more pained than I intended. "I'd like that a lot."

She nods, then gets in her car. I unlock my car door, and watch carefully as Callie drives away, making sure she gets out of here safely.

When I get back to my apartment, I park my car in the lot off to the side. The light's out again, and I frown. It's inconvenient, but I worry more for the other residents in this converted old house. I'm pretty sure Mrs. Finney is the youngest at sixty-five, and no one should be making the elderly walk around in the dark, especially as it gets colder.

It's made worse tonight by the lack of moon. It's a new moon, the sky dark except for the weak light of the stars.

I didn't have to look up the lunar cycle. I just know. Even after nine hundred years, I still know.

I trace the scar on my palm. New moons mean pain. They mean finishing the spell and cutting myself open all over again, knowing that there's no end in sight. I'd bleed all day, wanting desperately to stop the pain but knowing that would just mean my death.

But not anymore. I shake my head and look down, forcing myself to put the pain away. I don't need to be back there. I need to be in the here and now. And where I am right now is walking up to my barely lived-in apartment after dinner with someone who might genuinely be a friend.

Callie is something else. Kind and funny and welcoming in a way I'm not used to, and I'm actually looking forward to seeing her at work tomorrow as promised. And I'm a little sad I won't be getting in until after lunch, so she won't be coming by to annoy me about eating.

I've had plenty of friends before. I've seen the world and met people from every corner. Some of them I genuinely liked. Some of them I loved, even. Once upon a time, it was harder to stop myself from creating these friendships; I was desperate for that connection. But I have to be aware how temporary they are. Either they die, or I move on; it doesn't really matter in the end. The result is the same.

But I can't live my life avoiding that pain. I want to. I hate pain and I'll do just about anything to avoid more of it. But isolating myself is its own type of pain.

I'll make sure to say hi to her tomorrow. And I'll try to function like a normal human being and ask her if she maybe wants to have dinner again. She did say her husband goes out of town every few weeks, after all. Maybe pizza nights at Marty's can become a regular thing.

***

The next day is jam-packed. It's alright until school gets out, but then it feels like every high schooler in this town and the next has a major research project due, and they all frantically need help with the research, so I run around finding them books, and helping them learn how to find their own.

And I only recommend a horrifically out of print source to one kid, which I honestly consider progress. Remembering when things were written isn't a strong suit of mine.

Callie finds me around closing time, when I'm sorting through the piles of left behind reference books, gently pushing folded-back pages the right way and sorting them so they can easily be shelved later. "Busy day?"

"Did the entire high school show up today?"

"I think it was the ninth grade."

I groan. "They'll be back tomorrow. I think they said the project was due next week."

She offers me a piece of chocolate. I pointedly look down at the book still in my hand, but she shrugs. "I won't tell if you don't."

"Deal." It's a nice gesture, and it's pretty good chocolate, too.

We eat in silence for a second, and I take a moment to be grateful for her. Callie accepted me the moment I showed up here, and I need her to know that I appreciate it, no matter how bad I am at showing it. "Callie?"

She freezes. "Yeah?"

"Thank you. For everything. For making me feel included here."

Her eyes get somehow more knowing, like she can see right through me. "Of course," she says softly. Then, after a moment, she says, "Would you like to come over for dinner?"

12

Friends, I remind myself. *I'm making friends*. People make this world worth living in. Loneliness is the anathema of a long life. And I do want this; I want to be her friend, to know her, to have this connection. She's kind and she's caring and I bet there's more to it under the surface.

So I make myself nod, taking the leap. "I'd like that a lot."

She beams at me. "Perfect! Maybe not tonight. It's Blake's night to cook, and, well—"

"Not a good cook?" I guess. I can sympathize.

"He does his best," she says diplomatically, a fond look in her eyes. "But tomorrow night's my night. Nothing fancy, just dinner—probably spaghetti. Want to join us?"

Putting down roots in this town will just hurt more later. But for now—

"I'd love to," I tell her, and I mean it.

***

This town is small enough that Callie gave directions in landmarks, but then again, we navigated that way for the vast majority of my life, so I don't question it. I take a left past the only gas station, then drive two miles and turn left on the quiet little street past the big speckled rock. After that, I find her house on the right, tucked in neatly with a few others.

This is the type of place people go when they want the white picket fence life. Callie and her husband don't literally have the white picket fence, but some of their neighbors do, so I take it as implied. There's a garden that looks like it started as neat little garden beds right against the house but now sprawls over the majority of the yard. The evergreen bushes are the only things still living in it, but I assume that it's a riot of colorful flowers during the summer.

The house itself is painted a pale yellow with a bright-blue front door. It's all very *Callie*. It's the type of place straight out of a storybook.

I walk up the stepping-stone path to the front door, then knock, shifting the wine I brought under one arm as I wait.

After a moment, the door swings open. It's Callie, still wearing her celestial-patterned dress from work today, but now with an apron that says *I read banned books* over it. "You made it! Was it hard to find?"

"Not hard at all." I smile, hoping it looks normal enough, and Callie beams back, so I assume I succeed. "Thanks for having me."

"Blake's excited to meet you." She steps aside and ushers me in, closing the door behind me. I take a moment to peer around the house. While the outside was whimsical in a neat, contained sort of way, the whimsy is spilling out of every nook and cranny inside. There're plenty of plants, pictures on every available wall surface, and knick-knacks scattered around at all angles. I like it. There's something relaxing about being here.

It's definitely a contrast to my apartment, which is practically sterile still—I haven't bothered making it somewhere worth living yet. But this feels like a home.

And then a man, presumably Callie's husband, walks into the front foyer out of the kitchen, wiping his hands on a dish towel.

He looks like a pretty average man on the surface. He's not that tall, and not especially broad, but he looks strong, like someone who works out. His dark hair is shaved close to his head, his face slightly rounded, his clothes casual, and his smile soft.

It's his eyes, though, that stop me in my tracks. They're too bright. A brown that deep should never be that *bright*; I bet his eyes practically glow in the dark. They shine in a way that simply cannot be natural.

Every nerve in my body lights up as my muscles tense, ready to spring into action, to do something even when I don't know what to do.

Because I know what this is. I've spent nine hundred years running from people like this, keeping the supernatural as far in my rearview as I possibly can.

But here I am, standing in Callie's cozy little home, and looking into the too-bright eyes of a vampire.

Chapter Three

I can't fucking breathe.

A vampire. Here, tonight. I heard the door click shut behind me, but I didn't hear it lock. Could I get it open and get out before he comes closer? Would he chase me?

And then the thought hits me, a lurching pull in my stomach that makes me think I might actually throw up. What about Callie?

They're both watching me, those too bright eyes making my skin crawl. I force myself to breathe. Whatever I decide to do, I need oxygen in my lungs to be effective at it.

"Laurel?" Callie's voice cuts through my thoughts, drawing my attention to her. She *lives* here. With him. Does she know? Or is he lying to her? Does he feed off of her?

What kind of sick game is that? Not that I think supernatural creatures like that respect humans in the slightest—I know full well that they don't—but to actually get to her through marriage?

I have a half-formed impulsive urge to grab Callie's hand and run, dragging her away with me. Get us out of here, away and safe, because we can't stay here.

Would she go? Probably not. She either has somehow colluded with the vampire, or she doesn't know, and telling her that her husband is dangerous won't go well either way. She'd slow me down, and he'd catch us, and then where would we be?

He doesn't know I know, I remind myself slowly. I look human in every way, and no one would ever know there's anything weird about me without seeing living proof. I can do this slowly. I can be smart about this; I won't win if it comes to brute force or speed, but I'll win if I use my damn head.

"Nice to meet you," I make myself say.

"You too. Callie talks about you a lot," he says, studying me quizzically. Then he turns to Callie, "Hon, the sauce is done."

"I'll get it." She turns toward the kitchen, and I follow her immediately, not wanting to let anything separate us tonight. Of course, this requires me to walk right past Blake. I hold my breath the whole time.

He walks calmly behind the two of us, then sets the table while Callie starts plating up food. I stand there, useless and caught between the two of them, trying to figure out what is happening here.

Callie accused her husband of being a bad cook when we spoke yesterday, but it's now clear to me that she's not that much better. Likely, she's never had anyone around to criticize it, because I watch carefully while Blake eats. He definitely puts the food in his mouth, chews, swallows—all the things we think of as normal. But his expression doesn't change at all.

Does he even taste it? I know he doesn't need it. From everything I know, vampires can subsist solely off of blood.

But maybe I don't know everything. It's not like I ever asked a vampire, after all. I have a few sketchy records, stolen notes, and secondhand accounts that might mean nothing in the grand scheme of things. Maybe everything I know is wrong.

What he is is even more obvious now. Those too-bright eyes are a giveaway. And he doesn't blink as often as a normal person, and the flashes I get of his teeth are sharper than they should be. Not so sharp someone would think they're costume fangs, but definitely a touch past what's normal.

But he eats. And he watches his wife like she hung the moon and stars. And he asks me questions, which I do my best to answer so I sound like a normal, sane person. Keeping track of my own fake history is a herculean task.

"You alright?" Callie whispers when I offer to help her clear the table.

I study her face up close. She can't know. Can she? Callie is so *good*.

My mind involuntarily goes to the wives of serial killers who end up helping their husbands lure victims, sometimes even participating in the murder themselves. It's ridiculous—what, is Callie reveling in blood baths in her cute little dresses and pristine white sneakers? But I can't stop thinking about it.

Does she know who she married?

Is it better or worse if she does? And obviously, Blake hasn't killed her yet, so that's a good sign. But if he doesn't need to kill someone to feed off of them, then he could be drinking from her. Maybe in her sleep? Have I seen any cuts or bruises on her? They wouldn't necessarily have to be on her neck, either, and if he's experienced at this, he'd be smart enough to put them where they'd be hidden.

My brain is spinning, but I manage to nod. I don't need to make a scene right this moment. I can hold it together until I'm not here anymore.

"Headache," I tell her.

"Oh, that's the worst." Her forehead wrinkles. "You should go home and sleep. Are you okay to drive? Blake can—"

"No," I say hastily, because the absolute last thing on this planet I'll do is get into a car with Blake West. "No, I can get myself home."

She stares at me for a minute, and then nods. "Do you want some dessert?"

***

I do take dessert, getting a Tupperware container with a slice of supermarket chocolate cake, and I drop it into my car's passenger seat with shaky hands.

I need to drive away. I need to get my shit together enough to *move*, and I have to be able to operate a car safely while doing it.

I force a few deep breaths, and then I start driving.

I should get out of town. I should literally head for the town line, skip my apartment entirely, ditch the car, and catch a plane to who-knows-where right this second. I've done some version of that for centuries now.

Vampire, werewolf, witch, succubus, phantom, it doesn't matter—if I get even a whiff, I'm gone. It's the only safe way I know to live my life. I've been fucked over by the supernatural world too badly to risk it happening again.

Leaving town won't be hard. I'm actually very good at it, at ditching everything without remorse. But instead, I park my car at home, leave the cake in the passenger's seat, and walk back to Callie's house.

The five mile walk isn't fast. I didn't develop super speed when the witch did whatever she did to me. Still, I make it as quick as I can.

It's counter to everything I know to walk myself closer to danger. I've stayed alive and free this long by developing a skill for cowardice, and I don't regret it.

But it's never been put to the test like this before. I've never had someone I genuinely care about in the line of fire.

I've had people I care about in lots of dangerous situations. Malik had been in a mudslide and I'd been able to pull him out because I had absolutely no regard for my own safety. Dara had died of cancer and I'd had to watch her wither away. I try to do what I can, even if it's not always enough.

But I've never faced a friend of mine being in the proximity of the supernatural, and that's a threat I'm not sure how to face.

If I leave and something happens to her, could I forgive myself? I know they say time heals all wounds, and I have a lot of time. But I bet that one would stick with me.

They're in the living room when I get back, curled up on the couch, each with a book in their hands. I don't have the best view, considering I'm looking sideways through a window while hiding in their bushes, but I think I see Blake rubbing her ankle with a free hand, soft and slow.

There's absolutely nothing to prove that something weird is going on here. And it's not like I expected to come back and already find Callie dead, considering he's kept her alive this long. But it's so *normal*.

Well, what else did I expect? I didn't really think Callie was in on it—she's too nice, too kind to tolerate a man who hurts others. So it's not like I truly thought there'd be bleeding victims in their house.

I back out of the bush, ready to walk my way home so I can think this over in privacy. A branch cracks underneath my retreating foot. It's not that loud. It sounds like a gunshot to me, nervous as I am, but I doubt anyone else can hear it.

Blake looks up sharply, eyes zeroing in on the window as I duck down, trying to control my breathing. The keen, intense focus in those creepy eyes—well. That snapped everything back into place for me. It doesn't matter how normal he pretends to be. This man is dangerous.

Is it better to stay still and hope he thinks it was nothing, or to bolt away and risk being seen? Which way is safer?

I hold my breath, not daring to so much as twitch for several minutes, but no one opens the door, no one looks out of the window and screams. I'm safe. He wants to appear normal, and he can't do that if he shows his wife his superhuman hearing. I'm *safe*.

Slowly, and infinitely more careful this time, I back out of the bush and slink off toward home.

***

Blake is a vampire. There is a vampire in town. Not only that, but he knows my name. I ate dinner at his house.

The only logical next step is to run. To clear the fuck out of town and start over somewhere else.

I squeeze the scar on my hand, the phantom pain in my palm burning with the memories. I have no desire to ever be captured by the things that go bump in the night again.

What would a vampire do with me if they found out I could never bleed out? I shudder at the thought. The witch needed my blood for spells. A vampire would suck me dry for the rest of my life, an unending near-death experience. I refuse to be used like that again.

But... Callie.

You have to say goodbye to everyone eventually, I try to remind myself. People die and I move on. So what if I say goodbye a little earlier this time?

The argument doesn't hold much weight. I grit my teeth. I've never been put in this position before. I've lost friends over the centuries, sure, but I've never had to personally choose between what feels like life and death for them. Leaving them meant letting them live their lives, not signing their death warrants.

I can't leave. It's a realization that rattles me, but I know it's true. If I get in that car and attempt to run, I'll just turn back. I won't leave her like this.

Chapter Four

When I get to the library the next day, the daily newspapers have helpfully been left for me to find. I scan the top one, and see the story about the missing college student is still front-page news. They haven't found her yet.

I read the article, then stop cold, a sinking feeling in my gut. Sure, there are plenty of human predators out there. There are lots of ways for this young girl to get in trouble without needing to involve any supernatural forces.

But is it a coincidence that it seems to have happened outside a town with a vampire residing in it?

He has to get his blood somewhere. Maybe he miscalculated how much this girl's disappearance would stir up the local news. Or maybe he doesn't care.

I collapse into my desk chair and boot up the ancient computer, drumming my fingers on the keyboard when it doesn't come online fast enough. Old newspapers get digitized around here, and I only need a few months, maybe a couple of years worth.

I don't know how long he's been in town. I should have thought to ask Callie how long they've been married, so I'd at least have some sort of estimate—

The archives pop up. I take a quick look around, but my section is empty. If anyone asks me about this, I can pretend it's for an emailed patron request.

I start scanning the newspaper articles, working backward from today. I can start by looking at teenage girls, but there's nothing that says Blake has a particular preference. He might go for anyone. I should look for it all—any disappearances, any missing persons, and any bodies.

There was a mangled body found in the state park a little less than a year ago. The local authorities cited an animal attack, which is probable enough, but I know there's a different type of animal altogether lurking. Could this be from Blake?

I don't know enough to say for sure. I'm no expert in vampire kills. Two clean puncture marks to the neck? I could probably guess that's a vampire. But a body that was supposedly mauled so bad it looked like a bear did it? I have no way of knowing.

All of my information on the world I run from is second-hand. I've spent my long life acquiring information, piecing together legends and stories. I needed to know what to stay away from, after all. It's made me very good at research.

But none of that makes me an expert, and I don't know how to tell if a mangled corpse is the work of a vampire or not.

But what if it was him? Did he maul the body because he's sadistic, or was that some sort of countermeasure? How sophisticated is a vampire when they kill? Are they in full control of their body the whole time, or does the lust for blood take over?

I swallow, because that last bit is a disturbing thought. Humans bleed all the time, and if he can't control himself around Callie—

He has to be able to. He's done it so far.

Like thinking her name summoned her, Callie coughs lightly, making me jump nearly a mile in the air. "Bad time?" she asks.

She's a bright spot of color against the sepia-toned newsprint I've been staring at for hours. "No," I manage, surreptitiously looking her over. No new injuries. "How're you?"

"Fine. What're you working on?"

"An archival project," I manage to say. "I'm helping collect newspaper stories, I—"

She walks behind my desk and peers at the story, then shudders. "I remember that. Some tourist, right? Did they ever identify him? That's an awful story. Who the hell is requesting you gather information on *that*?"

"Some amateur local historian," I bluster, making it up entirely, but she seems to believe it. She makes a face, then pulls away from the screen.

"I like that the bloodiest thing my patrons want to know about is the T-Rex," she announces. "But we don't need to worry about that for a bit; it's lunch time."

Fuck. "I forgot lunch today," I admit, because packing one had been the last thing on my mind.

She stares at me for a moment. "I'll share," she says eventually. "C'mon. Let's go." I obediently follow her to the staff room, and she turns to look at me. "You feeling better today?"

"Yeah, just a headache," I confirm, because what else am I supposed to say? That I've been panicking for the last sixteen hours? That I'm pretty sure her life is in danger, and her husband is a murderer?

I force myself to take a deep breath. He probably is a murderer—he has to be getting his meals somewhere—but I can't prove anything. I only found the two stories, the currently missing girl and the dead tourist. Neither of those is proof.

Callie has leftover spaghetti from last night, and she portions some of it out for me on a paper plate after she microwaves it. I feel bad taking half her food when I certainly don't need it, but I know there's no arguing with her.

"So," I say, fighting to sound natural, "it was nice to meet Blake last night."

She beams. "Isn't he great?"

She's really under his spell. "Yeah, great," I say, particularly unenthusiastically and hoping she doesn't hear it. "How long have you two been married?"

"Almost four years."

Four years. Four years is a decent amount of time to pull off a con. I doubt Blake ages any more than I do, so he has to have some sort of extraction plan, right? There's only so much longer he can pull that off without her questioning it.

"How'd you two meet?"

If it was a subject that Callie was any less enthusiastic about, she might realize that I'm essentially pumping her for information. But it's obvious from the look on her face that she loves talking about her husband.

Because she loves him, my brain supplies. Somehow, the vampire has convinced her he's worthy of her love.

And that must mean—he loves her too? Callie doesn't seem like the type of person to settle for half-hearted love.

But does that make it real, or a particularly convincing act?

"Here, actually," she says, her eyes far away and dreamy.

"Does he have nieces or nephews or something?" *Please tell me there're no kids involved in this.*

She shakes her head immediately. "No, I got pulled to circulation to cover a lunch and he came in for a library card. And it was just—we clicked, you know? Anyway, he made up excuses to keep coming back for about a month before he asked me out. And then the rest is history."

"So he's not from around here, then?" I hesitantly ask, wondering how far I can push before she gets suspicious.

"No, he's another transplant. You could talk to him about getting settled in around here if that's something you're interested in? I'm happy to talk, but he's lived it for real. He'd be happy to help, I promise."

Great. My interrogation turned into her offering me the opportunity to spend more time with her vampire husband. Fucking fantastic.

And I've run out of things I think I can safely get away with asking. *Have you noticed your husband sneaks off for long periods of time? Does it coincide with fatalities? Does he ever come home with blood on him?* Those are not questions that will go over well.

"Maybe," I tell her, forcing a smile as I eat some of her too-mushy spaghetti. I'm not an exceptional cook—I've never needed to be—but seriously, how can she not know how mediocre of a cook she is?

"You should come to dinner again," she says, taking a bite herself. "You and Blake can chat then. Maybe tomorrow night?"

"Tonight Blake's night to cook again?" I guess.

She sighs. "He really is good at so many things. That's not one of them."

I imagine. I have no idea how a vampire went about learning to cook food. Is it something he learned just for Callie? Does he use it to lull people into a false sense of security?

"I'll come," I decide. If he didn't kill me last time, then he's unlikely to try this time. Maybe this time I'll be prepared, and I can get a look around. And then I can make a decision on whether I stay or go.

"Great! Any meal requests?"

Maybe pasta just isn't her dish. "Surprise me," I tell her. Dread is already building in my gut, and it's not from the thought of eating her food.

***

I know something is wrong as soon as I get to her house.

There's an extra car in the driveway. There's something in the air, a tension I can't quite place. Take your pick. Something is weird.

Every instinct in me screams to run. I force myself to take a few deep breaths and hold my ground.

I said I'd go tonight. I'm going to try to be brave for once in my life. I can do this.

With trepidation making my limbs heavy, I walk up the stepping stone path to the front door, knocking and waiting for whatever this tension is to reveal itself.

A woman answers the door. She looks a lot like Blake—same height, soft brown skin, slightly rounded face, and too-bright eyes—and she's staring at me like she knows too much.

"You must be Laurel," she says in a voice that sends shivers down my spine. "I've heard a lot about you."

Chapter Five

Another fucking vampire. I stand stock still, staring at her for a long minute, trying to figure out what to say. *Wrong door, sorry?* How about just bolting?

But then Callie is there, elbowing the vampire out of her way and saying, "Jesus Christ, Blaire, you have to let people inside. C'mon in, Laurel."

"I wasn't stopping her," Blaire says in that voice that's doing *something* to me. It's like it's reaching inside me, practically paralyzing me. "Just saying it's nice to meet her."

Callie rolls her eyes, then steers me toward her kitchen with a hand on my back, like I might have forgotten where it is. "Sorry, Blaire decided to stop by today, but she's nice, I swear—good company."

"Blake's twin?" I ask, sounding dazed even to myself. How did I forget there was a twin?

"Mhm. They got that twin thing going on. He was in a weird mood yesterday, she shows up today. Spooky sometimes."

"I can hear you," Blaire says, walking right behind us. "And I'm not a mind reader. I wanted to see my brother. Besides," she says, walking over toward the kitchen table, "all his moods are weird. He's weird. You'd have to be more specific."

"I heard that," Blake retorts, walking in through the slider door from the back yard. Only Blaire said most of it before he opened the door, and there's no way a normal human should have heard her clearly. Callie doesn't seem to notice.

"Just telling it like it is."

Callie looks her husband up and down. He's wearing ratty sweats, and there's a leaf sticking to one leg. "Go clean up, please."

He steals a kiss and walks off toward the stairs, and Blaire chuckles. "See, that's how you know he really is a man—picking the absolute last minute to start an absolutely irrelevant project. Only a man would rake leaves as dinner is starting. Transphobes can eat it."

"I heard that!" Blake's voice echoes from upstairs.

"You were supposed to!" she calls back, then smirks at her sister-in-law. "Got to validate him somehow."

"By working an insult in there?" Callie asks, but she smirks slightly, clearly not too upset.

"Is it an insult if it's true?"

"I feel very validated right now," Blake calls dryly. Callie doesn't react at all—how used is she to her husband hearing things he shouldn't?

I watch this back and forth like a tennis match, mind completely thrown by the absolutely *normal* way these people are acting. I'm not an expert on normal by any stretch of the imagination, considering I'm nine hundred years old and rarely have conversations with people outside of my place of work, but this sounds like any loving family.

Which would be great, if Blaire wasn't watching me like a hawk. She knows something.

I swallow. She can't know what I am. *I* don't know what I am. Maybe her brother told her that I was acting weird the other night, and she's trying to figure it out.

Yes. That has to be it. Nothing else. They can't know any more than that.

"Can you two set the table?" Callie asks. "The food is almost done."

I keep a wary eye on Blaire as I walk closer to the table, picking up napkins as I walk by. I don't know what I think will happen; she's not going to lunge at me in front of Callie.

"You just moved to town?" Blaire asks me, putting plates down.

"A few months ago."

She studies me and I fight not to squirm. What does she know—or think she knows? My hands shake slightly as I put down napkins.

"That's nice," Blaire says, sounding like it's anything but. "Where are you from, again?"

"Wyoming."

She raises an eyebrow, the little arch holding more judgment than I ever knew a single person could convey. "By way of England?"

Shit. I lost my accent long ago, or thought I did—it's close enough. I need to be a chameleon, and that means blending into wherever I am. But yes, sometimes a particularly astute person can probably still tell I wasn't born here.

How did she do that in just a few sentences? My heart is beating in my chest rapid-fire, like a rabbit facing down the fox. I remind myself that she can probably hear it and try to calm down. "My mother," I explain weakly. It's true enough; my mother *was* born in England. She just died there nine centuries ago.

"Ah." She couldn't make it more obvious that she doesn't believe me.

I fiddle with the salt shaker on the table, frantically scrambling for something to say. "And how about you?" I ask. "Where are you from, again?"

"Georgia." She doesn't break eye-contact, those too-bright eyes pinning me in place.

Is that true? I don't know. I can't tell what's true and what's a lie anymore.

"Hey, these dishes are ready to go on the table," Callie says.

Bless her. I turn away to grab it, thankful for the interruption. I feel Blaire's eyes on the back of my neck when I move over to the stove..

Blake wanders back downstairs wearing clean clothes, going straight to his wife to give her a kiss. I'm trapped between two vampires, one acting perfectly normal and one studying me like a scientific specimen.

I debate running away again. It's starting to seem like a more and more reasonable plan.

"Let's eat," Callie says, completely unaware of the tension in the room.

The uncomfortable energy in the air becomes oppressively strong as we all look at each other. Callie breaks it a bit when she starts to make her taco.

We all follow suit. Her tacos are as mediocre as her pasta.

"So, Blaire, how's... Joy?" Callie asks.

"Joyce," Blaire corrects, pushing food around on her plate. Apparently she doesn't fake eating as well as her brother. Or maybe she just doesn't like Callie's tacos. "And we broke up."

"Oh, I'm sorry." Callie sounds like she really means it, too, like, whatever this relationship between Blaire and Joyce is, she really cared about it.

Is Joyce another vampire? Is there an entire enclave of them near here? Did I manage to stumble on some sort of hotspot?

Blaire shrugs. "It is what it is. Never thought we'd last forever." She says it without a touch of emotion, like she couldn't be bothered less. Either she's a great actress, or she genuinely didn't care about Joyce.

My stomach lurches, and it's not the food. Oh, fuck, what if *dating* is code for finding a victim to steal their blood?

Is Joyce alive? I half-hope they say a last name, so I can look them up later.

Callie opens her mouth to say something, but Blake puts his hand on hers and shakes his head. He's not subtle about it, either, but Callie closes her mouth again.

So Callie turns her attention to me. "Eat more, Laurel," she says.

"No, I'm full, thank you though."

"You don't eat enough," she says. "Are you sure you're okay? You're so..." She trails off, clearly not knowing how to describe how I look, but I know what I look like. I'm too thin by far. My face is gaunt and has been for nine hundred years. The bags under my eyes are permanent.

I'll never gain the weight back, no matter how hard I try. Whatever made me like this, it froze me exactly as I was when the witch held me prisoner nine hundred years ago. Gaunt and starving. Dying. I'll never look healthy again.

But I can't explain that to Callie. I can't explain that to anyone present. So I force a half smile. "I'm fine, I promise."

Callie frowns, and Blake taps her hand again. Stopping her from asking more? Is it because he knows there's something odd about me, or just a social niceties thing?

Blaire continues pushing her food around her plate. She's deconstructed her tacos into a sort of taco salad, but I have a suspicion that's to make it easier to hide how little she's actually eaten. I almost point it out and let Callie pay

29

attention to someone else, but I stop myself. The last thing I need is to piss off the vampires I'm sharing a table with.

Like she can feel me staring, Blaire looks up, frowning at me. I hold perfectly still. Looking away too fast makes it look like I have something to hide. I count in my head. *One... two... three... now.* I slide my gaze back to my plate, forcing myself to breathe.

"How's the house?" Callie asks, and I turn before I realize she's not talking to me.

"The same as it was last time you asked, Callie," Blaire tells her.

Callie snorts. "Still not sure how you live there."

"I like my space. It's peaceful."

When Callie sees I've been left out of the conversation, she tells me, "Blaire's been renovating a cabin in the middle of the woods. It's one step up from a horror movie, if you ask me."

Or maybe it's a lot closer to a horror movie than Callie knows. A cabin in the middle of the woods—and didn't Callie say Blake goes to visit his sister often? *Fuck.* That sounds like a good place to hide murderous activities. And it'd be a good place to bury some bodies, too.

"It's perfectly nice," Blaire disputes. "Just because it's not Barbie's suburban dream house doesn't mean it's bad."

Callie opens her mouth to retort, but Blake squeezes her hand again, this time taking it in his and raising it to kiss the back. "She's got you there, babe."

"Barbie is a lovely role model for young people," Callie sniffs. "She exudes independence and joy and striving to meet your dreams."

Blaire turns to look at me, eyebrow raised, almost like she's saying *can you believe this shit?*—like this is a conspiracy we're in on together. I bite my lip, fighting to hold back a smile.

No. I can't be lulled into a false sense of security. The vampires can play house all they want. It doesn't make them safe, for me or for Callie. We're in constant danger being here.

I take another bite of my taco, just to break up the tension in the room.

***

30

When dinner breaks up at last and I can escape the house without seeming like I'm trying to run away, I sit in my car and ponder.

This is getting more dangerous. The number of people who can hurt me doubled, and getting out of town is the reasonable thing to do.

They seem so *normal*, is all. And Callie is married to one of them, and I do like her. She's a good person, a good friend. I don't know what to think.

So I force all of my instincts to shut the fuck up and be quiet, and when Blaire pulls out of their driveway, I follow her at a safe distance.

I don't know what I'm going to do. It's not like I have cadaver dogs to determine if they're stashing bodies in the woods. Maybe this supposed horror movie cabin will give me some clues, though.

Like what? I'm picturing blood on the walls, dismembered limbs littering the furniture. Something tells me that not even vampires live like that.

It's hard to keep a safe distance back, and eventually Blaire turns onto a remote road, unpaved and narrow, and there's no earthly way I can stay behind her without giving myself away. I need to make a decision; is it worth continuing to pursue this?

I park my car, pocket the keys, and walk up the road.

Thankfully, I come to a cabin a mile up the road. I'm not sure at first if it's Blaire's—it doesn't look entirely inviting, but it doesn't look like a horror movie, either. But then I see her moving through the front window, and duck behind a tree so I can continue to watch.

The place is made of faded wood. The front porch looks newer, and maybe this is what Callie meant when she said Blaire is fixing the place up. It's quite small; the one window in the front gives me a view of a small living room with a couch and a desk against the wall, and if I move four steps to the right, I can see the little kitchen. There are two doors in the back, leading to what I assume are a bedroom and a bathroom. And that's all.

I wonder if that refrigerator is full of blood. Judging by what I saw tonight, Blaire certainly doesn't use it to prepare normal food.

After a few minutes of Blaire puttering around, she sits on the couch and pulls out a laptop, a remarkably modern device at odds with her rustic little home. She boots it up and seems engrossed in whatever she's doing, and I start to draw closer.

What can I do here? It's pitch black, and even if I could see the ground, I doubt they left grave markers if they buried bodies. Still, I get closer, like I'm compelled to find out.

I need answers.

The door opens and I freeze, thankful there are still trees between me and the cabin. I hold my breath, watching, unblinking, as Blaire stands there and seems to sniff the air.

She holds perfectly still for a long moment, but then she walks back inside and shuts the door.

I've almost been caught by the vampire twins twice in the last few days. I need to stop testing fate and get my ass out of here.

I don't stop looking over my shoulder the whole way back to my car.

Chapter Six

It's cold, so *fucking* cold. Part of me knows it should be hot—I know exactly how many days passed since I got put in here, and it should be the height of summer—but perhaps you get cold when most of your blood is missing from your body.

The stench. The part of me who knows this is a dream, that tiny, rational part that always remains, knows that by the end, the stench had stopped bothering me. After a certain point, your body stops processing information like that.

But I smell it now. It smells like death, and it's a smell that will cling to me for years, decades maybe, or maybe I never shook it, and—

Her footsteps are light, light enough that I shouldn't hear them, but I do anyway, her delicate little steps sounding as loud as thunder, and I look up, and—

"Bleed for me, pet," she says, voice low and cruel. The pain starts before I do anything, and that's when I wake up.

***

Needless to say, I'm exhausted by the time I make it to work. I nearly send a patron to the completely wrong call number, despite the fact that I know the

Dewey Decimal System like the back of my hand. I can't sign into the damn computer because it takes me four tries to type my password correctly. And it takes me too long to realize that Blaire is staring at me from a few feet away.

I drop the books I'm holding and fail to catch all of them before they hit the floor. I heroically resist swearing out loud as I bend over to pick them up, and then Blaire is there, reaching for the books.

"Don't," I snap, my tone way too firm to be justifiable, but I'm too tired to moderate myself. Dreaming of having all my blood taken from me will do that to me.

I don't need a psychology degree to see the correlation, either. That witch might not have stolen my blood through fangs and biting, but she stole it all the same. And I'm never going to let that happen to me again.

"Just trying to help," she murmurs, voice so gentle you'd think I was a little kid she had to coax into doing the right thing. But she stands, offering me a hand up that I ignore. I don't need to touch her.

"What're you *doing* here?" I demand. "Don't you have work?" Do vampires have jobs? I didn't ask Callie what Blake does.

She shrugs. "Meeting Callie for lunch. And I'm a software engineer, and I work from home. I get to set my own hours mostly."

"Meeting Callie... oh." So, there go my lunch plans. Not that I remembered lunch today. It's becoming a bit of a habit, but I'd like to think I can be forgiven, given everything. And *software engineer*? How old is this vampire?

"Why?" I ask. I've never seen Blaire around here before. Nothing is going to convince me she has regular, casual lunches with her sister-in-law.

My throat tightens and my heart rate picks up. This probably isn't anything untoward—hurting Callie in the middle of the work day, when she'd be immediately missed at the end of her thirty-minute break, seems like a poor plan—but I can't help but think, *what if it is?* What if, after both siblings nearly caught me spying on them, they decided to cut their losses? What if this is my fault?

"Because Blake's birthday is next week," Blaire says, completely oblivious to what's going on in my head. "And Callie wants my help planning it."

I blink, trying to process that. "Isn't it your birthday, too?"

"Celebrating birthdays past the age of ten is stupid," Blaire says, which really isn't an answer.

"Okay, but your brother can celebrate his?"

"Have you met his wife? She has one of those birthday hats shaped like a cake. Every birthday involves more balloons than I knew existed in the world and a stupid cake." She rolls her eyes.

That does sound like my friend, and this conversation sounds way too normal for my liking. Not that I expected Blaire to walk in here and make public threats or reveal the existence of vampires, but we're talking about birthday parties.

"And you're... going to help her plan it?" I ask dubiously.

Blaire shrugs, leaning her hip against my desk. I bristle and almost tell her to get off, but that's plain anti-social, and I need to control my feelings. I can't give away that I know more than I should.

"Better to have one hand on the wheel," Blaire says.

"Ah, so you're here to pre-plan the humiliation a bit," I say, wincing when I realize that I'm bantering with a vampire who still looks like she's deciding if it's worth it to let me live. What is wrong with me?

"Seems like it."

I glance around, like I've somehow missed Callie in our immediate vicinity. "So, why're you over here?"

"She told me to wait. Something about the book report winners and a pizza party? She told me to come bother you for a few minutes."

How nice of her. Sticking me with the loose vampire who somehow always seems on the verge of causing trouble. Not that Callie knows that, of course. But now I feel responsible for this.

I can almost accept that maybe Blake is really in love with his wife. That he's somehow tamed by the tiny human in cartoonish dresses. But Blaire? There's nothing to tame Blaire.

I should re-check my newspaper archives for bodies, and include where Blaire lives in the search radius. I don't think I looked far enough north last time.

"How old are you both turning, anyway?" I ask, partially to make conversation, partially because I'm genuinely a little curious what the story will be.

35

She only pauses for a second. Most people probably wouldn't even notice. "Thirty-one."

"Nice." Thirty-one? I study her face carefully for a second, but the thing about both of the twins is they could tell me anything from twenty-five to thirty-five, and I'd believe them no question. Is that some innate vampire trait, or did they get lucky with that?

She nods. "I thought thirty-one would be smaller than the big deal she made about thirty, but, I swear, I think I heard her say the word *clown*."

"Really?" She could be fucking with me. But I could also see Callie doing that. It's really a toss-up.

She shrugs. "Guess you'll find out. I'm assuming you'll be invited. You seem to have wormed your way into Callie's life rather quickly."

It sounds like an insult, and she's staring into my eyes as she says it. Her too-bright eyes captivate mine, and I can't look away, spellbound.

A little voice in the back of my mind reminds me that there have been stories that vampires can mesmerize people with a long look. I force my eyes away.

"Wormed my way in?" I ask, looking down at my desk and moving the books so I have an excuse to keep my attention off of her.

"Well. Maybe that's the wrong word," she allows. I dare to glance up at her, and she's watching me still, brow furrowed. It's like she's trying to figure something out, and that's the last thing I want her to be doing. She doesn't need to learn anything else about me.

"Callie's a friend," I say slowly. "And you can tell her you don't want me at your damn birthday party."

Before Blaire can respond, Callie comes sweeping into my section, walking quicker than usual. "All good without me?" she asks, smiling at us both.

I can't exactly tell her that we're *not* good, and to not sic her sister-in-law on me again. That'd lead to too many questions, so I give her a noncommittal half smile and move behind my desk.

"C'mon," Blaire mutters. "Let's get this over with."

"Always a pleasure to hang out with you, too, Blaire," Callie says dryly. She turns to me, pointing. "You, don't forget to eat. And you," she says, turning to Blaire, "I have thirty minutes. Let's go."

Blaire follows her without argument, leaving me staring after the both of them. When they're out of sight, I sit behind my computer and begin to search for more records of missing persons and dead bodies.

***

My afternoon got a little busier after school, but I did still have time to search the newspaper archives. There're a few missing persons cases up closer to Blaire's house, scattered over the years. Is it her? Or is the natural consequence of Blaire living in the middle of the woods, where people are bound to get lost sometimes?

Callie finds me at the end of the day. "Blaire *liiikes* you," she sing-songs.

I snort, because she definitely does not. "What makes you think that?"

"She can't shut up about you," Callie grins, sitting on the edge of my desk. And that's a terrible sign, because the last thing I need is to draw too much of the vampire's attention. Between whatever she tried to do to me when she was here and her talking about me to Callie—well, I need to be careful.

"I think you're over-exaggerating," I tell her as calmly as I can, trying to make my pulse behave.

"I think she's going to ask you out," Callie predicts. "And also, that you're coming to her birthday, so I can prove it to you then. You'll see. She's into you."

"You can't invite me to someone else's birthday party." I might not be an expert on social niceties, but even I know that much.

Callie snorts and slides off my desk. "I didn't. She did. See you Saturday at seven." And she walks off while my head is still spinning.

Chapter Seven

What kind of gifts do you even get two immortal twin vampires? Blaire claims they're thirty-one, but I'm going to go out on a limb and assume that that's not actually true. Not that knowing their real age would help me.

When in doubt, go with books. I drive thirty minutes out of my way to find a decent local bookstore, and spend two hours digging through the stacks.

Maybe I should call Callie and ask what the twins actually enjoy. But that seems like the easy way out, so I stubbornly stay on my path, pick books, and wrap them in glittery bags before showing up at Callie's house just in time for the party.

There are a handful of cars in the driveway, so I end up parked on the street, walking up to the house across the yard. Blaire opens the door before I can even knock, a birthday crown on her head and a furious scowl on her face.

"Don't start," she warns.

"Callie's, what, five four and a hundred thirty pounds?" I guess. "And she wrestled you into that?"

"It's called keeping the peace."

"It's called being soft." I shouldn't tease the vampire. But in the crown, she almost looks like someone who isn't a threat, and she's making it so easy, poking at me like she is. I want to poke back.

Blake walks down the stairs, wearing the felt hat that looks like a birthday cake, complete with candles. I've seen Callie put the hat on kids before. I raise an eyebrow at him. "Don't start," he mutters, sounding exactly like his sister.

"She's already started," Blaire grumps, but steps aside so I can come in. "We're in the kitchen."

We apparently mean Callie, the twins, and three perfectly ordinary guys that Blake knows from work. Unless there are more people coming, I'm Blaire's only invitee, and I don't know how I feel about that.

Unless Callie was lying to me, and wanted to say Blaire invited me for whatever match-making scheme she has in her head. That's also a possibility, I suppose. I can't see why Blaire would want me here.

"Callie has birthday certificates, too," I point out, because I've seen her give them to kids. "You get those?"

"Don't be ridiculous," Callie snorts, putting food on the table, and I move to help her.

"They only go up to age ten," Blake says. "Believe me, she looked."

Chuckles break out around the room—apparently, the guys Blake works with know what Callie is like—and Callie raises an eyebrow, scooting the cupcakes pointedly away from her husband.

I can't imagine it's an effective threat, considering that he doesn't actually need to eat, but he apologizes and gives her a kiss. A sweet peck turns into his hand on the small of her back, dipping her dramatically until she breaks the kiss, giggling and clinging to him.

"Yeah, same." I start. I didn't notice Blaire stepping up beside me, also watching her brother and sister-in-law.

"I didn't say anything."

"You were thinking it," she says.

She has no idea what I'm thinking. I'm pretty positive mind reading isn't a talent anyone possesses.

I'm thinking that these two are oddly sweet, and if I didn't know anything else, I'd find them charming. I'm thinking that love is rare and precious, and that, for all the years I've been here, I've seen so few examples of really true, genuine love. Does this even count? I still can't figure out what Blake wants from Callie. Even if he does love her, even if nights like this are all he wants, what is his long-term plan?

But Blaire stands beside me and murmurs, "Yeah," before moving over to the table.

"Everyone come eat," Callie says, still staring into her husband's eyes, oddly breathless now. "I made all of Blake's favorites."

How did she determine what his favorites are? Has he been lying and randomly assigning certain foods as his favorites? Or does he actually like it for some reason?

"None of your favorites?" I ask Blaire.

She stares at me, and I have to wonder if I'm imagining the little smirk at the corner of her mouth. "I detest human food."

One of Blake's friends chortles, but my mouth goes entirely dry. Blaire is still watching me, and I can't figure out what we're doing.

Are we teasing each other? Does she already know more about me than I thought? Are we playing a game, testing how far the other will go? How far *would* I go, if it came down to it?

Everyone else grabs food, but Blaire ignores it, sitting at the far corner of the table while we all eat. Callie keeps looking at her, but Blaire stares at me.

This is probably lending credence to Callie's match-making scheme, but I shiver under her unending stare. I don't know what she thinks she knows, but she clearly has got some idea in her head.

This is really making me re-think the gift I bought. Unfortunately, it's too late to change anything.

Blake's friends chipped in to buy him and Callie baseball tickets, something I'm not sure either of them are at all into, but Blake thanks them nonetheless.

Blaire and Blake open up their presents from each other at the same time, both revealing two pairs of socks.

Callie rolls her eyes. "Every damn year." I look over at her, and she shrugs, clearly baffled by it.

But I'm not. Because once upon a time, a pair of new, sturdy wool socks would have been the greatest gift I could have imagined. Mending socks again and again and again is exhausting. How old are these twins?

Up next are my gifts. They open them at the same time, pulling out the books I painstakingly picked for them.

For Blake, I bought a new action thriller, something on the best seller list. Admittedly not the most well thought out gift ever, but most men tend to like those, so I assume it's a safe bet. And I know the hold list at the library for that book is like four months long right now, so it must be good.

He gives me a polite smile, but Blaire doesn't say anything, still staring at her book.

It's a YA vampire novel. Stupid? Maybe. But it had felt right at the time. Just a little jab.

She tried to mesmerize me with her vampire powers the other day. When I was shopping, this felt like fair compensation for that. My own little way to strike back. Now, it just feels dangerous and idiotic.

She's still staring at it, and the atmosphere is getting heavier and heavier.

Callie breaks it by reading the title over her shoulder. "I hear that one's good," she says. "It's popular in the YA section."

"Yeah," I say, unable to tear my eyes away from Blaire. "I heard that too. Thought it might be something you'd enjoy."

Blaire holds the book and stares at me for a moment longer, prolonging the awkward silence long enough that everyone else catches on and starts shifting uncomfortably.

"Thank you," Blaire manages. "I look forward to reading it."

Callie's gifts are next, but Blaire doesn't break eye contact with me the whole time.

***

I make my excuses not too long after.

What was I thinking? Just because Blaire and Blake have shown themselves to be relatively non-threatening doesn't mean I should push them. They are monsters. They drink human blood, they hypnotize people with their eyes, they're god-knows how old—just because they both come in a pretty package

41

that tricks the eye doesn't mean I should let my guard down. They are danger-ous.

That ominous thought sticks with me as I unlock the front door, walk up the stairs, and unlock the door to my apartment. I freeze as soon as I get the door open, the hairs on the back of my neck standing up. I've only survived this long because I trust myself, and I believe my instincts. Something is wrong here, and I prepare myself to run.

I somehow doubt this is regular-old robbers.

"Laurel," Blaire says, stepping out of my bedroom and into the moonlight shining through the living room window. "I think we need to talk."

Chapter Eight

My heart in my throat, I step back, feeling like a rabbit caught in the gaze of a predator. I wonder if it's better to freeze or bolt. Can I outrun her?

She didn't kill me right away, and she probably could have. Whether that's because she has an ulterior motive, or she likes playing with her food, I don't know. Either way, I'm not dead, and I have to take that as a win.

But if I run, and she catches me, then I probably will be dead. Every muscle in my body itches to turn tail and bolt, but I force myself to hold my ground.

"What are you doing here?"

She takes another step forward, and I move without thinking, until my back is pressed against my front door. "I think you know already, Laurel," she says, and is it my imagination, or does she sound tired?

"How'd you beat me here?" I demand—the stupidest, most possibly irrelevant question I can think about right now.

But Blaire responds like it's maybe more relevant than I thought, because she freezes, head tilting as she looks at me. Really looks at me. Looks *through* me, more like. "I think you know that, too."

I want to tell her that I don't know anything, but we both know that'd be a lie. I need to figure out what she already knows so I can plan how to play this.

She holds up the book I gave her. It looks so strange in her hands, at once perfectly ordinary and damning. I swallow. "Why'd you give me this, Laurel?"

I could say a lot of things. I could say, *what, a book?* Or I could say, *don't you know how to read?* I could be even more flippant, and say, *it's common to give gifts on birthdays.* But I don't.

I'm not going to solve this problem until I know what she knows. So I take a deep breath, force calm into my lungs, and say, "What are you, Blaire?"

I'm not brave enough to say it. I could; I could say, *I know what you are, Blaire.* But I hold back, watching. Waiting.

Is that cowardly? Maybe. But I need her to match me now. If I'm putting my cards on the table, then she needs to do the same.

Blaire falls backward like my simple question was a gunshot. Her hands tighten on the book, and I can see the cover starting to rip. "You know," Blaire whispers. "I don't know how you know, *why* you know—but you do." She stares at me. "How? I've never met a human who knows and survives it."

Human. There it is. The open admission that she isn't human.

"I know a lot of things," I tell her evasively, but I don't know how to tell her that I'm completely unsure if the label *human* even belongs to me.

Blaire tosses the book on the couch, clearly no longer in need of it, and starts to pace my living room. I shrink away, but with the door at my back, there's nowhere else I can go. She doesn't seem to even see me, almost like I don't matter at all to her anymore. She's too stuck in her own head.

She finally stops and turns back to me. "I thought I was imagining it at first. But you—I kept getting more obvious. And you kept going, too."

Maybe I shouldn't have done that. The book was stupid, and the comments I made were dangerous. But somehow, I don't think she's going to kill me for it.

"How'd you get here?" I ask her again, this time my voice softer.

She shrugs. "I ran and beat you here by about a minute. Callie thinks I'm up in their guest room, and Blake'll keep her from checking." She makes a face. "I think birthday sex was involved, so she definitely won't be checking."

"You... ran?" I *drove*, and she beat me.

"I thought we needed to have this conversation as soon as possible. And besides, it's not like you're unfamiliar with wandering through the woods alone at night."

Alright, fair. I fight not to blush. Sure, spying on someone is pretty shitty. But I think, in these circumstances, that I should be excused. "Yeah, about that—"

"What did you think you'd find, Laurel?" she demands, stepping closer again. When I flinch, she draws up short, her brow furrowed. "I won't hurt you."

"We both know you could."

She doesn't say anything to that. "How much do you know?" she asks after a moment, backing up so she's closer to the couch and giving me room to breathe. My hands find the wood of the door behind me, grounding myself.

"More than I should, and less than everything," I tell her. It's vague as shit, but I don't know what else to say.

"That's not an answer."

I shrug. It's the best answer she's going to get. "How old are you?" I ask her instead. She's not the only one who's looking for some information.

She freezes, then sits down on my couch like a puppet whose strings have been cut. She stares at her hands for a moment, but then looks up at me and says, "Blake and I were born in the late eighteenth century."

So young. I can't let that show, but that's all I can think about. The two of them aren't even three centuries old. And here I am, getting closer to a thousand years than not now.

"Were you born like this?"

She doesn't answer for a moment, then says, "What does *less than everything* mean?"

"It means I don't know everything." I get brave and take a step away from the door. "I'm not all-knowing. But I know enough."

"Turning vampires almost never works," she says, like it's a basic fact everyone should know.

I don't. I've been a lot more focused on knowing how to recognize and survive what's out there than on knowing the intricacies of their species. There's no need to know all the finer details if I just plan to run away.

"So, you were born," I surmise.

She continues to stare. "Blake and I *were* turned. It was a whole thing, but unless you were there—if you knew anything, you'd assume we were born."

"Excuse me for not reading the vampire encyclopedia." Blaire makes it too easy to be bold. Something about her draws it out, and I'm beginning to think it won't get me killed.

There's still time for that, though. I should be more careful.

"Is that what it is? Did the librarian find some arcane book somewhere? An actual vampire encyclopedia?" she asks, eyes brightening even more than usual like a dog with a bone.

"There are a lot of places where someone can learn something like this," I say evasively. "And yes, there are plenty of books."

"What does that mean? Laurel, I—"

"What do you eat?" I interrupt, because I don't want to talk about me. "Drink?"

"Drink. We call it drinking. And you know what we drink, Laurel."

"Say it." I need to hear it.

She watches me for a minute, and then nods. "Blood. We drink blood. But you knew that, Laurel."

"Do you kill people?"

"In the beginning, when we had poorer control. I haven't killed anyone in almost two hundred years, though. There are ways of getting a human to comply, and it doesn't hurt them."

That's better than I thought. Assuming she's not lying to me—and why would she, since she so clearly has the upper hand in this conversation—then this is the best news I've heard in years. The town I found is infested with monsters, perhaps, but they don't need to be monstrous.

There probably aren't bodies buried around Blaire's little cabin, then. That only leaves one more thing I need to know urgently. "What are you going to do with me?"

"Do with you?" she echoes, like the words are foreign to her. "What the hell do you mean, *do with you*?"

"I know," I remind her. "And you know I know. I'm assuming that's not your preference. So. What are you going to do?"

I can probably survive an attack. Maybe not if my blood is completely drained; I've never tested that before. But I've bled profusely and bounced back, and I have the advantage that Blaire doesn't know what I am. If she takes me down like she might any other human, I'll be able to walk away after.

And then I can never show my face around here again. I can survive an attack, but that doesn't mean I can eradicate an angry vampire. I'll have to run, and run far.

That's okay. I can live with that, now that I'm reasonably assured that Callie and the townsfolk are safe.

Blaire's head falls forward, like she lost the will to even hold it up anymore. "I'm going to assume you've known for a while," she mumbles. "And since you haven't done anything more than taunt me with some questionable taste in literature, and you haven't died yet somehow—nothing. You've known and you survived. I'm not going to be the thing that breaks that streak."

"You can just let me live?" I ask, dubious. That's never been the impression I've been given. Humans who find out find themselves dead.

She shrugs. "I didn't tell you. And you seem to be living just fine on your own. So, for what I'm going to do—I'm going to answer your questions, Laurel. Ask you not to say anything. And maybe have someone to talk to. Besides my brother, that is."

I study her face. She could be lying to me, I guess. Lulling me into some false sense of security, waiting for me to let my guard down before she strikes. But she really has no need to do that. Blaire is likely aware of how she'd dominate any sort of fight between us. She doesn't need me to be at any more of a disadvantage than I already am.

"Is Callie safe?" I ask, because it's the only question that matters.

"Callie?" Blaire asks, brow furrowed. "Callie is literally the safest human I've ever met. She has two vampires ready to defend her with their lives. My brother would kill and die for her, and I would too, since she means so much to him. She's safe. I don't know anyone safer."

"You're telling me that Blake would never get a little thirsty and hurt her?" I challenge.

Her eyes set like I've offended her. "I'm telling you he'd starve first. He'd cut his own heart out. He loves her. I don't pretend to understand it, the falling for a human thing, but he does. He adores her beyond measure and she won't ever

47

get hurt on his watch. And this is a ridiculous question. We take care of that need, Laurel. We're practically religious about making sure it gets done."

I think she's telling the truth. Is it stupid to trust her? I barely know her, and I've spent my life running away from things like her. But the way her eyes shine with sincerity, the way she talks about her brother—everything tells me she's telling me the truth.

"Laurel," she murmurs. "I need to know how you know. Please."

I consider her for a moment. "You were right. A book." A half-truth, and it'll have to be enough.

"Do you know other vampires?"

"Just you and your brother." And I sincerely hope those two are the only vampires I ever meet for the rest of my very long life.

Blaire stares at me, then huffs. "I'm used to being the one with secrets."

"Get used to it."

"Anything I can do to encourage you to share?"

Nothing that I think she'd be willing to do. I doubt I'd hold up to torture, but asking alone isn't getting what happened to me out of me.

"Do you want some coffee?" I ask her. If we're going to sit around talking about this, we might as well be comfortable. I don't have much food, but I do have coffee. It might not erase the bags under my eyes, but the caffeine does give me a temporary kick that I appreciate.

Blaire bites her lip, sharp incisor exposed. It's not a full-on Halloween fang, but it's definitely sharper than a human's incisor, and reminds me how stupid my question is. "I think I should go back; Callie can't know I left, after all."

I raise an eyebrow. "You think, on your brother's birthday, your sister-in-law is going to check on you in the night?"

"It's not really our birthday, you know—"

"Callie doesn't know that, does she?" I interrupt. "Now: coffee?"

"I won't drink it," she says after a pause. "But you're more than welcome."

Turning my back to her makes every hair on my neck stand on end, but I fight through it. Facing a vampire really isn't different than letting her be at my back; I'm fucked either way if she decides to attack.

When I have my coffee mug, Blaire gestures me toward the couch, and I sit at the far end, the closest I've been to her yet. She watches me while I take a sip, giving me a moment. "What did you want to know?"

I open my mouth and then close it again, because I have no idea. I have a thousand questions. I have no questions. I can't sort through it all, can't make it all click in my brain.

What even is important to know? She's a vampire. She swears she doesn't kill people, and that Callie is safe. She's less than three hundred years old, ancient by any standards except mine.

Blaire seems to accept that I have no idea what to say, giving me a wry smile. "I have to say, I'm not used to being the one with questions."

"No?" I ask. "It's been all clear for you since the minute you were changed? How convenient for you." Is that a little bitterness I hear in my own voice? Better reign that in, before the questions get more targeted.

"Fair enough. That was confusing," she acknowledges, a little furrow appearing in her brow.

"What happened, anyway?" I ask. "That you were turned, I mean."

She's quiet for a moment, and I think she's going to refuse to answer. But then she says, "Got sick. Modern medicine wasn't what it is today, and we were going to die. It happened," she shrugs, looking almost unbothered talking about her own death, except I can see the heaviness in her eyes. "Someone would catch something, and then everyone would have it, and you'd either get up and walk away from it... or you wouldn't."

My stomach drops. I know this story. I know how it goes. I lost more friends and acquaintances that way that I care to count. "And how do vampires factor into it?" I ask, because that's the piece I don't know.

"There was a man. A vampire, I guess, but I didn't know that—obviously. He'd shown some interest in me, and I was considering that. He'd clearly had money, and it would have done a lot for us, even if I didn't—well, it was an option. I don't know what he planned to do—maybe he thought he could keep it a secret, like Blake is. Or maybe he talked a big game but only really wanted a fuck. It didn't matter. When it was clear we were all going to die, he thought the turning was worth the risk—and it took. I woke up." She shakes her head.

49

"Not one in a hundred wakes up, but I did. And then I told him I wouldn't go anywhere with him until he saved my brother."

This story should end in tragedy. I know it doesn't—I saw Blake an hour ago—but it should have, and I can't figure out how it didn't. "And?"

"He gave in. Probably thought it was a mercy—might have been a quicker death than the sickness. But Blake woke up, too. And from there, we were the miracle twins. Paraded around in certain circles for years. Studied."

"And the vampire who turned you?" He'd turned Blaire, what, to make her his wife? Why is that the detail that's sticking with me?

"When you get old, novelty is like currency, and we were new. So he dragged us around, bringing us to vampire after vampire and everyone else he could think of. They poked us, prodded us, tested our blood and tissue and vampiric skills, convinced there's something special about us." Novelty has never been my currency, and I think bitterly about what a safe life someone must lead to think that way. Novel experiences mean danger in my life. I like my predictable little world.

She continues, interrupting my thoughts. "We're not special. We just lived. And eventually, he lost interest in me. Like I said, novelty, and it wore off. Anyway, that was a long time ago. And eventually we got sick of being prodded, and I got real tired of how some of them talked about Blake. *Transgender* wasn't a word we had to describe what he felt back then, but we all knew, and their disregard for him as a person pissed me the fuck off. So we left." She says *left* like there's something unsaid, but I don't push further.

That's awful. And achingly familiar, although I don't say that out loud. But I know full well what it's like to have a supernatural force choose you, poke you, prod you, change you.

"And then what happened?" I work up the courage to ask.

She shrugs. "We stayed under the radar for a long time. Kept small lives, small jobs. And then Blake had to go and fall in love, and here we are now."

"You aren't worried the people who hurt you before will come after you?"

"We're not novel anymore," she says like that explains everything. "Besides, we have friends now. We're not the dependent kids anymore, needing handouts to survive." She looks at me, really looks at me, and then says, "You don't have to worry, Laurel. Nothing is coming here to hurt you, or Callie, or anyone else."

And that's probably true. It doesn't mean I can let go of the vise grip fear has had on my heart for centuries, now.

She stands. "I should go. They *might* be fucking all night, but the last thing I need is for Callie to check on me for some reason." She glances toward my living room window. "You should lock that, by the way."

"It doesn't lock," I say tiredly, because I'd fought with it for an hour after I moved in. I stupidly thought living on the second story would be enough protection. Apparently, not from vampires.

"I'll go out the window again so your neighbors don't see anyone leave who didn't come in," she says. "And then… I don't know, nail it shut?"

"Not going to break into my house again?"

"Do I need to break in? Or would you answer if I knocked?" Somehow, the question conveys a lot more weight than I expected.

I swallow. "You can knock," I tell her, and she gives me a half smile.

Then, in a blur of motion, she has the window open and jumps out, landing in a crouch in the backyard, before disappearing into the trees.

Chapter Nine

I don't sleep well. The witch is in my nightmares, but Blaire and Blake are there too, in their own cells, and then Callie is there, and soon enough the knife is in her hand, cutting into her flesh, drawing her blood so she can become as fucked up as the rest of us, and—

I wake up before it can get any worse, and I don't fall back asleep.

Nightmares about what happened to me aren't new. *Time heals all wounds* is absolute bullshit, because nine hundred years hasn't given me closure. It's not uncommon for whatever current problem I'm dealing with to work its way into the dreams, either. Blake and Blaire showing up, and Callie being caught in the middle of it all, shouldn't surprise me at all.

And I'm not. I'm numb to it, and no better at handling it than I was all those centuries ago.

I sleepwalk my way through work, and as soon as my shift ends, I book it, walking over to the building where Blake works.

I stand next to his car, leaning against it as I wait for him to finish work for the day.

It's kind of mind-blowing that a vampire works as an accountant. Then again, I work as a librarian, and Blaire works in software. We're just three ancient creatures, doing what we can to keep up with the times.

To give Blake all due credit, he doesn't even pretend to look surprised when he sees me. "Not here," he says, motioning toward his passenger seat. I nod and get in.

"Blaire warned me you might be coming," he says once he slides in on his side.

Well, that's disturbing, because *I* didn't even know I'd be coming until long after Blaire left last night. "I didn't tell her."

"It's not a hard guess, Laurel. Where to?"

"Your house?" I shake my head. "Callie'll be headed home soon. Not your house."

"Your place," he nods, like it's a foregone conclusion.

I hesitate a second, but since Blaire was there last night, what do I have to lose? It's not like it's a secret location. "Left."

"Yeah, I know," he says, merging onto the road.

It strikes me suddenly that I have no idea how Blaire found my apartment last night. I certainly never brought her there. I never even brought Callie there.

"How?" I ask, suspicious now.

He shrugs, not looking away from the road. "I was pretty sure you were skulking around my home. Forgive me for wanting to check. You should get that window fixed."

At this point, I'm going to seal it in with concrete. "You broke in?" Not that there's anything interesting to find. I have the furniture that came with the apartment, my limited supply of clothes, and not much else. There's nothing that gives away what I am, but still. It's the principle of the thing.

"Yeah." He sounds totally unrepentant. "You would have broken into my house if you thought you could get away with it."

That's fair enough. He turns again, pulling into the driveway of my building.

"Second floor," I mutter, but I don't know why I bother.

"Even if I hadn't been here, I'd be able to follow your scent," he says, walking close behind me so he can keep his voice low.

"You can *smell* me?"

"Yeah. I always know who's nearby. I can pick you out of a crowd that way at a few hundred feet. For Blaire and Callie, probably even further."

Last night, I saw Blaire's speed. Both siblings have admitted climbing to my second story window to break in. Now Blake is telling me about these super senses, and I haven't forgotten whatever spooky thing Blaire's eyes did to me one time. I knew vampires were different from humans, that there's more to it than blood and immortality, but that is *a lot*.

"Anything else I should know about?" I ask, unlocking my door.

He walks in, looking around cursorily. "We can see in the dark. We get a pretty good read on someone's emotions through taste and smell. We can hear things way out of the range of humans. We're faster, stronger, and generally hardier." He turns to look at me. "But you could have asked my sister that last night, so I'm assuming that's not why you came to me today."

He's not wrong. Blaire did make it clear that I could ask her any questions last night, but there are some questions—urgent questions—that can only be answered by Blake.

Blake looks so much like his sister. There's something about both of their eyes that makes me feel like they're staring straight through me, and I don't like it. The very last thing I want is to be seen.

He sits down on my couch, and something about the way he sits strikes a chord in my brain. He's doing his best to keep his posture open and inviting, I realize. He's aiming for non-threatening.

I'm standing while he's sitting. It's my home, my turf. I'm sure this is meant to make me feel in control and safe.

It's not that I feel *unsafe*. I'm pretty convinced now that Blake and Blaire aren't planning to kill me. It would have been way easier to do it a while ago, and taken a lot less effort on their part. I'm as much a curiosity to them as they are to me, and I think that alone is enough to protect me right now. But for Blake in particular, he would never do anything to upset Callie. And Callie likes me. Therefore, he can't hurt me.

And that's the root of the issue. "Callie doesn't know about you," I say. It's not a question.

"She doesn't," he agrees. His voice sounds perfectly natural, but he won't look me in the eye.

"How can you do that to her? You're basically lying to her. You have no idea if she'd consent to this relationship if she knew. You're keeping some pretty pertinent details back."

Blake bites his full bottom lip, looking me over. "How long have you known?" he asks.

"Almost my whole life." It's a true statement, even if it is evasive. It's not my fault if he makes an inaccurate guess about how long my life has been.

He leans forward a bit, forgetting his open and welcoming posture. "You are the only human Blaire and I have ever heard of who has survived knowing. I don't know what it is, but humans don't survive this particular piece of information."

"What, it fries our brains?" I ask sardonically.

"Sometimes." He sounds dead serious as he says it, too. "Sometimes something in the human breaks, something that can't be put back together again. Other times, the human knows about what's out there, and they get involved when they're not equipped for it. They mess with the wrong person, they ask the wrong question—they end up dead, Laurel. I've never heard of a single other human surviving more than a few weeks. We are a curse on humans, and we ruin their lives."

"And you married one," I point out. I'm not saying it to hurt, but maybe he deserves a little sharpness. This is too big to keep from Callie, and if he can't justify telling her, then he shouldn't have married her.

"I know." His voice sounds almost fragile now, like anything I say will break it. "I angsted over it, believe me. Blaire told me not to do it, to leave her the fuck alone. She said we could leave town and move on if I couldn't stay away from her. But I—I love her, Laurel. From the bottom of my heart, everything I have—I love her."

"Not everything you have," I say.

He visibly flinches. "I prize her being alive over being informed. I'm sorry, but it's true."

"She's going to die," I remind him. "And you're going to live forever, basically. She's going to age and you won't. Her life is a drop in the bucket for you."

He looks more and more agitated as I talk, his brow furrowing and hands fisting. "Don't you think I know that?"

"You going to try to change her?"

"Not anytime soon," he says, voice getting rougher. "Don't ask me to think that far ahead. I know this is going to get bad. That I chose something that will be horrifically hard. But I love her. And I do think I can give her a good life. It's worth it. In the end, it's just—worth it."

"When you don't age?" I press, feeling like the villain here, but I need to know this. I need to know Callie is protected in all senses of the word. And aging has been the bane of my existence. I only get so many years in a place before I have to move on, before people get too suspicious. Blake has already been here for several years.

"Vampires can—it's called mesmer, and we can convince people of things for a while. I'll never pass as eighty, but I can probably go another ten, maybe fifteen years. And after that, Blaire and I agreed. We're reaching out to people again."

"Vampires?" I ask, surprised after the story from last night.

"Some. And witches, too. And anyone else." He's looking at his hands, so he doesn't notice the flinch I can't suppress. "Anyone who might know a way to fake it. A couple witches have some promising leads for me, when I'm ready for them. And I'll go from there."

He's thought a lot about this. And from the sound of things, he and Blaire have agreed to put themselves at risk so he can have this. "Alright," I say quietly, accepting his answer. It's awful and I hate it for Callie, but I hate it for him, too. Blake isn't doing this for a laugh; he's doing this because he loves her, even knowing he'll lose her. "For what it's worth; I'm sorry."

He shrugs. "Right now, I'm deliriously happy. I found the love of my life. And someday, there'll be a consequence. But right now, I can be happy."

And here I am, the asshole trying to make him miserable now. "Alright." Nothing about this is alright. "You should go home. Before you have to explain to Callie why you're late."

He nods, standing and walking toward my door. "Blake?"

"Huh?"

"I am sorry." It fixes nothing, but I feel like I need to say it.

He nods and leaves, nothing more to say between us.

Chapter Ten

I knock on Blaire's door that evening, and she looks entirely unsurprised to see me. "Human food is in the fridge," she says, stepping aside to let me in.

"You know that makes it sound like you eat humans," I tell her, just to be an asshole. I take in the main room of the cabin. It's exactly as small as it looked through her window, but it is cozier. Cold, yes, but Blaire did a nice job with filling it with soft furnishings. There's a big old couch and a few chunky blankets, and the whole place smells like fresh pine and a wood-burning stove. My shoulders relax just being here.

"Gross. Go see how I did."

"You really don't eat?" I ask, walking into what can charitably called a kitchen. Not that I'm one to judge, considering how rarely I put effort into my meals, but still. This is a two burner stove and a mini-fridge, and I'd bet good money that the fridge wasn't even plugged in until Blaire thought I might be coming over.

"We can."

"Obviously. I've seen it. But I'm guessing you don't, when you don't have to fake it."

Blaire comes into the kitchen behind me and leans against the counter. It makes the space crowded, but I don't mind. Blaire practically radiates warmth, and something about her presence makes the space feel more whole. "We don't need food," Blaire confirms. "Not human food, anyway. Or, well, *human* food—"

"—I get it."

"Yeah. We don't need it. And it seems like it's fifty-fifty if we even like it? Some vampires I've met tell me it's fine. They don't need to, but they eat meals if it's necessary. Some of them even like it. And then there's a subset of us who it tastes like ash to. That's me."

"Your brother?"

"Doesn't love it but doesn't hate it, thankfully for him, since he eats human food every single day." Blaire shudders. "I would never. Anyway. You better eat all of this, because I'd feel bad leaving food to rot but I'm not eating it."

There's a pre-made sandwich platter, the type you might get at a supermarket deli for a party, and I imagine Blaire in a grocery store, possibly for the first time in her life, walking around confused and settling for what looked like the easiest option. You think she'd realize the portions are too much for just me, and I make a mental note to tell her about prepared food if this is something we keep doing. I pull out two of the little sandwiches, and a soda Blaire has in the refrigerator door.

"I do have plates," Blaire says, reaching up to get one. "Mostly because they were here when I moved in."

"Thanks." I transfer my sandwich to the proffered plate, then go to sit at the tiny kitchen table that's more in the living room than the kitchen. At least it's close to the wood stove. I might not *need* to be as warm as a normal human, but it's fucking cold in here. Has Blaire seriously skipped paying for heat?

"Heard you talked to my brother."

"You two tell each other everything, huh?"

"The twin thing is real. We've been at each other's side since the day we were born. Yeah. We tell each other everything. So. What's the verdict?"

I shrug. "He's a good guy. I don't *love* that Callie is in the dark, but I get it. And she's happy."

"Yeah. They both are. I never got it, you know, how Blake could feel this way, knowing it would end. Wouldn't be me, ever. I've never been able to handle it, knowing how it'll all end up. But they make each other happy, so I pipe down and leave them to it."

"You ever tried?"

Blaire tilts her head, considering. "I date, sometimes, when I... you know. Get lonely or whatever. I don't let it get that far. I have no plans to play house with a human for thirty, forty years. It's not something I'm willing to do." She looks at me pretty intensely as she says it.

Sounds lonely, but who am I to judge? I've been plenty lonely in my life. Haven't I operated by the same rules?

"What do you do way out here for fun?" I ask her.

Blaire considers for a second. "You like movies?"

I saw the invention of cinema, watched the world go from black and white silent films to today. I've seen many of the best movies of all time, many of them right when they came out. "Yeah."

Blaire gets up and picks her laptop off the end table. She sets it in front of me, leaning over to unlock it, and then opening up Netflix. "Go ahead and pick something."

***

At some point, we migrate to the couch, and from there, I fall asleep and wake up in the pre-dawn light, cuddled into Blaire's side, my head on her shoulder. She's asleep when I first blink awake, her head tilted back, exposing the long, strong line of her throat to my too-hungry eyes.

I shouldn't be watching her like this. She made it perfectly clear last night that she's not interested in relationships she sees as doomed, and I'm not ready to tell her the truth about me. I've never told anyone. I don't even know how to say the words.

Her arm around me tightens. "Good morning, sunshine," she murmurs, eyes still closed, head still tipped back. "You sleep okay?"

Apparently. But now that I'm awake, I can admit it's freezing in here.

Frostbite won't kill me. It won't even make me lose my toes. But I can't ignore the cold like Blaire evidently can.

"Your fire burned out," I tell her, letting my eyes slide closed again and snuggling back into her side. For warmth, obviously.

But she tenses right up, making her much less comfortable to lie against. "Oh, shit. Alright, sorry. I can fix that."

"It's fine." The last thing I want is for her to move.

"It's not fine," she disagrees, trying to stand. "I forgot—human. You need proper heat."

It'd be so easy to tell her no, I don't. That she's worried for nothing. But then it'd get complicated, and I'd have to explain things I still don't understand. So I let her get up and watch through half-lidded eyes as she messes with the thermostat on the wall.

"You have to get cold too," I point out as I smell the tell-tale scent of a furnace that hasn't been used in a long time clicking on.

"Not really. I mean, I can tell when it is cold—the sensation is still there. But it doesn't bother me. It hasn't in a few centuries, so I practically forgot." She turns to me and smirks, saying, "Callie gets annoyed when Blake starts insisting she wear a jacket when it's too warm for it by her standards. But he's an over-protective asshole, and he can't tell the difference any better than I can."

Yeah, I can picture that.

"I'll do better next time," Blaire continues, finally moving back to the couch. Something inside me gets warm. *Next time.* She's thinking about a next time.

I don't know what this is. But it's not nothing, as much as it'd be more convenient for both of us if it was.

"Do you have to work today?" Blaire asks.

I turn my head to see my cellphone, poking it so the clock shows up. "Not for a while." It's barely after dawn, and I have a short shift this afternoon.

"What do you eat for breakfast?"

"You don't have to worry about me so much," I say, instead of telling her that I couldn't guess the last time I ate breakfast.

"Humans eat three meals a day. I'm old, but I remember that much."

"And I'm a grown woman. I'll take care of myself."

She huffs. "I'm asking because I want to hang out with you for a while longer, asshole. So, will you stay, or do you want to go and take care of yourself?"

Oh. Well, when she puts it like that. "I'll stay," I tell her. "I can eat a leftover sandwich." She'd bought an entire party platter, after all.

She tilts her head, watching me, then asks, "Wanna see something cool?"

***

I don't know what I expected. I had half a fear that it had to do with blood, or vampiric abilities, or something I want nothing to do with. But I had no idea that it'd involve getting into Blaire's ancient Subaru and driving thirty minutes east until we hit a remote stretch of ocean.

"Wow," I say, leaning against the hood of the car to look over the water. The ocean looks fathomless here, like a wide expanse that goes on forever. It's the same feeling that I got the first time I set sail to cross that ocean. I didn't realize the world is this big anymore.

If I look further up to the left, there's a lighthouse out on a rocky promontory, the single beacon of light spinning round and round. Surely lighthouses are just a beloved reminder of a bygone day at this point, but that kind of makes me feel right at home.

"Yeah," she agrees, resting her hip on the car next to mine. "Not bad, huh?"

"You come here a lot?"

"It's a quiet place." She starts walking and I fall in beside her. She's not exceptionally tall, but her legs are longer than mine, so I have to walk twice as fast to keep up. After a moment, she realizes and slows down. "The world is too loud now, I've decided. I know that makes me sound old as shit, but, well—I am. And the world is loud."

I know *exactly* what she means. Not that I'm telling her that, but still. She begins to climb down the rocky cliff, navigating over the big boulders to get closer to the water, and I follow suit, watching where she puts her feet so I can do the same. "I've been meaning to ask you something," I say when we're halfway down.

"Okay, shoot."

"Vampires and the sun. How does that work?"

"Are you asking if we burn up in daylight?" she asks. The corners of her eyes crinkle up, amusement plain on her face.

I thought of immortal faces as immovable as marble before all this. It's nice to see the laugh lines Blaire has.

"Well, obviously not." The sun is fully up now, and she hasn't caught on fire. I've seen Blake in the daylight, too. And I think Callie would notice something is off if her husband slept in a coffin all day and only walked around at night. "But, is there any truth to it?"

She shakes her head, now at the bottom of the climb, walking on the rocks right along the water. Some of them are wet, no doubt splashed when the tide comes further in, but the ocean spray isn't too bad right now. "I've never met someone who knows so much and yet so little."

"Rude." I finish climbing down, planting two feet on the ground.

She looks at me sideways. "Was that climb too much? Sorry. I sometimes forget—we didn't get to do much as humans. It was a long time ago, and travel was hard. So most of my experiences have been *like this* and I sometimes forget that we're not the best barometers of reasonable behavior."

"It's fine," I brush off, although if she's planning on taking other humans here, I probably should tell her to stop. It can obviously be done, but one wrong move and I'd likely have broken my neck. "Now, sunlight."

"We don't die in the sun."

"Obviously. What *does* happen?"

She shrugs. "Not much. We're stronger at night, in a way. Not physically, that doesn't change. But if you're going to mesmerize someone, literally make them see and believe what you want them to, then darkness is the way to do it."

That makes sense. "So, if I'm running from a vampire, wait until dawn."

Blaire snorts. "Like it matters to you. Mesmer doesn't even work on you."

I stop. "Wait, really?"

"Really. I tried." She must see something on my face, because she hastily continues, "Not maliciously. But you were freaking Blake and I the fuck out, back before you and I talked. So that day I came to the library, I tried."

"It was daylight," I point out. "Maybe you were just too weak."

If I expected her to take offense to being called weak, I'd be disappointed. "Maybe," she allows. "But you shook me off easily. I think it has to do with you knowing what you do. Maybe it's acting like a layer of protection."

"Maybe."

"I never tried it again. And Blake's never done it on Callie. He'll have to someday, if he's going to pretend to age, but that's the only reason why he would. I swear."

And I believe her. I know that she and Blake aren't malicious, and I'm sure Blake will wrestle long and hard with that when the time comes. I'm more stuck on the fact that it failed to work on me. Maybe Blaire is right. Maybe it's a product of me already knowing who she is and what she can do.

But maybe—maybe it's one more thing that makes me different. I don't know why it would be—other than my inability to actually die, I didn't get any other enhanced supernatural abilities. Not that I know of, anyway.

Blaire turns so the sunlight catches her just right, making her skin glow as mist from the waves burst around her. She looks like a painting.

"Everything alright?" she asks, frowning now. Those laugh lines are gone, and I irrationally want them to come back.

"Everything's fine," I manage to tell her. It's as fine as it ever is, at any rate.

Chapter Eleven

B eing back at work is jarring.

I like my job. I genuinely think I'm good at it, and this is a nice library to spend time in. And while the idea of never working again is appealing to some, I know I'd grow bored without the work.

But there's a certain separation here, like there's some line I didn't know about that's now been crossed. There's the world of *here*, and there's the world of whatever Blaire and I are doing.

We're not doing anything, I remind myself. She's a vampire and I'm whatever the hell I am. She's made it perfectly clear that she doesn't want a relationship that she sees as doomed. And if I want her to know otherwise, then I'd need to be brave and tell her the truth. And I still haven't figured out how to do that.

Maybe that's stupid. Maybe in the grand scheme of things, after all I've learned about her and whatever this is building between us, this shouldn't be that hard. But it is.

Being back at work is a distraction from ruminating on that, at least. For the first part of my day, patrons keep me busy enough that I can't think, and when it gets quieter around lunch time, I make work for myself. There are plenty of projects that have been on the back burner since long before I got here, and now seems like the perfect time to tackle them.

I'm printing new barcode stickers for some of our more worn titles when Callie finds me, blurring that line between work and Blaire once more. "I heard you had a good night," she practically sing-songs.

"Where on earth did you hear that?" If things were normal, Callie would be the friend I'd tell about my confusing feelings. But things aren't normal, and I'd never be able to explain why everything is so complicated.

"Blake and Blaire talk constantly, you know," she says. "And Blake tells me everything. He can't help himself. I don't think he could keep a secret if his life depended on it."

Shit. I pretend to be interested in the barcodes for a moment so she can't see the reaction on my face.

It seems cruel not to tell her. But Blake had been clear; he doesn't have another way to protect her. And maybe he's getting the worse end of the deal; after all, he's the one who has to live with it when she's gone.

"It was a nice night," I allow. I don't know how to define it, and I hope she doesn't ask too many more questions.

Unfortunately, she seems determined to torment me. Or, knowing her, more likely to match-make me, but she's only going into this with half the story, and she's hopelessly out-gunned here.

"Blake is going to visit Blaire tonight," she says abruptly. "Want to come over for dinner?"

I didn't know that, and I fight to keep my face neutral. Because it's not that Blaire owes me an accounting of her movements, but if Blake is coming to her, does that mean they're going to drink? Did they plan that after I left, or was that always the plan?

And what does it mean, exactly? I've still only gotten the vaguest answers.

She doesn't owe me more, I remind myself. It's not like I've been entirely forthcoming, either.

And Callie is still waiting for an answer. "Dinner sounds good."

Dinner sounds like mediocre food and giving her a chance to interrogate me, but with the way she smiles, I don't have the heart to say anything other than *good*.

***

Dinner is take-out, which I try not to look too excited over. "Did you stay at the cabin?" Callie asks over lo mein.

"Mhm."

"I've only been there a few times. Isn't it freezing?"

"Pretty cold," I agree.

"You should get her to stay at your place. Get her to get out of the woods more."

I privately think that Blaire would hate that. This is a pretty small town, but everything about her tells me she needs more space than this provides. Like she said, the world has gotten loud recently, and I respect her wanting to have some quiet away from it all.

Blaire would hate her neighbors knowing any more about her than that she exists.

Then again, only one of my neighbors knows me, and that's because Mrs. Feeney is a library patron who loves the senior book club. I don't have many interactions with her at work, but I know she recognizes me. Not that it comes up often; I'm also not one to socialize with my neighbors.

"Maybe," I tell Callie, because I can't let on how much the cold doesn't bother me.

Blaire and Blake are together tonight, presumably drinking blood. Is that a silent activity, or is there room to talk? Is Blake right now reminding his sister about the pitfalls of dating a human?

We're not dating, but that doesn't matter right now. Something is there. I don't know the details, but it's there. And I either have to tell her the truth, or let it all go.

What, I'm going to keep pretending I'm human, and have her watch me heal instantly the first time I get a paper cut? Have her watch me forget to eat for days at a time and expect her not to find that concerning?

"I told you she liked you," Callie says, smiling as she watches me.

"You did." And fuck her for that, for putting this idea in my head. "It's not anything real yet, Callie," I remind her before she starts planning a damned wedding.

She shrugs. "It always starts that way, doesn't it?"

Sure. But I imagine it just as often fizzles out as it becomes something more, too. Not that I say that to her. That would hurt her feelings, and there's something about Callie that makes me never want to hurt her feelings.

Chapter Twelve

When I leave work the next day, Blaire is leaning against her car in the parking lot, mirrored sunglasses hiding most of her face as she waits for me.

I stop and look her over. She's wearing a black leather jacket, roughed-up jeans, and combat boots. Her arms are crossed over her chest and her hip propped against her car, and I wonder if she's ever driven a motorcycle. She certainly looks the part.

I'm debating bringing it up as I get closer, but then she says, "Dinner tonight?"

"You're going to feed me?" I ask when I'm right next to her, sure that no one can hear me. It wouldn't do to have anyone hear how skeptical I am right now.

"I've heard humans like drive-thrus," she says. She pauses for a minute, but then says, "But only if you want, obviously. I don't want to mess up your plans."

Like I have any plans. Like I *ever* have plans. I've had more plans here in this town than I have in decades, and they all revolve around Blaire and her little family, so she'd know full well if I had any plans.

"I'd love to." And it's true. I don't know what's coming next, but I know I'd rather spend the evening with her than anyone else.

"Awesome." She opens her door and gestures for me to open the passenger door. I debate mentioning that I too have a car here, but decide against it.

Nothing will happen to it in the library parking lot. "Tell me what drive-thru is good."

I don't have much of an opinion on that, so I end up at the first drive-thru we see, and I eat chicken nuggets as Blaire drives us to her cabin. "How was last night?"

She glances over at me for a second, looking away from the road like she needs to see my reaction. I keep my face carefully neutral. I surprise myself by genuinely wanting to know more about this. I expected to be at least a bit disgusted, but that's definitely not what I'm feeling.

Well, not unless she confesses she really has been killing piles of humans every few weeks with her brother. That's a line I won't cross.

"Last night was fine," she says gruffly. "Routine, really."

"What does it look like?" I ask. "What do you do?"

She shrugs, clearly uncomfortable now. One hand taps repeatedly at the steering wheel, thumb drumming a rapid beat. Maybe it's her heart rate.

Do vampires have heart rates? I haven't been close enough to consciously check yet. Then again, I think Callie would have noticed by now if her husband didn't have a beating heart.

"These days, we get dressed up, go to a club. A place where inhibitions are low and people are already primed to let you get close to them, maybe even put your mouth on them. You get good at finding the ones especially susceptible to mesmer after a while. They don't feel a thing. They lose a little bit of blood, might be a little light-headed later, but I assume they usually attribute that to the alcohol."

That sounds both shockingly easy and surprisingly humane. "These days?"

The drumming gets faster. "We've tried different things. And in the early days, I admit our control wasn't as good." She shudders. "The man who changed us, he didn't watch us as well as he should have. And he was too focused on what a scientific *marvel* we were to realize that we were also just plain thirsty. People died, and I regret that. But we learned."

What must it be like, to wake up in a body that has urges you never expected? I know all about having a body that doesn't match what I once had, but at least I still feel like I did. I don't suddenly crave blood.

"That must've been hard."

Her eyes flick to me like she's trying to gauge my sincerity. "It was. But also, we killed people. So it should be hard."

My mind involuntarily goes to the witch who drained me for all I was worth without a second thought. Who would have easily discarded my corpse and slept fine if I wasn't like this. And it makes sense why I was so scared of creatures like Blaire for so long, but I've so horrifically misread her. She's good. Not perfect, but good.

I settle further back into my seat. We're on the twisty road through the woods that leads to her cabin now, so we'll be at her house soon. I finish my food so I don't bring any human food into her home.

"I hope it's better tonight," Blaire murmurs when she parks, and I raise an eyebrow, but she doesn't elaborate. I have no idea what she wants to be *better*. As far as I'm aware, everything was fine last time. More than fine, really.

But when she unlocks her front door, the answer is obvious. This place is *warm*. And not the warmth of a fire, either.

She's turned the heat on high enough for a tropical garden, and I find myself giggling. I didn't even know I could make that sound. "You really can't tell what's a good temperature, hm?"

Her brow furrows. "Did I mess it up?" She pulls off her jacket and sets it on the coat stand by the door, but it looks like she's just going through the motion, like it's something expected, like she could be comfortable with or without it. Unlike me, who is two seconds from pulling off all my clothes.

"Show me the thermostat?" I ask, and she shows me the little device by her bedroom.

I peer at it for a second—it's not like I'm an expert with this technology—but I figure out how to turn it down and set it to a much more comfortable sixty-eight degrees. "There."

"Don't all the humans up here only get happy when summer rolls around?" she asks, looking over my shoulder.

"Maybe? I assume some people live up here because they like the winter. You all have a lot of it."

"Then what's wrong with summer temperatures? Or are you one of those humans that likes the winter? Is that why you moved here?"

Oh, not a topic I wanted to tread into tonight. "This is a pretty standard temperature," I tell her instead of answering. "People mostly feel comfortable like this. So—the more you know."

"Huh." Then, seemingly losing interest now that I've assured her the problem is fixed, she goes back to the main room and sits on the couch, already reaching for her laptop. "Movie night?"

I want to ask her if she brought me here just for movies. I'm not brave enough to. So I nod, follow her, and I'm asleep against her side before the first movie even finishes.

***

When I wake up, there's sunlight streaming through the little window right in my face. I groan and try to turn over, but there's Blaire, taking up more space on the couch than she has any right to.

She starts when I bump into her, an arm involuntarily tightening around me. "Next time," she mutters, voice deliciously rough with sleep, "we sleep in the damned bed."

Next time? My heart starts beating faster, and I fight to control it. She can definitely hear that. She's probably preternaturally able to sense increased blood flow or something.

"I'm not working until this afternoon," I tell her. "And it's a short shift. Want to go to the ocean again?"

I'm desperate for any excuse to stick around. I think she might call me out on it, but after a moment, all she does is nod.

***

Of course, by the time we make it to the cliff's edge, it's starting to rain. "Should've checked the weather," Blaire mutters, glaring out the windshield like it personally offended her.

"We can still walk," I tell her, looking around. The rain isn't terrible, really. Honestly, it's more the churned up waves that are making the storm look bad.

"You'll be soaked through."

It won't be the first time or the last. It's not like I'll get sick from it or anything, and I know full well she can't, either. We came all this way. I'm not turning back just to go back to her place and have our time together end. A storm isn't something to be scared of.

"We'll be fine. It's barely raining, anyway," I protest.

Blaire pointedly looks out the window at the storm clouds growing thick and fast, but nods, even if her expression is still uncertain. "If you're sure."

"I'm sure." I open the car door and step out before she can question me more. The view of the water through the mist of the rain is spectacular; the fog hangs thick and heavy, and occasionally the lighthouse will break through as the bulb spins, turning the mist an orange glow.

Other than the rain and the waves, it's quiet here in the way Blaire said she likes. I know the lighthouse is probably run on some high-end technology, but from here, it still feels like the old-fashioned lighthouse, like someone is up there lighting lanterns to protect traveling ships. Like there's a place where the two of us can still connect with those long-ago times we left behind.

The waves are higher than they were the last time we were here. They crash against the rocks, making the mist heavier over the water. I get closer to the edge, looking out to take it all in.

"What're you looking for?" Blaire asks as she steps up behind me. She stands closer than she needs, our shoulders practically brushing. I don't pull away.

"Nothing." I don't know how to describe it, the sense of quiet. It's just her and I here. The world is smaller, more contained. I close my eyes, letting the mist soak into me, and inhale the salt air.

I don't care about the ocean this much. I've never been on a beach vacation in my entire life. The ocean is a means of sustenance and travel, and that's it. But here, now—well, it's Blaire.

If only I could untangle what that means.

"Let's walk over to the lighthouse," I propose.

Blaire looks at me dubiously. "You're going to freeze, Laurel."

"I'll be fine." I literally stood outside during a Russian winter once, all night without so much as a coat. Was I cold and miserable? Absolutely. But I was fine the next morning. "You coming or not?"

Blaire snorts. "Yes, you crazy human. Let's go."

The wind picks up some more as we walk, but the lighthouse isn't that far away. I ground my feet, digging them into the dirt as the path gets narrower. Eventually, the dirt gives way to rocks, perched in ways that look precarious but have probably stood through storms across the centuries. I watch my feet, wanting to avoid stepping in the cracks. I'll survive a twisted ankle, but that doesn't mean I want one.

"Let me go first!" Blaire calls from behind me. "I can steady you."

That's a sweet gesture, if entirely unnecessary. This woman let me climb down the cliff a few days ago, barely aware that it might be difficult for a human. And now, here she is wanting to hold my hand while I walk over a few rocks.

I turn to see her, wanting to reassure her. She steps through the mist like a vision, the now-driving rain soaking her clothes to her skin. "I'll be fine; you worry too much—"

I step backward and feel it the moment it happens. I scramble to get a handhold, but can't grip the slick rock, my arms windmilling in the air, desperate to regain my balance. But it's no use.

There's a loud, gruesome crunch when I hit the rocks below, bones breaking. I lose my vision, splitting pain making me keen as my skull no doubt cracks open. Then everything is cold and numb, and then everything is gone.

Chapter Thirteen

I wake up.

If I was thinking rationally, I would say it's inevitable. I always wake up. I always bounce back. It's a fact of life as much as anything else, and a fall off a cliff isn't going to be what does me in.

It still hurts, though.

The first thing I register is an absolutely numbing cold, which might be a blessing in disguise. This weather is acting like a giant, natural ice pack, and it'll hopefully help tame the soreness from my injuries. I'll feel good as new soon, but not yet.

The only thing I can feel, though, is icy-cold hands cupping my face.

I shift my neck experimentally. I'm pretty sure I broke it, but the damage is healing. I can move it, and the bones don't make that ominous cracking they do when they're not fully healed yet.

Sound comes back next. I didn't even realize that I couldn't hear anything, but now I hear the waves and Blaire's frantic pleading that's almost drowning them out. "C'mon, c'mon, I can still hear your heartbeat, Laurel. I'll get you to a hospital, you'll be fine, you're going to be fine, I promise, I—"

Sight comes back last. Or maybe it's the colossal effort of opening my eyes that takes so long. But when I finally force them open, my entire field of view is

Blaire, bending over me. Her face is wet from the rain, but I think it might be from tears, too.

We're still on the rocks at the bottom of the cliff. Blaire hasn't moved me yet, no doubt worried about moving someone who probably looked like they had a broken neck. Fuck, I hope she didn't call an ambulance. I hope that's so far out of her realm of experience that she wouldn't have even thought about it. It would be so awkward to explain why I'm alive to them.

"I told you I'd be fine," I tell her. Getting enough air to talk feels like stabbing knives into my lungs, but I force myself to draw another deep breath. Blaire looks wrecked, and I can't allow that. I'm *fine*. It's all fine.

"Fine? Laurel, I told you to let me go first, that fall is like fifty feet, and—"

"You going to blame me, or help me up?"

"You shouldn't move, we don't know what's broken—"

"Nothing's broken." I sigh. "Blaire, think logically. I should have smashed my skull open. The rocks should have cut me to pieces. You see anything still bleeding?"

It's silent for a minute. "The rain," Blaire tries weakly.

"Not quite." I have no idea how to say this. I suppose this is what I get—I had an opportunity to tell her without it being a *thing*, but I was too much of a coward. Now I don't have a way out, and I can't soften the blow for either of us. "Could we—I promise I'll explain, but I need you to trust me that I'm fine and help me up."

Blaire hesitates a second, but then nods stoically grabs me underneath my arms, hauling me upright.

I grit my teeth so I don't scream. That'll ruin the image of being alright, but I was definitely over-selling my condition. I won't be alright for an hour or so more.

My legs buckle as soon as Blaire lets me go. "I thought you said you were fine," Blaire accuses, immediately pulling me into her side. I sink into her warmth, letting her take more of my weight.

"I will be. I'm better than you expected, right?"

Blaire gives a bitter, strangled laugh. "Laurel, I truly expected you to be *dead* when I saw you down here. Anything is a step up."

"I'm hard to kill." I try to subtly test each limb, stretching and flexing. The pain is like being pricked with a thousand needles, but I don't let that stop me. Everything moves still, and that's what matters.

"Laurel, what the fuck is going on?" I pull away from her enough to look at her, to see how frantic her eyes are, how lost she looks. I have to fix this.

But not here. "How'd you get down here, anyway?"

"I jumped. *I* can take a fifty foot fall."

I want to retort that, clearly, so can I, but now isn't the time. The wind is only getting worse, and I'd much rather be achy and in pain just about anywhere else. "You know how to get back up?"

"No, I didn't make a damn extraction plan when you looked *dead*, forgive me—" Blaire takes a deep breath. "The rocks are easier to climb further back."

Turning my head to look over there hurts, but I know better than to mention that. "Easier for you, maybe." I really am going to have to tell her someday that all this climbing of the rocks around here is not something she should ever have a human to do. I've only been willing to do it because I know I bounce when I fall.

"Can you hold on? If you're capable of holding on, I can do it while carrying you. If not, it's about a mile that way to the public beach and road access. I can carry you."

I flex my fingers, testing them. "I can hold on."

"You sure?"

"Yes," I snap, but it's not Blaire's fault that I'm a freak of nature that Blaire doesn't yet understand. What's the worst that could happen? I fall again?

Gratifyingly, Blaire takes my word for it, and I'm scooped up seconds later. She walks toward the cliff's edge, arms cradling me. "You sure you can carry me? While climbing, I mean?"

"You're pretty small. A human could probably do it," Blaire mutters, letting me down onto my feet so she can help me scramble onto her back. I wrap my arms around her tightly, ignoring my protesting bones. I'd rather not take a second tumble today.

Blaire is quick about it, at least, deft and sure of every handhold and foothold as she moves. The rain is driving now, all but blinding me, and it's all I can do to hold on. I'm not even sure if Blaire can see through the rain, or if she's using some other enhanced sense, but she gets us up the cliff with no issues.

When we get to the top, Blaire helps me slide off her back. I try to regain my footing, but Blaire doesn't let me, scooping me up in a bridal carry again, walking to the car while she clutches me tight enough to make me think she's worried I'll disappear.

She doesn't say anything, and I don't either. The only sound is the driving rain and crashing waves, and they get louder and louder inside my skull while I desperately search for what the hell I say to her when I finally have to talk.

Blaire places me in the passenger's seat and even buckles my damned seatbelt for me, then rushes around to the driver's side. She cranks the heat all the way up even though it's still blowing cold air, and then she turns to me, her eyes still frantic but now set with a deep determination to match. "Tell me what the hell is going on."

I don't have a good answer. But if I haven't thought of one by now, then the truth is there's probably no good way to say it, so I take a deep, shaky breath and force the words out. I owe her this much.

"I don't know what I am. But I can't die."

She stares at me for a moment, looking like a buffering video while she processes that information. "What do you mean?"

"I mean I can fall down a cliff and walk away. And I can break bones and be better in a few minutes. Stab wounds don't stick. I don't need to eat. I might not even need to breathe, but muscle memory doesn't let me turn that off. I won't get frostbite and I can't catch any diseases. I'm nine hundred years old, Blaire, and I look exactly like I did back then."

Pale, and sickly, and small. I know people notice and I know people talk about it. People wouldn't be surprised if I told them I was dying. Because I was, once. And then I couldn't.

"You can't—you don't—what are you?" she asks.

And that's the question. "I'm me. I don't know. I was born human. I feel like I still am. Mostly, at least. Except for the not dying thing."

"That's not possible. That's not a *thing*. I've never heard of anything like you." She practically growls it, frustration bubbling up.

I'm sitting in a car with a frustrated vampire but I am not afraid. Not anymore. I've somehow moved beyond fear, into some sort of zen calm that feels too similar to numbness for my liking.

"And yet," I tell her calmly, watching her carefully, "I exist. And you don't know everything, Blaire."

She growls again. "I was the little poster child for supernatural marvels, Laurel. I was dragged around and introduced to a whole host of people who gawked and asked questions, and they introduced me to their marvels in turn. You're telling me you're so unique that not even those collector freaks heard of you?"

"Why do you think I almost ran a dozen times when I realized what you and your brother are?" I challenge. The car is starting to warm up, finally, but the heat can't cut into the deep ache settling inside me. It's nothing I can't handle, and I fight not to show her. "I did everything I could to stay away. I know there are things out there who want me—maybe as a spectacle, maybe as worse. And I won't do it. I've made a good life out of running away, Blaire."

"You didn't run," she murmurs.

I jut out my chin. "No. I didn't."

"You didn't tell me, either," she continues, voice still quiet and laced with hurt.

"This is the first time I've *ever* told anyone," I say. "I've never had to say it out loud before. I didn't know how."

She deflates a bit. "I get it; you're the first person I told, too. I'm not mad, Laurel. It's just—it's literally unbelievable. I've never heard of anything like you, not even once."

"I haven't heard about anything like me either, if that helps." And believe me, I looked. I turned over every stone I could without announcing my existence to the world.

"It doesn't." Blaire shifts the car into drive. "Keep talking. Let's find a place to get you warm."

Despite her order to keep talking, I don't really know what to say. I watch her, hoping for more of a reaction, while she stares intently out the windshield. Maybe I could say she's being extra careful while driving through the pouring rain, but honestly, it seems like she's avoiding me.

But if she needs a minute to process this, then I owe her a minute.

"Where are you going?" I finally ask, because this isn't the way back to her house.

"Hotel," she grunts.

"You live thirty minutes away."

"And you're freezing."

I bite my lip, unsure if I should correct her or not. I'm cold, but not freezing. I can't freeze, not in any way that matters. But if this is what makes her feel more in control, then I'm not going to stop her.

"You're wet too," I say.

"I can't feel the cold," Blaire dismisses. "You can. We should get you warm."

She drives past two motels, both clearly closed for the season. The third one has a swinging *vacancy* sign, and Blaire turns sharply into the lot, parking right in front of the little office. Practically no one else is here.

The woman behind the desk looks at us with pity. "I have a dryer back here, if you want it," she says after handing Blaire a set of keys.

"Thank you," I tell her. "We might take you up on it." Then again, if my clothes aren't dark with rain water, she might see the blood on them. I'd probably be better off throwing these away.

But it's not like I have anything to change into, so we're going to need to make it work.

She gave us the room right next to the office, which means we can stay under the awning and don't have to get any wetter. Blaire looks it over as soon as we get inside, inspecting every inch like she's some sort of forensic expert looking for a clue.

For my part, I grab one of the scratchy towels in the bathroom and start doing what damage control I can.

When Blaire is done checking under the beds or whatever she was doing, she turns to me. "Gimme your clothes."

"I told you; it doesn't really bother me. You can stop thinking of me as fragile."

"But you can still feel it. C'mon. Hand them over."

I don't know how I feel about the first time I strip in front of her being in this context. I don't know how I feel about thinking there will be more times, either. But I take them off, using the duvet off the closer bed to wrap myself up like a burrito. Maybe she was right about how cold I was, after all. This is a thousand times better already.

Blaire averts her eyes and doesn't look at me until I hand her the bundle of sopping wet clothes. "I'll be right back."

It's totally irrational, but as soon as the door shuts I worry she won't come back. Like she's decided I'm too much, and that abandoning me here is her plan to get out of dealing with all the nonsense about me. It's not a terrible plan. Oh, I could make it back home eventually, but I'd take the hint first. I know where I'm not wanted.

Of course, Blaire reappears less than five minutes later, standing in the doorway and staring at me in a way that makes me think perhaps she also worried that I wouldn't be here when she got back.

"I need more, Laurel," she says, shutting the door behind her. "Make this make sense to me."

What a tall order. Still, I have to try. "A witch made me like this. About nine hundred years ago. I'll tell you everything I know, but I don't know much. I don't really know how it happened. I don't know how to reverse it."

"Alright," Blaire says slowly. "You said a witch did it. I've never heard of that, but I don't know a ton about witches. So—start with them."

The witch is the last person on the planet I want to talk about, but I owe Blaire this much. "I can't imagine she did this on purpose," I tell her. "And she has no idea I'm alive. I worked very hard to keep it that way."

"*Had* no idea you were alive," Blaire corrects. "Witches don't live forever; they barely live longer than humans. If this was nine hundred years ago..."

I shrug. "I haven't kept track of her. I've tried *very hard* to stay the hell off of her radar. It's why I leave town whenever I get even a whiff of the supernatural, why I almost bolted when I met you and your brother, why I was so cautious around you all. But she held me hostage so I'd make her a spell for immortality. It required blood, and a lot of it, and she wasn't willing to give her own blood. That's why she needed me; she bled me dry over and over and over again. And it worked on me, clearly, so I could assume it worked on her."

The witch drank that damned spell every single day. And I'd been the one to painstakingly brew it for her. How many times had I been forced to do it?

At least twenty, more than five times what any who came before me managed, according to the witch's old taunts.

I don't say any of that, but Blaire seems to sense that there's something I haven't told her. "What did she do to you?" she asks quietly. "It must've been something, if you've been avoiding her for nearly a millennium."

"She kidnapped me. I was walking home, and then—she took me. And she made me brew that spell for her. Not just me, either—there were others. She cut into me again and again and again, and I bled for her, and the pain—that spell only didn't kill me because *nothing* can kill me. I was forced to give her too much, Blaire. All my blood. My pain. I barely slept. I was with her for over a year and a half." I fight to stay in the moment and not slip away into the memories.

Blaire sucks in a breath, her face pained. "How'd you escape?"

"I hope I killed her," I murmur, this one single memory from back then something I want to hold on to. "I doubt it, though; I don't know fully how the spell was intended to work, but if it's anything like what I somehow ended up with, the wound would have healed."

"What did you do?" Blaire asks.

"I stabbed her. She came to cut another girl up. An ear, I think she wanted, for some spell or another. She came into the cell when I had a knife for cutting my own arm, for the blood, and I took my opportunity." I close my eyes. I've forgotten probably too many things over the years, but not that day. The adrenaline made everything brighter, sharper. The blood more red, the sun outside more bright. The screams of the girl I left behind unforgettable.

Blaire watches me for a moment. "I know very few witches," she admits, "but I've never heard about any magic like that."

"Like you said. You don't know many witches," I point out.

"Well, no. But that's a lot, Laurel. You're saying there's a crazy spell to keep a witch alive forever, but your witch is the only one who knows it?" She shakes her head.

"Maybe," I say tightly, trying to bite back a retort. I don't know why we're debating this when I'm here as living proof.

Blaire seems to be thinking along the same train of thought. "You drank her spell? This is the effect?"

"I never drank it. Never, not even a little. None ever got in my mouth by accident, either. I just brewed it. Twenty times, or thereabouts. She said I lasted the longest. That no one else had survived brewing it so many times, the blood it took, the pain it caused the brewer. I imagine it must've, somehow, already been working in me."

"I don't know much about spells. But I know a few witches. I could ask them."

Even the word *witch* makes my body brace to run. "I'd prefer it if you didn't." I'd prefer never to come face to face with a witch, any witch, ever again, although I don't say it. "I know I don't have the answers, but I can live with what I know. It's gotten me this far."

Blaire laughs, the sound low and rough. "Yeah. Blake and I wondered, you know. Made us a bit frantic, trying to figure it out. You weren't supposed to be *alive*. Humans don't know what you know and live. We've never seen it; it never works. But it makes sense now."

"Does it?" What I am is a lot of things, but I've never described it as making sense.

Blaire leans forward a bit. "I don't know what exactly you are, Laurel, but I don't think it's entirely human."

"Should I be offended?"

"Offended?" Blaire stands up and full-on laughs. It sounds cold; not as cold as the water on the rocks, but cold enough to tighten my spine. "Laurel, I have been working myself into *knots* about falling for a human. I'm not my brother; I can't tolerate it like he does. I don't want to know my partner is going to die and I won't be following them, that our time will be so short. I promised myself I wouldn't, and then there was *you,* and I..." She shakes her head, and starts to pace. "When I saw you, over that cliff, when I jumped down and I could smell your blood and your heartbeat was fading and your whole body was broken and crooked, I wanted to try to turn you into one of us. Which wouldn't be fair, because we hadn't talked about it, and the odds of you even surviving it are terrible anyway, but I wasn't going to give up hope until I exhausted every option because the thought of living without you now is more than terrifying."

She stops pacing and turns fully toward me, reaching out her hands like she wants to touch me before dropping them. I want to reach out to her, to take her hands, but it's like I'm spellbound to this spot, unable to even blink. "Call it selfish. Maybe not being human is offensive to you, I don't know. But I can't describe—I am so *damn glad* that you're going to live." She laughs a little, a disbelieving little sound. "You're going to live, Laurel."

"Yeah, I am," I promise softly after a minute. I stand, making sure to keep the blanket wrapped around me so I don't wreck this moment with nudity. I think my heart might pound right out of my chest, but I wrestle it into submission, needing control over this moment. "I'm not offended, or bothered. I didn't ask for this—I guess you didn't either—but being here with you makes me not mind so much."

Blaire's hands are overheated and a little rough when she grabs me, one cupping the side of my face, one clutching me by the back of the blanket, pulling me into a desperate, hungry sort of kiss.

I kiss her back, eyes closing as I sink into her, her warmth, her taste, the steady sureness of her body against mine. The hand not holding my blanket closed grips her sweatshirt, because there is no way in hell I'm letting her go anywhere now.

Chapter Fourteen

We stop kissing when Blaire's phone alarm goes off. She makes a face, shutting it off while she apologizes. "That's your clothes," she tells me. "Let me go get those for you."

This time, I'm somehow not worried that she'll vanish. I can feel the press of her lips on mine, the taste of her, the warmth of her hands, and I know she'll be back.

She comes back quickly with my clothes, holding them away from her still-wet body.

"Your turn."

She flashes me a grin big enough to show off those too-sharp incisors. "If you wanted me naked, all you had to do was ask." But she goes to the bathroom, coming back out in a towel with her clothes in hand once I'm completely dressed. The towel isn't substantial enough to cover much, revealing pretty, strong legs. I force myself to look away.

I give her my blanket, which she swaps for the towel while I go to start the dryer on her clothes.

Thankfully, I must not have bled too terribly; the stains on my clothes aren't that noticeable, so the nice woman at the front desk doesn't see them and call the cops on us. Either that, or this motel gets way worse traffic than I assumed.

Blaire is sitting on the bed when I get back, wrapped up in the blanket so only her face shows. "How're you feeling?" she asks me. "You're looking better than earlier, but I'm not going to lie; you looked awful."

"Relationship fifteen minutes old, and already insulting my looks," I tease, butterflies flipping in my stomach. Is relationship the right word? How does she feel about that?

She doesn't argue my word choice, but that might be because she's too focused on getting an answer to her question. She raises an eyebrow at me. "I mean it, Laurel."

"I'm fine. I'm always fine," I dismiss, sitting down on the bed next to her.

"Laurel."

The way she says my name makes my heart beat faster. Firm, determined, and entirely focused on me, no one's ever looked at me like this before.

"I'm fine," I tell her. "Just a little soreness, and that'll last for a few hours. Everything else is healed."

"You've experienced something like this before?"

"Not even the first time I fell off a cliff. I always bounce back, Blaire. I promise."

Blaire's next breath is a little ragged, but she nods. "Alright. Okay."

"Not a delicate human you need to worry about."

"No. You're not. Promise it's just soreness?"

"Promise."

"Still nothing to sneeze at," Blaire decides. "You should lie down. Rest, maybe?"

I go completely soft in a way I'm not used to, like my entire body has melted. "I'm going to be fine, Blaire. Besides, if I lie down, you'll have to go get your own clothes, wearing nothing but a blanket."

"I've done worse," she mutters, but she doesn't try to force me to rest. I don't need it; I really am feeling much better.

"Did you call your brother the minute I walked out of the room?" I ask. I wouldn't be mad if Blaire did. I just want to know.

"No. He's with his wife and I don't want Callie to hear something she shouldn't. But please don't ask me to keep this a secret."

"I won't," I promise. "I won't make you choose between us, Blaire. I know he's your brother."

She exhales deeply, relief evident. "We've looked out for each other for our whole lives," she murmurs. "We have been through everything together. I didn't want now to be the time we're not honest with each other."

"Tell him. So I don't have to, please. It was hard enough to tell it once."

Blaire nods. "As soon as I know I can, I will." She pauses for a minute, clearly lost in thought, then, "Do painkillers and that stuff work on you being sore?"

"You don't need to go find me anything. It won't work, anyway."

"No? You sure?"

I gesture to my own face. "You've all noticed. I'm not actually tired, Blaire. Or starving. I just look it, because I've been frozen for nine hundred years. Nothing new affects my body. It'll go away soon." I stop, a thought occurring to me. "Can *you* take painkillers?"

"No. Our blood is different, our organs are different. We won't metabolize any of that stuff correctly." She tilts her head. "I've accidentally drank from a human I didn't realize was high first. I think I might have gotten a residual hit off of them, for a minute or two. It was an experience, I'll tell you that, but it didn't last long."

"Interesting."

Blaire reclines deeper into the pillows. "Let's stay here tonight. Already paid for it. I don't really want to move."

"I have to work this afternoon."

"I think, after falling off a cliff, you should call out."

"I'm fine," I remind her for what feels like the thousandth time. Not that I'm opposed to her asking—it feels nice to have someone genuinely care. But still, it's not needed. "I'm absolutely fine to work. You could stick me in an x-ray machine right now and I'd look fine." Probably. I've never actually tested that; I don't exactly go to the doctor.

She seems unimpressed with that response. "Laurel. Call out. Rest."

I almost argue back, but she keeps watching me, and I don't put up too much of a protest. I don't know if it's her firm tone or the fact that I really do want to stay with her, but it's sounding like a better and better idea. I call and let the library director know I won't be there, and by the time I'm done, Blaire is fully on her back, curled up in bed in such an inviting way that I can't resist joining her.

The blanket we've both used as clothing is slightly damp, but she's warm and I fit right into the curve of her body. She squirms for a minute, to the point where I worry she wants space, but all she does is wrestle one arm out of her blanket cocoon so she can put it around me.

My eyes slip closed. I probably need the sleep, considering all the healing my body did today. And I feel good here, at peace in a way I so rarely do.

When the alarm on my phone goes off, signaling that the dryer is done, I have to persuade Blaire to let me go. "Don't need clothes," she moans.

"And when we leave tomorrow?" I ask.

"That's a tomorrow problem," she murmurs, not even opening her eyes.

"I'll be back in five minutes."

The arm she has around me tightens. "That's not a good deal, Laurel."

I twist around so I can kiss her, hard and quick. Like I suspected, her grip loosens, and I wiggle out. "Be right back!" I tell her as cheerfully as I can manage, liking the way she stares after me, open-mouthed and wide-eyed, as I walk away.

Blaire demands snuggles once I'm back. I make her dress so we can ditch the damp blanket, and then we cuddle until we fall asleep in each other's arms. There's a part of me that wants more. There's a bigger part that's glad for this and doesn't want anything else right now.

***

We fall asleep like that eventually, and I wake up in the morning to discover I'm all alone. I check my phone groggily, seeing five alerts flash on my screen.

The first is from Blaire, time stamped fifteen minutes prior.

> Went to find you some human food.

The second is from Callie.

> Heard you called out sick, you okay?

I respond to that, putting together a half-formed thought about Blaire looking after me. I don't need her to worry.

Then there are three texts from a number I don't have saved.

> What the hell?

> This is Blake, by the way, Blaire gave me your number.

> I'm somehow both shocked and not shocked? Like this is impossible but also explains so much?

They'd all come in in the last ten minutes. I save his number, then respond.

> Should I take that as a compliment?

I drop my phone beside my head, then settle back into the pillows. There doesn't seem to be any real need to be up, not until Blaire gets back with food.

I did it. I told Blaire about what I am and the world didn't end. In fact, it might have even gotten better. My lips still tingle a bit.

Blaire wants to be seen, to not be alone, to have something that can't be taken away from her. And I get it. I really do.

The world always felt unstable. It's a product of running as much as I have; I don't collect too many things, don't bond to too many people, because I know full well that it can be taken away at a moment's notice. And there's still some of that, some lingering worry that this could all be taken away. But it feels more real than anything has in a long time.

It's just a few kisses, I remind myself. Not a marriage. Not any sort of promise.

Still. Blaire said she didn't want a relationship that time could take away. And now she knows that I'm not going anywhere. What does that make us?

Like thinking of her summoned her, Blaire walks in holding a grease-stained paper bag. "Good morning. Please explain why humans like this stuff."

"Is *this stuff* hashbrowns?" I ask, sniffing overly obviously to inhale them. In my defense, I don't have a super nose like she does.

"Apparently."

"Because they're delicious. And you're missing out." One positive outcome from whatever happened to me is that I got to live long enough to taste foods I'd never even imagined in my old life.

"I have to work today," I tell her.

"Call out."

"I'm not calling out two days in a row. I know you latched onto the whole work-from-home thing, but I haven't done that yet, and I don't want to mess up this job." I like being a librarian. It feels like somewhere I belong, and I'm damn good at it.

She heaves a theatrical sigh, flopping onto the other side of the bed and handing me the bag. "Alright, then. Let's get you fed and get you home."

I open the bag to reveal hash browns and an egg sandwich. "Did you talk to your brother?"

"Mhm. He texted you?"

"Seems to think this makes a lot of sense, actually." I bite into the hash-browns.

She rolls her eyes. "Yeah, well. He would. He's been on and on about how you can't exist. And I've kind of agreed with him, to be honest." She eyes the food like it might bite her.

"I'm sure you ate a potato at some point in your life," I tell her. "You know they're good." I pause a moment, then ask, "Why is my existence so weird?"

"I told you: because humans don't survive the concept of knowing us," she says matter-of-factly. She sounds so confident when she says it, too, like there's no room for argument. "They either run head-first into something they shouldn't and get themselves killed, or it breaks their brains a bit. You've heard ghost stories, Laurel."

"They're *stories*."

"And some of them are based in reality. People die from this. Keeping it from humans is in their best interest. It's why you shouldn't have existed—at least, until we learned you're not actually human."

"I don't know what I am. But I feel human." I frown. I've thought about it before, sure. Humans don't live as long as I do, don't heal up from their injuries like I do. But I don't know what to call myself if I don't consider myself human.

"You're nine hundred years old," she reminds me, and that's fair.

I consider all that for a second, then say, "So, we're all putting Callie at a lot of risk then."

Blaire groans, her head falling back. "Why do you think we take such care to keep her from finding out? We know this is serious, Laurel. But Blake fell in love anyway." She sits there for a moment, still as a statue, then admits, "I never got where he was coming from until now. Don't get me wrong, I like Callie. I just didn't get the risk."

My heart flutters like a hummingbird in my chest. That's remarkably close to saying she loves me. She's not, I know—it's way too soon for that. But it's close.

"Well, as you said—I'm not human. So it doesn't apply," I remind her when I get my voice back.

She hums, neither agreeing nor disagreeing. "Eat your food," she says. "If you're going to make me leave you at work, then we have to get you fresh clothes first."

Chapter Fifteen

"You feeling better?" Callie asks, leaning her hip against my desk.

I think she's dressed as a character today, although for the life of me I don't know which one. She's wearing a tutu and has her hair teased out, and somehow, she makes it all look effortlessly natural.

It's jarring being here after everything. She's asking me such a mundane question, but between the last time I saw her and now, so much happened. My life fundamentally changed. And I'll never be able to tell her about it.

I take a second to process what happened and how much I can tell her. "We went out for a hike and I took a spill." That's one way to put it. "I was sore, a little banged up, so Blaire convinced me to stay in bed and take a break. But I feel fine today, I promise."

"Mmm, good. I'm glad. I worried when I didn't see you, you know."

She probably did, because she's a damn good friend. And I am *this*, this thing that invades her life, keeps the truth from her, and piles up more and more untruths every day.

I'm seized by the urge to tell her, but I stop myself. Humans *die* when they know, Blake and Blaire told me. And the look on Blake's face when we'd discussed it, the pain of knowing what he'd backed himself into, loving a human...

If he'd made these choices to keep her alive, then I can damn well stick by them. Even if it hurts a bit.

"I'm fine," I tell her, hoping she doesn't notice the pause. "I always bounce back. Anything interesting happen around here yesterday?"

She rolls her eyes, but leans down conspiratorially. I look around quickly, but all my patrons nearby aren't paying any attention to us. "Oh, you know it. Absolute chaos when the Girl Scouts were here. They're little sharks. I think I bought fifteen boxes of cookies."

"Good ones?"

"Thin Mints only around here."

"Very nice. Save me a box."

"Oh, don't worry. They'll be back next week, and I'm sure they'll get to you then. No one is going to escape their clutches."

I snort at that description, because the Girl Scout troop that meets here are all fourth graders.

"I have to get back. Just wanted to check on you." She steps away from my desk, then turns back. "Come to dinner tomorrow night. I'll tell Blake to call Blaire. Or you can, by the sounds of it."

I flush. I can't help it, not when she talks about it like it's so normal. She can't know how monumental yesterday was to me, to her, to us—to our relationship. But something in her eyes tells me she knows something big happened.

"I'll be there," I say, and she gives me one more knowing look before she walks away.

***

When I arrive at Callie and Blake's house, Blake opens the door and pulls me into a hug so tight I'm worried he'll crack some bones.

I stiffen. He's never touched me before, and he's not being mindful of his strength right now. This is weird, right?

He must realize I'm not hugging him back—I don't think I could move my arms even if I wanted to, with how tight his hold is—and he lets me go.

"What's that for?" I ask, rolling my shoulders to test my movement.

"You've made my sister really happy," he murmurs. "She cannot shut up about you."

I can feel the burn of my face flushing and try to school my expression into an unimpressed look. "Because I'm sure you've been the model of restraint for the last few years."

Blake laughs. "Fair enough. It's payback. And I'm damn happy for it." He takes the bottle of wine I brought with me. "Thank you."

"I haven't done anything."

"You've changed Blaire's life." He hesitates, then looks around. He must be looking for Callie, because he only starts talking once he sees she's still out of earshot. "She's been fine. Just kinda going along, you know? But not living, not really. And you've given her something she never found anywhere else."

It's sweet, but I deliberately don't think that I'm going to live forever, and Blaire will live forever, and Blake will be the one who is left alone someday. And really, given the span of our lives, that someday isn't too far in our futures. Callie has *maybe* seventy years left, if life is exceedingly generous to her. That's nearly a third of Blake's life so far. It's barely a fraction of mine.

"Trust me: it's all mutual," I tell him. I'm definitely not bringing any of that up. I look closely at him, trying to see if there's any sadness in his expression, but he genuinely looks happy for his sister. He's really living in the moment, focusing on the now, just like he told me does that time we talked.

"Stop hogging my girlfriend!" Blaire calls from the kitchen.

Girlfriend. Is that what we are? She says it so easily, and it makes my heart beat faster. *Yes.* I want that. I like the way that sounds.

"Yeah!" Callie echoes.

"We're coming," Blake calls, rolling his eyes.

Blaire is standing over by the kitchen table, like she can stay away from the food if she tries hard enough. She really, genuinely, is disgusted by it and can barely hide it. She must truly love her brother to keep coming to these dinners.

I give Callie the wine, stepping up next to her to see what she's cooking. "Ravioli?"

"Mhm. I made it myself!"

That'll make this interesting. "Need any help?"

"Go help your girlfriend set the table, since it seems like she's forgotten how."

Blaire is standing there with a pile of plates, napkins, and silverware on the table, so I walk over and begin to set it out properly. "Hey," I murmur.

"Hey." Her voice is a little deeper than usual, slightly husky, and it sends a shiver down my spine. *Fuck.* I want her. I want to spend time with her. As much as I enjoy Callie and Blake, I wish we were at the cabin, just the two of us.

Her hand trails over my lower back as I bend to place a plate at the far side of the table. Clearly, she's thinking the same thing.

Blake clears his throat pointedly, and my whole body shoots straight. Right. We're in his house.

Still, he's the one who *just* said how happy he is that his sister is happy. He can't get mad when we act like it.

"I think Blaire can handle setting a table," he says.

Blaire didn't seem to twitch at all when her brother turned his attention to us. She slides her hand from my back to around my stomach, pulling me back toward her in a way that has me biting my lip. This isn't fair. We need to be somewhere alone.

I shouldn't have gone to work yesterday. I should have let her convince me to call out a second time, so we could have had this all day.

"I think it's a two-person job," Blaire informs him, fingertips digging into my stomach in a way I didn't know would be hot until I experienced it. *Fuck.* "And I don't think you get room to judge."

"Making ravioli might also be a two-person job," I offer, because seriously, I need a minute here, and I could do without him watching us.

"Yeah, come help me with this," Callie tells him, even though I'm pretty confident she doesn't need any sort of help right now. Still, he goes to help her, no doubt taking his own opportunity to feel her up. As soon as he turns, Blaire pushes me up against the table.

"Hi," she says again.

"Hi." Does my voice sound breathless?

"Come back to my house tonight."

"Sure thing." Do I have to work tomorrow? Yeah. Is the drive going to be so much longer if I'm all the way at her place? Absolutely. Is that going to stop me? Not a chance in hell.

There's some sort of echo in the back of my brain repeating that this is *forever*. Not that I'm saying Blaire and I will be together forever—it's way too early to assume anything like that—but it's that we *could* be together forever. I've never had a relationship like that before.

I've probably never had a real relationship before, honestly. Just little dalliances, distractions when I was lonely. People I cared about, absolutely, but no one I could let myself get that close to. I had secrets to protect, after all.

But not here. Blaire knows all of it, and she's still here. Blaire will stand the test of time. I can let her in in a way I haven't been able to for anyone else.

I can't say it's forever. But I can say that it feels real in a way I'm not used to.

The table is set. Callie isn't one for fancy place settings, so there's really no excuse to keep fiddling around with it. I straighten fully, stepping out from where Blaire's boxed me in, but give her a long look while I walk over to help get food on the table.

The raviolis are chewy in a slightly off-putting way, but they're not terrible. Callie did a good job with the filling, at least. Five minutes into the meal, I see Blaire give her brother a firm look, and he reaches over to squeeze Callie's hand, drawing her attention while Blaire surreptitiously slides half her food onto my plate.

Goddamn. Now I have to eat it all, and quickly, or else Callie will notice. I'll have to remind her that I don't need to eat either, not really, and I'm not going to be her human garbage disposal for the rest of our lives.

I shovel two raviolis into my mouth before Callie turns back around.

"Baby, tell them about next weekend," Blake tells her, still stroking his thumb along the back of her hand.

"What's next weekend?" I ask, pushing the remaining raviolis around my plate.

"Our fourth wedding anniversary," Callie says. "I'm thinking of a small party on Friday night."

Blaire sets her fork down, clearly grateful for the distraction. "It's been four years?"

Blake gives his sister a hard look. "Yeah, Blaire. Four years."

"Damn." She says it so flippantly that I have to suppress a laugh, but I know she's being serious. Time feels different when you get older.

But I see the way Blake is looking at Callie, all soft, dewy eyes, and think he found a way to slow it down for himself. He's holding and cherishing every moment with her.

"So, a party?" I prompt.

"Yeah. Friday night. Our anniversary is technically Saturday, so we're going to go away for the weekend. There's a nice little cabin we're renting; it'll be lovely. But Friday, we're going to have some people over. I'm assuming I'll see you both?"

The way she says it gets to something in me. It's the expectation of it, the casual way she assumes I'll be there. I've known her barely any time at all, but Callie clearly sees me as someone so ingrained in her life that she doesn't even think of me not being at her party. I wasn't at that wedding four years ago, and I've only been in the most recent moments of her life. But she still wants me there.

I look around the table. Blake, Callie, and Blaire. This is the most comfortable I can ever remember being in my too-long life. This feels like *home* in a way I never knew how to define before.

"Of course we'll be there," I say. "I wouldn't miss it for the world."

***

After dinner, I drive to Blaire's house, following her car down the remote roads until at last we're alone together.

The woods are alive with noise, chirping and rustling, our footsteps crunching the leaves underfoot. Somewhere above us, the moon is nearly full. I can't see it, and didn't see it when I was driving here, either. I just know. It's one hell of an internal clock that I never wanted to develop.

"What do you get someone for their fourth wedding anniversary?" I ask Blaire instead of sharing where my thoughts went. She holds open the door, and I walk inside, taking in the little living room that looks exactly the same as when I left.

"Why would I know that?" she asks, plopping onto the couch. "Blake's never been married before, and I pay attention to very few other people. Besides, aren't you the researcher here?"

"I'll look it up." There is probably some sort of etiquette book on the subject I can find at the library tomorrow. I kick my shoes off, then sit on the other end of the couch, swinging my legs up. Blaire tugs them into her lap.

We're silent for a minute, and then Blaire murmurs, "Four years."

"That hard to believe, huh?"

"It's going too fast." The whimsy of a few minutes ago is gone. "I know she's still young, but every year is one year closer to the end, and he's not going to handle it well. I don't—I worry about him, Laurel. It's not easy, but there are ways for a vampire to die, and I'm worried he'll take one." Her eyes close for a second. "We keep in contact with a few people from our world. More so lately, now that Blake's looking for magical ways to mimic aging. And I know they all think this is some passing fancy of his, that he'll love the time he has with her and then get over her. But he won't."

I squeeze her hand that's still on my ankle, not knowing what to say. It's not an unfounded fear. She knows her brother better than anyone on the planet, but even I can see it in his eyes; Callie is the love of his life.

"You'll have to be there for him," I say, then decide to take the risk. "We'll have to be there for him." It's presumptuous to think I'll still be around, but then again, I'm not going anywhere. I'm Callie's friend, and I'm their friend, too. Even if at some point, I'll have to leave Callie's life—I don't have any mystical vampire mesmer to help her not see that I never change—that doesn't mean I'll ever forget her.

Blaire squeezes my leg. "Did you ever have siblings?" she asks, voice a little hoarse.

"I had three sisters. I never got to find out what happened to them. I hope they lived long lives." I hope they lived any lives; my memory of the time *before* is admittedly dulled by distance and pain, but I remember a lot of hungry nights and lean days.

"I'm sorry."

They're people I grieved centuries before. Blaire is grieving something that hasn't happened yet, but that looms in front of her, practically inevitable. I don't know which one is worse.

"We'll go to their party," I tell her softly. "And celebrate them, because they're happy. And we'll let them be happy. For as long as they can."

"Yeah. For as long as they can," she echoes.

Chapter Sixteen

I don't go home after that.

I go to work, but I turn around right after and come back here. We don't talk about it; there's nothing to talk about. I just do it.

We sleep in the same bed, hold each other close, tease and talk, and we kiss like we can't believe the other is real sometimes. Nothing else yet.

I think we're both still a little stuck on the *believing this is real* thing. But it doesn't matter; we genuinely have all the time in the world.

Blaire clears her throat while I eat the protein bar she must have bought for me while I was at work that first day. There's been a box here, without any comment, but she pushes it toward me until I eat every morning. For someone who hates all human food, she sure is a mother hen about it.

"Yes?" I ask, swallowing a bite.

"Blake and I are going to get blood tonight."

I do some quick math in my head. "Isn't it a little earlier than usual?"

She shrugs. "Not by much. And he and Callie are going to do their long weekend, so this makes sense."

"Of course." Of course it does. Here she is, buying me protein bars when I have a strong suspicion she's never stepped in a grocery store in her life before meeting me, and I'm barely thinking of her getting her needs met. I'll have to be better about that. "So... I should stay at my place tonight, then."

Blaire nods, but there's something in her eyes. She hesitates, then offers quietly, "Unless—did you want to come with us?"

I pause and consider it. It's an offering and I know it. I highly doubt Blaire's ever invited someone to this type of thing before.

It's blood. From everything she's told me, she and Blake have a system that's relatively humane for this, but still. Blood.

I don't think Blaire understands exactly how much blood can hurt me. Not like a human who faints at the sight, but the soul-deep, burning ache, the memory of the worst pain I ever felt, again and again and again—it comes back to me every time. I told her the witch made me bleed, but I didn't go into too much detail. It hadn't felt relevant.

If I say I don't want to go, then she won't say a word. She'll probably never bring it up again, and this will be a *thing*, some sort of permanent barrier between us.

No, I'm not doing that. I'm not going to put something between us, not when we're trying to build something on the premise that we're the first people *ever* in each other's lives that require no barriers. I'm going.

"What do I need to bring?" I ask her, crumpling the protein bar wrapper in my tight grip.

"Do you own club clothes?"

***

I do not own club clothes. I've never, in my very long life, owned anything even approximating club clothes. And Blaire's clothes are never going to fit me. Even with her still being relatively short, she's solid muscle everywhere that my body is sunken and thin.

So I end up leaving work, driving for thirty minutes to the mall, and buying my best approximation at clothes that'll blend in at a club.

I end up in skin tight jeans with the thighs ripped to shreds for some reason, a shirt that barely qualifies as one, and boots that thud when I walk in them. I try hard not to sound like I'm old in my day-to-day life. Just because I was born before most humans can fathom doesn't mean I have to sound like it. But

100

I know I sound like a grandmother when I think to myself that I don't really *get* what the kids are into these days.

When I make it to Blaire's cabin again, she's waiting on her little porch, completely heedless of the cold. She's dressed not too dissimilar to me, except for in place of the flowy cropped top I have on, she's wearing something that qualifies as little more than a bra with her leather jacket over it.

And suddenly, I get the point of these clothes. Forget the grandmotherly thoughts; I'm fully with the youth on this one. She looks *good*.

She looks like someone I want to beg to stay home with. Judging by the way her eyes flick over me, she might be thinking something similar. "That's—you had that?" she asks.

"Went shopping today," I tell her, walking up to the porch. "So, how does this work?"

"We drive to the club, go in. If you get a drink and give me half an hour, I'll be done and we can do whatever you want."

Half an hour. Is that all it takes? "Alright. I can handle that."

She gives me a sharp look. Fuck. Shouldn't have said *handle*. I'm going to have to watch my mouth.

I can *handle* it. It doesn't sound like I'm going to actually have to watch her make anyone bleed, and regardless, this isn't the past. This isn't what happened to me.

She stares at me for a minute before she says, "I'll drive," so I follow her to her car and press my thumb into the scar on my palm, feeling the phantom pain there again.

Blake gives Blaire an unimpressed look when we walk in. "Your thought was, what, *I like the girl, so I should make her watch me flirt with someone else?*" He turns to me. "Callie told me like six times about the new book she's going to be reading with a glass of wine tonight. Wouldn't that be a better use of your time?"

It might, actually. But I need to be here tonight. This is something that I need to see.

"Shut up, Blake," Blaire says, all faux pleasantness despite her cutting words. She turns her full attention to me. "How do you feel about posting up near the bar?"

I feel like I'll get knocked over in that crowd, so it's maybe not the best idea for me to fight my way through. And it's not like I need a drink, either. "I'll get a table," I tell her, scoping out a few standing tables at the edge of the room.

She looks at me for a long moment, then nods. "If you want to go home, or leave, or anything else, then get me. No harm, no foul."

But it would be harm, because this is literally her sustenance, and if she can buy fucking protein bars for me, then I can sit in a too-loud club with too many bodies for a half hour.

Blake checks my shoulder as he walks by. "Sit back and watch the show, Laurel. You'll be fine." Then he fades off into the crowd, joining the thrum of bodies.

"You're okay?" Blaire checks again.

"I'm fine." Mostly. This isn't on her to solve, and I *will* be fine.

And if they're coming to clubs like this and not triggering mass panics and urban legends, then it's clearly a pretty subtle thing. No one is bleeding out here tonight.

"I'll be back," Blaire promises, and then she joins her brother in the crowd.

I keep an eye on her, watching that jacket dodge through the crowd. It's a damned good thing she doesn't truly experience temperatures, because I can't imagine wearing a jacket that heavy in the sweating, writhing mass of people here.

I might see Blake, once or twice, but he slips in and out, insignificant in light of what I'm really watching, what I can't take my eyes off of.

Blaire can *dance*, apparently. Can dance well enough that a half a dozen people around her notice too, and give her their full attention.

I don't know what her criteria is—maybe she looks for a scent, or something in their eyes, or maybe it's random—but Blaire chooses one of them, a man, and draws him in.

I can't see Blaire's face, but I can sort of see the man's face through the chaotic darkness. He's wide-eyed and captivated, like Blaire is suddenly the center of his whole world. Like she's gravity, drawing him in.

I imagine Blaire's eyes are sparkling a little brighter than normal, that mesmer pouring off her in waves. The man bends to it easily, unable to do anything but watch Blaire and nod at whatever she's saying.

Someone brushes past me to get to their table, and I curve my body away, trying to keep space for myself even when I don't move my head an inch. I have a show to watch.

The man nods after a few moments, and Blaire's fingers walk up his shoulders, and then her arms wrap around his neck.

My whole body tenses, the muscles in my neck tightening. This must be it. So far it has been easy, tame even; things people don't want to see their girlfriend doing, unless they know it's all an act, but nothing disturbing. But surely the actual act of drinking blood will bring about some stronger feelings. I'm bracing myself for disgust. I'm hoping I can push down any fear.

The scar on my palm aches, memories of twenty cycles worth of blood pouring from it plaguing me. If I could bury them, I would. I don't begrudge Blaire her blood, but I can't let the past go.

And then Blaire leans in, mouth going to the man's throat, and any onlooker would think it's a kiss, a tease, nothing more. He tips his head back and stops dancing, and Blaire's hands go to his back, supporting him. I hold my breath.

And then, barely a minute later, it's over. Blaire pulls away, and the man blinks at her. He seems confused, but that's definitely not pain on his face.

Blaire holds him for an extra moment, likely until he gets his feet under him, and then turns away from him.

I blink, my attention divided between the human—still a little uncoordinated but seemingly no worse for wear, and even beginning to dance again with someone new—and Blaire, who is moving throughout the crowd, clearly looking for a second target.

Nothing about this feels like I expected it to. This isn't fear inside me, that's for sure. I watch Blaire dancing through the crowd, light on her feet and quick, touching a person here and there, looking into eyes, then moving on, looking for something specific.

She finds another one, a woman this time, and it's clear Blaire is supporting her entire weight as she drinks, the woman's hand fisted in the front of Blaire's jacket, as if to keep her from leaving.

Blaire breaks away after a minute, holding the woman up until she's steadier, and then she looks over at me. She finds my eye, and my breath catches. Her eyes are sparkling just as much as I thought they would be, her gaze intense.

She smiles wickedly, doing something to my damned heart. I half expected to see blood on her face, but of course there's not, not a single wasted drop.

The clawing in my belly from earlier is gone. Instead, it's replaced by something else, something warm and heavy that makes me want to keep watching.

So I smile and raise an imaginary glass, as if I'm toasting her.

Blaire nods, and begins to make her way closer. She takes her time about it, working her way through the room, still looking for one more target. I wonder if I should be offended by that. Most people probably would be, if their girlfriend looked at them like that, and then went to go stare deeply into someone else's eyes.

The feeling I'm experiencing isn't anger, though, or fear. No, it's definitely not that.

Blaire finds someone in the crowd again, another woman, and this time I can clearly see Blaire's face, the tilt of her head, the look in her eyes that makes me lean as far forward as I can.

And then she leads the woman over closer to me, one hand on the small of her back, and never drops my eyes. I swallow, and refuse to look away.

She even has the gall to *smile*, slow and mischievous, as she leans in, latching onto the woman's throat. I can't hear her, but I can see the woman's mouth fall open in what I can only imagine is a moan. Apparently being bitten and having your blood sucked out of your neck feels really fucking good.

Blaire keeps eye contact the entire time, even as she pulls away, even as she supports the woman for an extra second, even as she gently nudges her on her way.

And then she walks over toward me.

"Come here often?" she teases, voice low, and I snort, the spell broken. I shove her in the arm.

"Fuck off," I say, but I can't help grinning. Blaire's smile shifts, less seductive and alluring but no less powerful.

"Are you done?"

"Nice and full."

"Good for you. Think Blake will mind if we leave now?"

104

She looks across the room, and I think I see her mouth move, but I don't hear anything. Fucking vampire hearing. "I told you we could leave whenever you wanted. Let's go."

I don't think I'm entirely imagining the stares on us as we walk out—Blaire clearly made quite the impression on people tonight. But I couldn't care less. Her hand is drifting from my lower back to my ass, her warmth pressed into my side. We're both thrumming with an undeniable energy.

She might come here and do what she has to do, but she's walking out with me. And I don't want anyone to forget that.

There's something electric about it all, about Blaire's grip, about the swagger she has when she walks, about the eyes on us. And I can't take my eyes off her either, looking up at her as we push past the crowd and walk out the door.

The night air is cold, but I ignore it, instead turning to Blaire. I step in her way, halting any movement, and grab that jacket by the lapels like I've wanted to all night.

Blaire turns and pushes me against the wall of the building, leaning closer. Her grin isn't the seductive, practiced one she wore inside, that she wore for other people. No, for me, she smiles a little goofy, a little hungry, and I can't resist for another moment.

Blaire presses her whole body to mine, leaning into the kiss, and it feels like if she doesn't kiss me, she's worried she'll die. Like she needs this, like this is as life-giving as the blood was. My body thrums in response, a hum under my skin that feels like it's going to explode its way out.

Blaire breaks away for a minute, kissing the corner of my mouth, then my jaw, and finally along my cheekbones. "Is it the blood or the way you've been seducing people all night that's making you so hot for it?" I dare to ask, words biting off in a moan as Blaire bites at my jaw. She doesn't break skin, and it's really the barest little nip, but I suddenly understand completely why all those people folded under Blaire's touch. I tilt my head to the side, inviting more.

"It's you," Blaire says, breath fanning across my face. "Watching me like you have been." Her hands come up to grip at my hips, dragging me closer. I move easily, rocking my hips into her. We're out in public, pressed against the wall of a busy club. It's cold and the alley we're in smells a bit like piss. None of that matters. Nothing could take this away from me.

105

A little thrill shoots through me, sitting in my chest and expanding, warming me from the inside.

Blaire deepens the kiss, moving one hand on the wall and one into my hair, her knee working its way between my thighs. I rock against it, helpless to resist.

I break away to laugh a bit—I can't escape the realization of how *young* some of the people we just saw are, and here we are, ancient by all comparisons, acting like teenagers. Blaire doesn't even seem to hear my laugh, instead kissing down my neck.

I go still. I saw Blaire bite three people, and she went for the neck every time.

Blaire must notice. "Relax," she murmurs. "I've already had my fill." But she takes her lips off my neck, trailing kisses along my jaw and back to my mouth. As soon as her lips are gone, I relax back into her, letting her thigh support my weight. "And I won't bite you. I promise."

I release one of the lapels on that damned jacket to get a hand on Blaire's already-bared stomach, then make my way up to play with the band of that sad excuse for a shirt. I want to touch her, to know her, to *have* her. I want pieces of her she hasn't given me yet, to know I was here, to know I matter to her more than any of those people inside.

"You're shivering," Blaire murmurs near my ear, her breath a tickle that sends shivers down my spine.

"It's cold out here," I reply, pushing my hands flat against Blaire. "And you're warm." I drag my nails over Blaire's skin. "Even more than usual."

"It's the fresh blood. Does that."

"Mm. Fun vampire fact. Are you going to tell me facts or kiss me?" I don't care about vampire facts right now. I care about her hands, her mouth. I care about her warmth in an entirely different way.

Blaire sighs before she leans in, tugging me into another kiss, softer this time, more gentle. It might feel like an ending, but the way her hands are on me, I don't think that's what it is. "Maybe somewhere less cold. I don't want to find out if you can lose a finger to frostbite."

"Haven't yet."

"And you won't tonight either."

I let Blaire pull away from me, albeit reluctantly. If she wants to go somewhere else, I'll follow her. I'm beginning to think I'd follow her anywhere. "Fine, killjoy. Take me home, then?"

Blaire takes my hand, despite her previous insistence that it's cold. She doesn't seem to mind anymore. "Sure thing."

Chapter Seventeen

I keep my hands to myself in the car, not wanting to find out if those enhanced reflexes are good enough to keep a car steady. Crashing a car would delay me in getting what I want tonight.

"You okay?" Blaire asks quietly, completely misreading my silence. Or maybe not misreading it, but needing some confirmation.

"I'm great," I tell her. Then, after a second, "I want to be home."

She steps on the gas a little harder. "Soon."

Blaire barely parks the car before I have my seatbelt undone and the door opened. I start walking toward the house, but she catches me before I make it five steps, lifting me around the waist quicker than I can even process.

Strong arms grip my waist, then slide down to my ass. I lock my legs around her instinctively, and she carries me like it's nothing. I make a mental note to ask if the fresh blood in her system makes her stronger, but the thought is chased from my mind when she slams me into the side of the house, inches from the front door, and then her mouth is on mine again, causing my mind to go entirely blank.

"I thought you said you wanted to have sex inside," I whisper when she pulls back. I have one hand on her face, fingertips stroking along her jaw, but I cup her chin and make her look at me when she starts trying to kiss down my throat again.

"Frost bite," she says, as if in a daze and remembering the concept exists now. "Right. Yeah. We want to avoid that."

"I need to know that you know that no one is getting frostbite outside in this weather, when there's not even any snow on the ground."

"Well, we'll never find out for sure, because we aren't going to test it," Blaire says. She steps away from the wall, still keeping me perfectly supported.

"Fuck, you're strong."

"You're too light."

Probably. It's not like I can do anything about it, though. "Blaire. Take me inside."

She doesn't need any more encouragement, shifting so she's holding me up one-handed while she fishes out her keys from those skin-tight jeans, then unlocking her front door and letting us both in.

I expect her to put me down on the couch, but she skips the whole main room and beelines directly for the bedroom, dropping me on the bed while she stands, eyes raking over me and taking me in.

Here. Real. I wish there was a way to reassure her without outright saying it, but I know exactly how she's feeling.

"Blaire—" I sit up on the bed, needing her, but she's still frustratingly out of reach.

And then she's on the bed with me, my hand on her jacket and hers on my waist, sliding slowly under the stupid shirt I'm still wearing. I shiver.

"You make me crazy," she tells me, voice low. "I'm fucking starving for you, Laurel."

Starving. Maybe it shouldn't sound that good, not after I literally just watched her eat, but it sends a shiver down my spine nonetheless. I'm fucking starving for her too, hungry for more.

The fingers under my shirt have discovered that I didn't bother to put a bra on—it's not like there's much there for a bra to hold—and her blunt nails momentarily dig into the skin of my ribcage. "Laurel—"

I slide her jacket off her shoulders. It's definitely served us well, but I need it gone for what I have in mind. Maybe I can convince her to wear it to bed some other time, but for tonight, I want to see her.

The jacket pools around her elbows, stuck there while she won't stop touching me. She's stroking my skin, feather-light and slow, a tease of a touch that creeps higher and higher—and then back down. I have no doubt she can hear the way my breath catches, backing off again and again to see what it does to me.

"Blaire—"

She shifts her weight onto her hip, kneeling slightly closer to me now. "Yeah?"

"Did you have plans to do this tonight, or—"

Her grin is sensual, and slow, and shows off her too sharp teeth. "Patience, Laurel," she murmurs. "Haven't you heard that good things come to those who wait?"

How long have I been waiting? A few hours? Or is it the last few days, or the weeks since I met her? Or nine hundred years, looking for a person who's *real* in a way I've never had?

I don't argue with her, though. Something tells me she'll just go slower.

As if to reward me, Blaire pushes up my shirt, moving it up, up, up, until it's around my head and then gone, leaving me bare from the waist up.

"Fucking gorgeous," she tells me, although honestly it sounds more like she's talking to herself, reverential and quiet.

I feel it, though, even if she isn't saying it to me. Under her eyes, I feel happier with myself than I ever have been. "Blaire—take your jacket off." I hope it comes off like an order, something she'll actually do instead of teasing me further. I'm looking for a little parity around here.

She lets it drop off her arms, discarding it on the bed, leaving her lean stomach bare, her breasts barely covered by that shirt that might as well be a bra. I take her in, eyes hungry and finally invited to look their fill.

"Gorgeous," I tell her, needing her to hear it, too. Then I lean forward, one hand on her belly, the other on her shoulder, and I kiss her jaw, then down her throat, across those stark collarbones, and down to her breasts, kissing what I can reach without taking that bra off.

Her breathing is getting heavier, her chest moving with each inhale under my lips. One of her hands finds my hair, pulling it loose and then twisting it up in her fingers. She tugs lightly, probably inadvertently, but I groan.

"You like that?" she whispers, like it's a secret and anything that disturbs the moment might break us. I get the instinct, but honestly I think we could get struck by lightning right now and not get distracted. A train could crash through the living room and we wouldn't stop.

"Mhm." I suck at her skin, nipping at it with my teeth. She won't bruise and I know it, but that doesn't stop me from trying to leave a mark. She tugs on my hair again, experimentally, like she's cataloguing results. I groan when she tugs, leaning into it.

"Laurel," she rasps, her free hand coming up to trail along my bare back, feather-light touches snaking down my spine, "I want to—please tell me I can—"

"We still have our damn shoes on," I tell her, which is what comes out when I intend to tell her *yes*, and then tell her to get me naked as quickly as possible.

She gives me the ghost of a smile. "Well, we'll have to fix that, won't we?"

My boots have a convenient zip on the side, so I have them off and tossed across the room quickly, but Blaire has to actually unlace her combat boots, so I sit back and wait, popping the button on my jeans while I watch her.

When she finally has her boots off, she starts to work at her pants, unhooking the button fly and revealing another tantalizing strip of skin.

"Let me—" I reach for her, and she lets me brush her hands away, stroking each inch of revealed skin while I work her pants past her hips.

Her thighs are soft as silk, and I wonder what it would feel like under my mouth instead of my fingertips. I let that thought win, leaning in to kiss her thigh when I have her pants worked down past her knees.

"If you keep doing that, we'll never get anywhere," Blaire grits out when my lips trail higher, closer to the black panties she's still wearing.

"I consider this getting somewhere," I tell her, not lifting my head. She shivers from the brush of my breath, and I want to do that over her clit.

She's still too dressed, between her bra and panties and the pants she hasn't quite managed to kick off yet. Half of me is in a rush to get her naked. The other half is too busy enjoying the way her breath hitches when I use my hand to push her knees slightly wider.

"You're a menace," she accuses.

"And you're wet for me, aren't you?" I ask. It's a guess—I don't have any supernatural senses, and her panties are dark enough that I can't tell—but it's an educated guess.

I haven't done something like this in so long, and it's never been like *this* before, so open and honest. I've been hungry, I've been needy, and I've been scratching an itch for company—but I've never wanted like this before.

I want to know if she's wet for me. I want to be a menace who makes her clench her thighs and grab my hair.

"So fucking wet," she agrees, spreading her knees of her own accord. "Laurel, baby—"

"You had your mouth all over a ton of people tonight," I interrupt her. "It's my turn."

She moves her hand from my hair to my chin, tilting it up so I'm looking at her. Her look is intent, like she's trying to figure out how serious I am about that.

I'm dead serious about having my mouth on her. I'm less serious about my complaint about who she's had her mouth on; I just want my turn.

"Alright," she concedes. "Have your way with me, then."

I plan to. I plan to make her scream so she can't even string a thought together. And here I have her, laid out on her bed, thighs already spread for me.

I trail both hands from her knee to her hip, slow and light, watching her shiver. She stares at me like she can't take her eyes off me, which is gratifying even if my attention is primarily on my hands.

I lean down, getting comfortable between her thighs, and run my nose from her thigh across her still-covered pussy.

She smells delicious, and she's definitely wet. I can feel it soaking into the fabric, the wet, welcoming invitation practically calling to me.

Well, fuck. Who am I to ignore it?

I reluctantly pull back enough so I can work her panties down, drinking in the sight of her like a person in the desert dying of thirst. She's fucking beautiful, a sight that would make an artist weep. Her dark hair, neatly trimmed, frames the pretty pussy she shows me when she spreads her thighs wider.

"Beautiful," I tell her, because she deserves to know. And then, without giving her another moment, I lean in to have a taste.

"*Fuck me*," she curses, and I'd tell her that I absolutely plan to, but my mouth is busy, tongue tip teasing at her clit while I use one hand to press down on her lower belly, holding her in place for my tongue. She tastes delicious, and when she lets out a little whimper, so at odds with everything I've heard from her before, I know I can't stop until I've made her come all over my face.

"That's it," I whisper after a particularly loud moan, voice caressing right over her folds, which sends her cascading into another moan. Her pleasure is a loop, feeding me so I feed it right back into her, pushing us both higher, higher, and—

The angle isn't right. She's getting close, I can feel it, can feel it in the way she bucks underneath my hand, but she's not there yet. She's been teetering on the edge for several minutes, and while that sounds like a fun idea for later, right now, I really want to feel her come.

I give her a finger, sitting up as I slide into her wet, warm heat. She whines again, reaching for me. "Two seconds," I promise her, feeling her clench around my finger as I use my free hand to reach for a pillow. She figures out what I'm doing and raises her hips so I can shove it under her, leveraging her up in order for me to get back to work.

"Come for me, Blaire," I murmur into her pussy, finger still inside her. I turn back to her clit, returning to the same rhythm I had before, and put my hand back on her stomach to hold her exactly where I want her.

I'm not an idiot; I know Blaire is a thousand times stronger than I am. I'm not really holding her anywhere. But she lets me move her and position her, trusting me to give her what she wants, and that's a heady feeling.

It takes two particularly firm sucks and a slight crooking of my finger, and then Blaire is bowing up, her warm, wet come soaking my face as I keep going, doubling my efforts so I can see her through it.

She pushes me away, and I'm gratified to feel her fingers shaking as she shoves. "Laurel—"

"Why'd you stop me?" I ask, moving like she asked but not going far. Her soft thighs are wet now, glistening, and I'm tempted to start the process all over again, to make her make a real mess of this bed.

Blaire growls, low and threatening, but I chuckle. "Because, smartass, I still don't have you naked. And I want that."

Who am I to argue? I wiggle my jeans off, cursing myself for deciding to buy the tightest pants possible. Most jeans fall off my hips after I unbutton them, but I have to work these down my thighs.

"Fucking pretty," Blaire murmurs, leaning forward to see me closer. I know for a fact that her vision is a thousand times better than mine, so this *old lady who needs her glasses* routine is definitely a ruse, but it brings her closer to me, so I'm not going to protest.

And then I'm in the air before I know what's going on, once again hoisted up like a sack of flour. "Blaire!"

She squeezes my thigh, hoisting me higher and encouraging me to wrap my legs around her. "Just because I'm not fucking you in a freezing, dirty alleyway doesn't mean I won't give you the full experience."

I want to ask what that means, but then she's pushing me against the bedroom wall, sliding me down until I'm straddling her thigh again, just like I was in the alleyway. I whine, the pressure too good, too perfect. "*Fuck,*" I hiss out, rocking slowly against her thigh, chasing that feeling.

Eating her out made me desperate for it, and I'm so fucking close. I've been worked up since the club, since I watched her dance around, seducing people while watching me, and I'm hungry for it now.

Like she can read my mind—or maybe she's still thinking about the club, too—Blaire leans in and kisses the corner of my mouth, then down my jaw, and finally to my neck.

I freeze, not moving an inch. I stop my hips. I think I might stop breathing altogether. Her lips are poised on my neck, barely brushing the skin. She freezes when I do, and we hang there, suspended.

I don't know how I feel about this. I don't know if it's good or bad, if I want it or I need her to stop. I don't want to bleed—I've been forced to bleed plenty, and while I know I can handle the pain, I hate the idea of it. But I remember the look in her eyes, the way she moved out on that dance floor. Maybe I want to be a part of that.

"It's okay," she whispers, cutting straight through my thoughts. "I'm not going to bite you." She backs up, and I still don't know how I feel, but I know

I don't like her moving away from me. I grab her shoulders, refusing to let her move too far. "I don't need your blood, Laurel. I don't want it; you've bled enough. I just need you. I won't touch your neck again."

"You can—" I begin, but she must hear my uncertainty, because she shakes her head.

"No. Absolutely not. The humans I drink from, they never know it's happening. It doesn't hurt them. It would hurt you. Maybe not physically, although honestly I don't know—if you resist my mesmer, maybe it would. But I can feel how tense you are." She grins, wicked now. "The point is for you to be less tense, baby. Otherwise, I'm not doing my job right."

"Blaire—"

"Shh," she says, and then slowly, tantalizingly slowly, pushes her thigh against my cunt.

"*Oh*, fuck," I hiss. She's clearly done with the conversation, and I'll decide how I feel about that later. Right now, I need her to make me come.

She leans back in, using her body to press mine to the wall, caging me in. I melt against the wall, against her thigh, losing any control I might have had left of my body.

"Next time we go to the club," she says, voice low and intense as it shivers down my spine. I like that she's assuming there's a next time, that this is something we'll keep doing. "I'm going to make you dance with me. Going to pull you close and get you hot and bothered on the dance floor, then pull you into a corner and make you come right there, see if you can be quiet enough that we don't get noticed. What do you think? Think you can handle that?"

Oh *god*. I can barely think, my body on fire as I rock against her thigh. I don't know if she'd actually do that, but I do know she could. She could absolutely make me come like that. I close my eyes, picturing it. She'd tease me on the dance floor, back me into a corner, and then slip her fingers into my pants, and—

"Ah, ah," she scolds. "Watch me, Laurel."

She's going to kill me. I open my eyes, watching her intense stare watch me back. Her dark, too-bright eyes seem to stare right into my soul. In this partially dark room, they almost seem to glow, and what would have terrified me a few weeks ago is somehow even hotter now.

"You're close." She says it like a statement, like it's just a matter of fact, and she's not wrong. "Come for me, Laurel. Get there."

I grind against her thigh, chasing that high, and when Blaire moves one hand from my hip and gives me her fingers to rub my clit on, I can't hold back anymore, spilling over that edge like a dam broke.

I ride her fingers and thigh, chasing the high, riding the aftershocks while sparks fly behind my eyelids. I don't know if I make sound or not, but I do know Blaire does, a low, approving hum that somehow sends my pleasure even deeper.

When I finally stop moving, Blaire carefully lowers her thigh, giving me space to breathe. And then she raises her fingers to her mouth, sucking them obscenely, tongue tantalizingly teasing over each digit like she absolutely needs to get every single drop.

"Better than blood," she rasps, voice low and wrecked in a way that makes me want to go all over again.

The hand still holding me up tightens on my hip, which is great, because I'm not one hundred percent sure I can stand. I test it, grounding my toes into the floor, and when I'm reasonably assured my balance is steady, I step forward, crowding back into her space again.

I trail my hands up her stomach, up her chest, across that stupid shirt that's still on, and then around the back of her neck. "Is that all you got?"

She clutches my hips with both hands. "Oh, baby, you have no idea," she promises, voice low and wicked, and I shiver, waiting for her to show me what she's got.

Chapter Eighteen

E verything is slick with blood.

My hands, the knife, the cauldron, the floor. Blood stains every surface. Most of it is mine, although I'm sure someone else's blood is mixed in too. There's a nagging thought in the back of my mind that someone died here, and recently, but I can't think of who.

Lots of people die. The witch kills a ton of people, treating all of us like expendable spell ingredients, and it's just some weird quirk that means I've survived this long. How many months is this now? I can't remember. Too many.

It's so cold in here. I don't remember it being this cold—isn't the fire lit under the cauldron? Did it go out? My heart races; if I let that fire die, if the spell fails—well. I don't know what she will do to me.

Blood starts pouring from my hand, the sharp ache of the wound ripped open tearing through me. I frown, looking down at it. Did I cut it open? I don't remember cutting it open.

"It's nearly time, pet," a soft voice croons, making every muscle in my body tense like nails on a chalkboard. *Her*.

But when I look up, it's not her face. This isn't the witch who's tormented me. I can't place it, can't figure it out—

Like a bell ringing in my brain, Blaire's name comes to me, and I force myself awake, heaving and panting as I sit upright.

I can't breathe. I can't fucking breathe, there is no air in this room, and everything hurts. Is this what dying feels like?

There are arms around me. It takes me a second to realize they're warm, and they're helping to chase away the chill.

Blaire, again. My brain starts to slow down, actually processing what's going on. This is Blaire holding me, warm and strong and smelling like the simple, fresh soap she uses. It's not back then. *I'm* not back then.

It was just a nightmare. A miserable, awful nightmare, and my brain is cruel to me. I grip Blaire's arm, needing to chase away the dream and the cold.

One of her hands strokes my back, moving up and down in slow, soothing motions. "Baby…"

"Nothing," I manage to say. "A nightmare."

"Laurel—"

"Nightmare," I re-iterate. "I get them sometimes, Blaire. I'm nine hundred years old. It'd be weird if I didn't."

Her arm tightens around me, and I sink into the squeeze. "Are you okay?"

"It can't hurt me." I'm okay. I'm *fine*. I haven't been there in nine hundred years. If the witch is still alive, she's been far, far away from me for a long time now.

"Not what I asked."

That stops me short, and I take a deep breath. Blaire cares about me. If that wasn't obvious enough last night, or in the last few days, it's becoming more and more apparent now. Blaire cares, and I owe her something for that.

But not the truth. I'm not going to tell her I saw her face. That can go with me to my grave.

It's not her fault that blood-drinking apparently triggers something in me. She didn't do anything wrong, and here my brain is, shoe-horning her into the worst moments of my life.

"I'm cold," I admit, because it seems a safe place to start, and she's always so damned worried I'm going to freeze or something.

"Are you okay with me getting up? I'll turn the heat up."

I nod, and try not to overreact when she lets me go.

She comes back what could be two minutes or two hours later; I'm not really in a position to keep track. But either way, she wraps me in her arms again, holding me close.

"Do you think you can sleep again?" she asks.

I have no idea. I want to, though. Sleeping in her arms sounds nice.

"I want to try," I tell her, expecting her to lie back down to get her rest. But instead, she pulls me into the cradle of her arms and rubs my back, the slow, methodical, soothing movement lulling me back to sleep.

***

When I wake up with the sun shining in my face, I'm torn between the two realities. One, I had an ugly nightmare that would be better forgotten. And two, Blaire and I had sex last night.

The thing about my immortality is I never get the pleasant, achy soreness after good sex. I never had sex before what happened to me, so I don't have a point of comparison, but I've read enough books that assure me that I'm missing out on the feeling.

No soreness. No hickies. Blaire even brought us both a washcloth last night, so there's essentially no proof at all of what we did together.

No proof, that is, except the vampire who is still on top of me, her heavy arm pinning me to the bed like she's worried I'd flee while she slept.

"Blaire—"

"No," she says firmly, face pressed into the pillow and voice muffled. "Wake me in two hours." When I squirm again, she groans and squeezes me tighter. "You don't even need to go to work today. You were up half the night. Fucking sleep, Laurel."

All that is true, but we do have that anniversary party this evening, and we haven't even bought a real gift yet. Not that I want to go shopping at six-thirty in the morning, but we don't have all day.

And besides, after everything last night—the good and the bad—I kind of want Blaire again. If I've lost all reminders of having sex with her, then I'd like a few more, for however short a time I get them.

I snake out from under her arm. She grabs at me ineffectually, and I can't tell if she's letting me go on purpose or if she's really that tired this morning.

Well, I know a way to wake her up.

"Shame you're still sleeping," I tell her, laying across her back, stroking the skin of her side with one hand while I press kisses to the back of her neck. "We could have had some fun."

She moves before I can even process it, flipping me onto my back and hovering over me. "What'd you have in mind?" she demands, and I grin.

***

When we're done, I'm the one who wants to go back to bed, but Blaire has remembered both our agenda for today and her weird obsession with feeding me food that she finds disgusting. She looks at the eggs she apparently bought like they might be radioactive, but she pushes me to cook them and keeps nudging me to eat.

"Once again, not eating won't kill me," I remind her.

"Not dying isn't a high bar," she shoots back. "Eat your damn food. If you can come with me and watch me eat last night, then I can put up with the noxious smell of those eggs."

"You have to have eaten eggs before."

"Yeah, well, it's been a while." She rolls her shoulders and neck, like she has to shake out soreness I know for a fact that she doesn't feel. I wonder if it's a holdover, a habit from when she was still human that's still stubbornly holding on.

"About that, actually—" Blaire begins.

"About eggs?"

"About last night," she clarifies. "We got a little distracted—"

"Is that what we're calling it?"

"Smartass," she accuses. "We got *distracted*, and I didn't really get to ask you—were you okay with that?"

We're both thinking about the same thing, when I froze last night when she put her mouth on my neck. I want to brush it off, dismiss it as nothing, but I doubt she'd let me get away with it. We both know it's something.

"I'm not scared of you, Blaire," I tell her, because I think that's the most important thing for her to hear.

"But you're scared of being drank from?" She says it clinically, almost detached. There's no judgment, and I don't think she's trying to form a plan of how she can drink from me. Even though that might be easier for her than going to clubs and finding people on a regular basis, I don't think she's even imagining a future where she drinks from me.

It's slightly reassuring, but I feel the bristle of annoyance inside me that I *still* need this level of care. Blaire is a good person. Blake is a good person. They're vampires, and that doesn't change that fact. Why am I sliding all the way back to the fear I had when I first met them?

"I don't think I can properly explain how much blood the witch took from me," I tell her. "Over and over and over again. It didn't stop. And I try not to let it get to me. I bleed, I heal, I know how it goes. But sometimes—well, sometimes I remember."

That's putting it mildly, but I don't want to put a finer point on it. I can handle this.

"Laurel—" she swallows. "I'm sorry."

"You didn't do anything." If nothing else, I need her to know that much. "It's in the past. And I'm not *scared*." I feel like a child even as I'm saying it, but it's true. I don't know what I am, but I'm not scared of her.

I don't want to keep having this conversation, but I know she's probably not going to drop it entirely. "Last night, when I offered you my blood—you said you can't mesmer me."

"It doesn't work on you," she agrees, nodding slowly.

"Can you not drink from someone without it?"

"I mean, I could. Just like you *could* take a bite out of a live cow. But I'm puncturing someone's neck with my teeth, Laurel. It hurts. I much rather be able to anesthetize them to the pain."

There's a story in there and I know it, an experience she doesn't want to remember. I don't push. "You know I don't feel pain the same way a normal human does."

She stares at me. "Laurel, are you really asking why I *didn't* bite you? I think we can both safely agree that it would have been a colossally bad idea, given everything. Also, you do fucking feel pain; don't lie. You heal faster, but you feel it first."

Damn her. We haven't been together long enough for her to read me like this. "If I could feed you—"

"I don't need you to fucking feed me," she snaps, but the sharp tone of her words is contrasted with her sliding her chair right next to mine. "In case you didn't notice, I have a pretty strong system. Blake and I figured it out, because we had to. You don't need to save me, Laurel. I don't need you there if it's too hard. You don't have to suffer for me."

Well, fuck me. I blink, letting that sink in. "Alright," I tell her quietly, processing that.

My hand aches like I ripped the cut open all over again.

"Eat your breakfast," she murmurs. "We can talk about this later."

Blaire makes me eat every bite. We don't talk, and I worry that I've somehow broken things between us, but I don't think I have. Blaire doesn't change how she acts, anyway.

***

After I finish the damned eggs, I look up what we should get for an anniversary gift. It turns out, the appropriate anniversary gift for a fourth anniversary is flowers.

We go out and buy a giant bouquet of flowers. And then Blaire adds a five hundred dollar gift card to some resort up the coast to encourage them to go away again, this time to the beach.

When I raise an eyebrow at the gift card, she shrugs. "I make decent money," she says. "Cyber security software actually pays well. And besides, what's the point if I don't spend it on Blake? Giving him more moments with Callie is important."

That's sweet, and incredibly thoughtful, and I'm sure Blake will get that aspect of the gift even if Callie doesn't understand it.

I'm holding the bouquet of flowers while Blaire negotiates doors for me, opening the car door and then getting the front door of Blake and Callie's house.

We're not late, but we're certainly not the first ones here. There's a rumble of conversation, different groups talking over each other.

"What a crowd," Blaire mumbles. I almost want to ask her who's here—and if any of them are supernatural—but it doesn't feel like I should ask that with humans around.

It's funny, because two months ago if I ended up in a party with supernaturals, I'd chew off my own leg to get away. But now, I trust Blaire to protect me if it's needed.

And then I hear a laugh and every muscle in my body locks up. I'm rocketed back in time, blood and pain and the sure certainty that things would never, ever get better—

It's like the flowers fall in slow motion. I look through the mess, and sure enough, there she is. Slight. Blonde. Almost elfin, with a pointed chin and nose and a regal air that hides a monster underneath.

I don't think. I don't pick up the flowers, I don't hide behind Blaire, I don't come up with an excuse.

I just run.

Chapter Nineteen

When I stop, it's because my legs physically give out. I'll be alright in a few minutes, but this level of exhaustion means I ran hard.

I don't know how far I went. I don't know how long I've been running. All I know is I left all of that so far in my rearview that I'll probably never see it again.

Wherever I am, there's a lot of snow here already, soaking into the knees of my pants and chilling me. North, then. I must have run north.

I *trusted* them. I trusted them with my life. I thought there was goodness in the world, that I could find someone like me. That I could have someone who really knew me, who knew the secrets and would be able to survive them beside me. But no, because they know that witch. Not just know her—they casually invited her to their home.

Callie couldn't have known better, some distant part of my brain reminds me, but I honestly don't have it in me to care. It's like my insides have been scooped out, leaving me hollow. I have nothing left to give.

I lie down in the snow. Might as well; it's not like I have anywhere else to go. I can't go home, and I don't have the energy to find a new place to go yet. Here is as good as anywhere.

The snow is falling harder now, heavy sheets landing on me, burying me under it. The cold shock of snow is almost a relief, and I close my eyes.

I don't know how long I lay there. Losing time seems to be something I'm doing a fair amount of, but why bother trying to fix it? What does it matter?

I should move again, because it doesn't matter how far I've gone; it's probably far too easy to track me. Do they care enough to do that?

My gut sours. Was this all a plan to lure me back to her? It would have been ridiculously overelaborate, and there were probably easier ways—but still. I can't shake the thought from my head.

Pushing myself up out of the snow bank I've apparently entombed myself in, I shake the snow off and look around, trying to get a clue to where I am.

Snow, and trees. If I look up, I can see the moon, and the sight of it sends my heart racing.

If I've started going north, then I should keep going the same way, put more distance between me and them.

Blake and Blaire have both proven that they have exceptional noses. I'm not an expert at evading trackers, but I can think of a few ways to dilute my scent. The mud clinging to me from sleeping in a snow bank is probably a good start.

I probably look like some feral thing, but I really can't care right now. Maybe I am a feral thing; maybe this is what's left when you pull back my attempts to act like I have a home.

I pick the direction I think is north, and I start walking.

***

I walk for days. The sun rises and sets, the weather changes, and I keep on moving. I'm not even sure where I am, because I've been avoiding towns. At this point, everyone is a potential threat in my brain, and I don't know how to turn that off.

They're her *friend*. They invited her to their house; they laughed with her. How long have they known her?

Did Blaire put it together? Did she know that her witch and mine were the same? Did she keep a great poker face when I had that awful nightmare and talked about what she did to me?

If she was that good of a liar, then I'm an idiot. An idiot and a fool.

Maybe I won't ever know the answer. It's not like I can go back and ask, not if the goal is to never see any of them again.

That fucking hurts to think about. For once, leaving wasn't a persistent thought at the back of my mind. I began to truly believe that I could stay. That I belonged somewhere. And it hurts like hell to give that up. But I'll push through it, because what else am I supposed to do?

Tears track down my cheeks as I keep walking, freezing to my face. It's never hurt this much to leave somewhere before. I've lost friends, and I've given up homes I loved. But I'd always known when it was time to go. Not this time, though. This one hurts so bad that it's almost the worst pain I've ever known.

My stomach is twisting, eating itself, but I don't let the hunger stop me. I can be hungry. It doesn't mean anything in the long run. Nothing about my body—not hunger, not exhaustion, not aching muscles or my fucked-up heart—matters in the long run.

***

I'm once again in a snowbank, exhausted, unable to even keep my eyes open another second. It's like my body's quit, like I can't handle any of this anymore.

And when I fall asleep there, I dream.

I dream about Blaire. Of sitting on the cliff over the ocean by the lighthouse with her. This time, there is no storm, no driving wind or biting rain. The air is warm and the sea breeze a soft caress against my skin. It's the summer we never got to have.

I've wrapped my arm around Blaire's waist, letting my hand caress her hip, and Blaire leans her head onto mine. "We should stay like this," Blaire murmurs, and I hum in agreement.

The sun sets around us, lighting the ocean up vibrant reds and oranges, and we don't move even as the moon rises above us. I can smell the salt, hear the waves. Mostly, I feel Blaire's warmth and weight against me, feel her solid, real, there. Something I can hold onto. My heart beats faster.

And that's when I wake myself up from the dream, cold and lonely and decidedly without Blaire as I dig myself out from this snowbank. I'm simultaneously chasing the heat of the dream and repelled by it. That's a fantasy, and one I can't get back.

Why'd they have to know the witch? And how could I have been so wrong about them? I've considered myself a pretty good judge of character. I've had a lot of practice at it, after all.

So that leads to the question; how did I get tricked so badly? Was everything they said to me a lie?

How did it even work? I picked that town. I moved there. If they were luring me in on the witch's behalf, they got luckier than anyone could possibly hope.

And Blaire—she'd been truly shocked when she learned about what I am. She was shaken, and I'd believed her when she said she hadn't known something like me was possible. Maybe she's a really good liar, but that doesn't seem right either.

But she's a vampire. And she's flat-out admitted that vampires can do that mesmer thing that she does to the humans she drinks from. And she said it doesn't work on me, but how can I trust anything she says?

No. That's not true. Because I know the one time she tried to do it on me, I felt it, and I felt it fail, that day in the library before we were being honest with each other. Unless that was also a very clever ruse, then the mesmer doesn't work on me.

This is all too confusing. I pull myself to my feet and start walking, picking a direction at random. I'll think better if I'm moving, or at least that's what I'm telling myself.

If Blake and Blaire were working for the witch, there were a ton of earlier times to retrieve me for her that didn't involve waiting until the party. Even if they genuinely didn't know what I was until I fell off that cliff, there were still plenty of opportunities. I followed Blaire right into that club, after all. I was alone with her so many times. It would have been easy.

But that's not what happened. My head spins, unable to put it together.

The only explanation is that I'm missing something. Maybe they don't know. Maybe they have no idea that their friend is the same person who tortured me long before they were ever born. Maybe this is all somehow some giant, cosmic mix-up.

But *why was she there?*

Blake invited three people to his birthday party, three regular guys who he knows from work. They were probably there again at the anniversary party, although it's not like I got a chance to look around. But it's kind of telling that he invited three humans that he barely knows. Blake and Blaire aren't the type of people to have many friends.

Didn't Blaire tell me that, after being shown off like prized pets when they survived their transformation, the two of them had withdrawn from most of the supernatural community?

Does that make it better or worse, I wonder? On the one hand, maybe they don't know the witch well at all. On the other, maybe she's such a close, personal friend that she's an exception to the rule.

This is driving me crazy. I can't do this, can't keep wondering if it was real or not. I either have to let this go, or—

Well, I either have to let this go, or I have to find out for sure.

Everything in me rebels at the thought. I've lived all of my very long life honing the art of running away. Why fight the danger when I can simply avoid it altogether? I've left towns and budding friendships behind without a single thought for far less than what I saw at that house that night.

But Blaire—well. She's Blaire. And that might be what makes all the difference.

***

I mull it over for two days. I walk, and walk, and walk, muscles exhausted, stomach twisting with hunger, and still I can't get the damned thoughts to leave me alone.

Blaire, who held me after that nightmare. Who cradled me and cried when I fell off that cliff. Who would make me eat eggs even though everything about them was repulsive to her. Who refused to drink from me because she could tell without me having to explain—without me even fully understanding it myself—that it would trigger something painful in me.

That Blaire wouldn't betray me. And that Blaire wouldn't lie to me.

My mind made itself up, and I know I'll never be able to let this go. If I run now, I could start a new life. I could find a home, a job, a semblance of purpose—it's not like I haven't done it hundreds of times. But I'd never be able to forget Blaire, and this, and wonder what it all means.

So I'm going back.

I won't be a complete idiot about it. I won't walk back into town and go back to my apartment. I'll try to be subtle, to see what I can see before I announce myself. Honestly, if I could remember Blaire's number, I'd call her and make her come to me, somewhere away from town and everything she knows.

Fucking cellphones. Turns out, I'm fine after sleeping in a snowbank. The cellphone, not so much. Modern technology has come so far just to be so limited.

I could just turn around and start walking back, but there are problems with that plan, too. For one thing, I have no idea where I am, which means I have no idea how far back it will be. For another, I'm sure I look like some sort of creature who rises out of a swamp to eat children, and that isn't exactly a good way to stay inconspicuous.

So I find a pond, break the thin ice on it, and dip into the frigid water, holding steady as my teeth chatter and extremities freeze. This is going to really put to the test whether or not I can get frostbite.

Once I've deemed that enough of the mud has sloshed off, I haul myself out, and then, shivering, find a tree to sit in, trying to warm myself up while I wait for my clothes to dry. It's a rather futile process—I guess ice might technically be considered *dry*, but it's not much of an improvement—but at least I'm not coated in mud anymore.

It's time to figure out where the hell I am. I start walking again, finding the nearest town and making my way through the streets.

I go to where I always go; the public library will have everything I need. The sign tells me the name of the town, and then a quick Google search tells me where the hell that is. Like I suspected, I walked into Canada at some point, but I am surprised by how far west I managed to get. I'll have a hell of a walk home.

Well, it's not like I have money on me. I'm not booking a flight, that's for sure.

I do some casual research on the best way to get home—although it's not like search engines are equipped to give great walking paths across hundreds of miles across international borders for a person more than capable of navigating hostile terrain. I'm interrupted in my efforts by a librarian slowly sliding into the seat next to me.

"Hi," she says, voice gentle, like she thinks I'm a cat about to spook. "Do you need any help?"

I think of what I must look like; clothes worn down by the elements, and river water on its own never got anything clean. I bet I still have dirt on me, and although the ice definitely melted in this warm building, it's not going to take a genius to figure out that I've been sleeping outside. Paired with my usual sickly demeanor, I'm sure I look a fright.

I look like the type of person you ask if they need help. I look down, embarrassment coloring my cheeks. *Fuck.* My first human interaction in who-knows how long, and this is what it is.

She's kind. She means well, too, and I know librarians. If I say I need help, she'll have a list of services ready to contact with me before I can blink. But I can't do this right now.

I shake my head, willing her to believe my half-hearted denial.

"Are you hungry?"

I am. I haven't eaten since the eggs at Blaire's place. And I *know* I can go perpetually without food, but that doesn't mean it's pleasant. Walking back into town has been like waking up, returning to feeling human, and the hunger claws at me.

She doesn't seem to need an actual response from me. She's gone before I can blink, and then back with what I'm sure is her own lunch.

"Take it," she murmurs.

I manage to summon words, speaking for the first time in who knows how long. "You're not supposed to eat in the library."

She gives me a smile, seemingly delighted by my response. Maybe she's delighted I talk at all. "I think we can make an exception. Go on, eat."

I could eat a horse right now, but I don't need all her food. I open the container and mentally portion the salad in half, sticking the plastic fork she hands me in what I'm now seeing as *my half*.

It's gone in what feels like seconds.

"Keep eating," she tells me, but I shake my head.

"I shouldn't. I'll get sick." That's a bold-faced lie, but I don't want to eat more of her food.

"Can I call anyone for you?" she asks, accepting the container back when I offer it to her.

Oh, if only. It'd be so much easier if I could borrow a phone and be done with this.

I'm memorizing Blaire's number when I get back. Modern technology made me complacent, but no more. I'm going back to old-school habits and memorizing every phone number I come across.

If, I remind myself. *If* I can go back. *If* she's not in league with the witch.

I remember I was asked a question, so I shake my head. No, she can't call anyone for me. If only it was that easy.

I look at her properly for the first time, taking in the freckles and kind eyes. "Thank you," I tell her. "For everything. But I got what I came here for." And more. This gentle reminder that people are *good* might be exactly what I need.

The worried look on her face doesn't ease. "Are you sure?"

"I'm sure." I swallow. I wouldn't usually give more information, but it feels right to tell her, somehow. "I'm going home." Nothing has ever felt more right than calling it home. I fight to temper that expectation. I have no idea what's coming, after all.

I don't ask her name, even though a part of me desperately wants to. I don't give her mine, either. She'll just be the kind stranger who checked on me and fed me when I needed it.

I gather my things and leave the library.

***

This time, I count the days. I walk with more of a purpose, too, moving consistently in the right direction and with a sense of urgency. It still takes me two weeks to get back.

I dip in a stream again, trying not to look like a monster covered in mud. My teeth chatter for hours as I keep walking, refusing to lose time for anything.

I debate getting clothes, but I'd have to steal them. I've done it before, and while I'm not an exceptional thief, I've had enough practice to know that I could get away with it. But that would involve stopping.

It's like I have some sort of homing beacon when I get close enough, because I find the cabin with unerring accuracy. It's about midday, so Blaire is probably home, working. I cautiously peer through the window.

Blaire is there. She looks the same, really. Same soft skin, same short hair, same intense gaze. I know her body is like mine, in the way that time changes it very little. But even so, there's something off about her. Something leaner, something slightly frantic.

My heart skips. Is that because of me? Did she miss me?

Her eyes shoot up from her computer screen, and my heart freezes in my chest. *Fuck*. Did she hear my heartbeat, or did she scent me? It doesn't matter either way. I need to decide if I'm ready to see her, and fast, because—

The cabin door fling open, and then I'm like a deer caught in the headlights, completely frozen under her gaze. And just like that, I know I won't be leaving. There will be no regrouping, no coming back later.

Blaire crumbles in front of me. Her legs wobble, and she clutches the door like it's single-handedly holding her up. Her eyes rake over me, again and again, like a woman desperate to believe and reluctant to let herself be fooled.

"You came back." Her voice is hoarser than I remember.

"I did," I agree. Now isn't the time to mention that I don't know for how long I'll be here.

"Can I—will you—come here. Please," she croaks.

There should be a part of my brain that's reluctant. There should be a part of me that worries. After all, I ran hundreds of miles away because I was worried she was turning me over to my worst enemy.

Maybe it makes me a fool, but all that is gone. There's just Blaire, and here and now, and I don't want to be away from her for another second.

Chapter Twenty

Blaire walks me into the cabin like she's afraid I'll disappear, touching me the whole time.

Her touch feels electric. Like sticking my finger in a light socket, like grabbing a bolt of lightning—the circuit has been closed. It hurts, but it's good.

"Laurel, baby," she murmurs, touching my hand, studying my fingers. She hasn't looked me in the eye since we got inside. "You need—what do you need?"

So many things. A shower. A meal. Sleep in a real bed. But answers. Mostly, I need answers.

There's no good way to ask this, so I just do it. "Do you know her?" I demand.

Blaire's eyes dart up to me for a second before she looks back at my hand. "Who?"

"The witch. The witch who your brother invited to his anniversary party," I bite out, the pain of it all coming back now, like a fresh wound all over again.

I'd felt so safe, so ridiculously safe for the first time ever. And they'd pulled the rug right out from under me.

"There were a couple witches there," Blaire says slowly. "And I didn't exactly stay at the party, so—give me a little more, Laurel. I'll tell you if I know them."

"Blonde," I say, voice whip-sharp. "Taller than me, shorter than you. Pointy little face. Angelic. Likes cutting people open for horrific spell ingredients."

Blaire blanches. "Laurel, are you—what are you saying?"

133

She knows what I'm saying. "Do. You. Know. Her?" I demand, words sharp and staccato.

"Madge? I—sure. I met her a few times in the last couple years. I told you, Blake's been looking for ways to artificially age himself; she's one of the witches he went to, and I went with him to vet her—what does she have to do with anything?"

My lungs are so tight I'm shocked I can get any air at all. A spell. They've been planning to buy a spell from her, and who knows who died to make that spell. Someone always dies for it. If I learned nothing else from my time with the witch—with *Madge*—then that's it. Someone else always suffers.

But through that panic, I can discern one other thing. Blaire isn't lying to me, or at least, I don't think she is. She's a better liar than I've ever encountered if she is.

"Blaire," I say, putting as much feeling into her name as I can. It feels good to say it, grounding in a way I can't quite describe, but it still hurts in a strange way. "She's the one. She's the one who did this to me."

Blaire looks me in the eye again, perfectly still for a long moment before she shakes her head. "She can't be," she says. "You said you stabbed her. Killed her."

"I said I *hoped*," I nearly snarl. "But I was a weak, starving, *dying* human thing and forgive me for not succeeding against an immortal."

She's still shaking her head. "I told you; witches aren't immortal. They don't live that much longer than humans. She's dead by now, Laurel."

"And I told *you*," I snap, impatient now, because why doesn't she understand the gravity of this? "She made me brew a spell for immortality. She's been hurting people to keep herself immortal this whole time."

"For nine *hundred* years?" she asks skeptically.

"Apparently, if she's now selling spells to your brother." I'm a ball of tightly coiled rage, and it's not all necessarily directed at Blaire, but I can recognize that she's taking the brunt of it. "Call your fucking brother," I demand. "I want to know what he knows. I want to know where she is."

I don't know what I'll do with that information, exactly. Stay far away from her? Kill her? Both sound impossible. But if Blake knows something, then I need to know it too.

Blaire considers me for a long moment, and then nods slowly. "Alright, Laurel," she murmurs. "Whatever you want." It's too calm, too placating, and that somehow feels worse against all my anger and sharp edges.

She dials her brother and doesn't even bother with a greeting before she snaps, "Get here. Now." She doesn't wait for a response, so confident he'll come without any explanation at all.

She puts her phone on the table, sliding it closer to me like she needs me to see it, like she needs to keep everything in plain view of me.

"He'll be a little while," she says. "Do you want to—I don't know. Do whatever you need? Shower, food, change of clothes?"

All three things sound heavenly and critically important. "I haven't showered in a while," I admit. I refuse to count my dips in icy streams.

"You know where the shower is. Feel free to borrow any of my clothes," she says, and I feel her eyes on me the whole way to the bathroom.

When I emerge from Blaire's bedroom wearing sweats I cuffed five times and cinched the drawstring as tight as it will go, she's sitting in a kitchen chair she dragged to right outside the bedroom door.

I raise an eyebrow. "Afraid I'll run again?"

"The thought had crossed my mind."

It had crossed mine, too. I'd like to think I won't bolt, though. For one thing, there's no sense in going anywhere until I have the answers I want. For another, even just a shower and a change of clothes has made me feel more human, more grounded. Running off with no plan again is sounding less and less appealing.

"I can put your clothes in the wash," she offers.

"I think they're better off being burned."

She gives me the ghost of a smile. "You said it, not me."

"I'm sure you could smell it." Honestly, looking back, it's slightly surprising that she ran *toward* me when she smelled me instead of running away.

"You've been outside this whole time?" she asks instead of answering.

She knows the answer without me saying it. "Running away requires, you know, *running*."

"So you haven't been eating, either," she surmises, springing up from her chair. She moves away, although she doesn't stop looking at me.

"Not in a bit," I admit.

She rifles through one of the cabinets. "Blaire, you know I'm fine—"

"No," she snaps, the most emotive I've heard her since I've been back. "Goddammit, Laurel. You are not *fine*. I don't care why you ran, alright? We'll sort it out and find the truth when my brother gets here. But for now, you're going to do the bare minimum to take care of yourself if it fucking kills me."

I freeze, then accept the protein bar when she hands it to me. "Everything else went bad," she mutters, not looking at me again. "Eat your fucking protein bar."

I do as she asks. I'm a little afraid to see what would happen if I don't.

Not that I think she'd hurt me or anything. Even when I worried that Blaire was conspiring with the witch, the theoretical plan always fell apart because I couldn't picture her hurting me. She went through so much trouble to *not* drink my blood that night when it would have been so easy for her to do so. I would have let her, and we both know it. A person who intends harm doesn't take care of someone on that level.

But I worry what will happen to *her*. She seems like she's a breath away from collapsing entirely, and if I were in a better place, I might stop and deal with that. I might take the time to help her, to ease her fears. Unfortunately, I can't be that person until this mystery is solved.

***

By the time I finish the food, Blake's headlights are shining through the windows. I stiffen. Either this man knows who he colluded with, or he's had the wool pulled over his eyes in a colossally fucked up way. He let that witch near his wife.

My stomach twists into knots when he knocks on the door.

He doesn't wait, opening it, and flicking his eyes back and forth. "What the fuck, Blaire?" he demands, and then his eyes land firmly on me. "You're back?"

That's anger in his voice, cold and sharp, and I flinch back from it. I think, given everything, I'm the one with grounds to be angry, but apparently he's found something on his own to be mad about.

"I'm back." I keep it short and don't offer any additional information. He owes me some first.

"After what you put us through—after making Callie cry, after making Blaire go out of her mind—that's it?"

Oh. I get it now, where this anger is coming from. I made Callie cry, and for him, that's an unforgivable sin.

It's pretty bad in my eyes, too. I never meant to hurt either any of them.

Fuck, *Callie*. I've been so caught up in my own fears that I haven't thought of her, but I left her in that house with a witch who chops up humans with no protection. I did that. If she got hurt, that'd be on me.

Blake doesn't act like she's been hurt, though, at least not physically. But I made her cry, and that's enough of a crime.

"Blake," Blaire says, voice soft but firm. "There's something we need to ask you."

"And you," he says, rounding on his sister. "Letting her back in. Acting like she didn't hurt you."

Blaire ignores his outburst, an admirable feat given that it's shaken me to my core. I did that. I hurt them all.

"The witch at your party. Madge. Where is she?"

"How should I know?" he tosses out, crossing his arms and leaning against the door. "It's not my job to keep track of people. She's just someone I might hire some day."

"Then give me her phone number," Blaire insists. "Let me track her down. You know I can."

Well, that's a skill I didn't know she had. "You can?"

"Just because I'm not supposed to use the software I design doesn't mean I can't," she says, not looking away from her brother. "I wrote it; I can work it. Assuming she didn't break her fucking phone like you did."

That is... oddly disturbing, but I'm not about to quibble about privacy laws right now.

"Why does it matter?" Blake demands. He turns to me. "You're not seriously saying you came back because you need a witch for something?"

"I've never in my life needed a witch," I say with more venom than is perhaps warranted.

"Blake," Blaire says firmly. "Madge. Give me her number so we can put this to rest."

"Put *what* to rest?"

"Laurel thinks—" and I don't miss that, don't miss that this is my belief, that Blaire clearly doesn't agree, "Madge is the witch she knew nine hundred years ago. The same one who made her like this."

"That's not possible."

"You've both said, and yet neither of you are the one who nearly died twenty times to help her brew a damned immortality spell."

The room gets very quiet with that pronouncement. "Alright," Blake acquiesces. "We'll look into this. And then we can talk about how you're going to make this up to my wife."

I bite my lip, because he's not wrong, but I can't even begin to think about that until we know where that damned witch is.

"Phone number," Blaire prompts her brother, and when he gives it to her, she types on her laptop for a few minutes. Blake stares at me the entire time his sister is looking at the screen, like now it's his job to make sure I don't bolt.

A restless, frenetic energy rises underneath my skin, and I can't name it. I'm scared, but not so scared I want to run. I'm not running away from the witch—for the first time, I'm running right toward her. What I'll do when we find her, I'm not sure yet.

"I know where she is," Blaire offers quietly. "Or her phone, at least. I have an address."

She looks at her brother for a long minute, then looks at me. "You don't have to come," she offers.

A part of me is relieved to hear that. A part of me wants to seize the opportunity and stay far away. But what's the point in sending them otherwise? They don't believe me. They're not malicious about it, but they think I'm somehow mistaken, that this is some reaction blown greatly out of proportion. And if I don't go and show them the truth, then I might as well leave again.

"I'm coming," I tell her, lifting my head and hoping she can see the determination in my eyes.

She nods slowly. "Alright. Let's go, then."

Chapter Twenty-One

I know what they're both thinking, They're thinking that this is a cute little house and that there's no way an immortal, immoral witch lives here. They're thinking that when we finally arrive at this quiet, cozy cottage a few miles off the main road, I'll realize how wrong I've been.

And I admit, it's kind of a setback. When I was younger, she hadn't put up such a nice front about where she was living. Maybe nice homes were in shorter supply then. But that doesn't mean that I'm in any way unsure.

I know who I saw. I know who she is and what she's done, and I've had nine hundred years to dwell on all that.

"Let's see, then," I say, moving toward the door. There's no car here, and when I get closer, I can see the dust on everything through the windows. She hasn't been here in a while. Something in me eases. We're not looking at a confrontation today, then.

The door isn't locked, and I let myself in, taking in the dust and musty scent of the room.

The cellphone is on the counter. Blaire's eyes latch onto it as soon as she follows me in, eyes narrowed. Her posture tightens, and I think she might finally be beginning to believe me.

"Something smells off," Blake announces.

"No shit," I say. "She hasn't been here in ages and left her phone. Not a totally innocent thing to do."

But he's already shaking his head. "No, like—Blaire, tell me you smell it, too?"

She takes a jagged inhale, then nods. "Death."

Well. That's ominous. I look around, sure there'll be something. The space isn't very big, though, and there's not a lot of spots for her to hide anything.

My eyes lock on the door to the left. It's the only closed door in the place, so I walk over and open it to reveal a staircase descending into the dark. I turn to them with an expectant look.

Both twins stare at the door, their eyes wide, and I know I've found it, whatever it is.

There doesn't seem to be a light, so I hold onto the wall as I make my way down the stairs, Blaire and Blake right on my heels.

"Fuck me," Blake whispers, stopping before he gets all the way to the bottom.

I want to ask what he means, but Blaire answers before I can, turning her phone flashlight on and shining it around the room.

Blood. The whole room is soaked in blood, stained into the cement floors and the walls. I can smell the decay, the viscera, and I lean harder against the wall. I know this scent. I know this place, even if I've never been here.

"Believe me now?" I ask, forcing myself to breathe evenly. "She kills people. She's who-knows how old and the magic she does is *wrong*. She tortured me, she made me this, and she's still doing it."

"How many people..." Blaire doesn't finish her thought, but we all know what she's thinking.

"A lot." She was very clear that no one had survived even a fraction as long as I did. Which means she's running through bodies. I have no idea how long she's operated out of this area, but if Blake went to her when he was trying to make plans about how to fake aging, she's probably been here killing people for a while.

I jolt. That college kid. The one who went missing, who I blamed on Blaire and Blake until I knew better. Was that her? Is this her blood?

Are there more missing people? I didn't find an obvious trail of bodies when I looked before, but the number wasn't zero. And she could be pulling them from anywhere. And I haven't looked in a while; she could have grabbed another one when the college student died.

Fuck. Everything is a swirling vortex of chaos inside my head, the present horror show in front of me mixing with the nightmares of my past. I blink, the world going in and out of focus, not helped by the darkness pierced through by the phone light and swirls of rust-colored blood.

Blaire holds me up before I even realize I'm falling. "Laurel?"

"I'm okay," I murmur, although we all know it's a lie. "I'm—I'll be okay."

"Let's get you out of here," she says. "No need to stay down here."

"I'm going outside," Blake announces, walking up the stairs to get out of our way.

I feel gross sitting in a chair that the witch might have sat in, but Blaire gently pushes me into her kitchen chair, crouching in front of me. "What can I do for you?"

I shake my head. "Nothing. I need—I don't know," I realize abruptly. I have no idea what'll make me feel better. I want to not be here. I want this not to be happening. I want to have answers.

"I'm sorry I doubted you," Blaire says like she can read my mind. "As soon as Blake's back, we'll start calling people. We don't have a lot of friends, but we'll tell everyone we know, and have them tell everyone they know. She won't have anywhere to hide."

That's a romantic notion, but I know how reality works. "She doesn't just kill people for herself," I say. "I don't know what she would have done to make that spell for Blake, but I've seen her make spells, Blaire. She chops people up. It's what she would have done to me when I wasn't useful anymore. It's what she did to the one before me and probably the one after and a thousand others who she kept in cells like mine. And people bought those spells from her. She had a business."

"Not everyone is like that."

But enough people are. Enough people will protect her. And even if they're not sadistic themselves, even if they don't enjoy the violence that way—if she's selling something they think they need, then they'll let her continue on unaccosted forever.

Blake marches back in. "There are bodies buried out there," he says. "Old, so the smell isn't fresh, but if you really look—I don't know how many. I don't really want to know."

We probably owe it to those people to find out, to find them so their families can lay them to rest. "We should call someone," I manage to say. "The humans. Let them find the bodies."

The twins share a look over my head. "What if they get too curious?" Blaire asks.

"What are they going to find? Did she leave behind spellbooks or something? They'll have found a serial killer." When they don't say anything, I add, "That's a lot of bodies."

"She's right," Blaire declares, squeezing my knee. "We call, then we bail. And then we start telling everyone else what a piece of filth has been living in our midst."

***

She makes the call on Madge's cellphone, leaving it on the kitchen table. It'll give the location to any law enforcement that cares to look and won't be traceable back to any of us. Then we drive.

Blaire drove out here, but without saying a word, she slides into the back with me, leaving Blake to drive us back to the cabin. Blaire pulls my legs across her lap, touching as much of me as she can like she's worried I'm going to disappear.

The car is quiet and tense until we make it a good way away. No cops have shown up on our tail, so at least we got away before anyone got there.

"If she abandoned that place, she already set up a new one," I tell them after a while. "She can't go without that spell, and it requires constant maintenance. Someone is spending every second of every day brewing that thing for her. She needs a stable base. Somewhere she can hold prisoners without other people noticing."

Blaire nods tightly. "Alright. We'll tell people to keep an eye out."

Blake meets my eyes in the rearview mirror. "I'll tell everyone I know," he promises. "I'm sorry, Laurel. I'm sorry it happened and I'm sorry I was an asshole when you came back. And I'm sorry I didn't see through it and let her in my house."

I shudder thinking of how close she was to Callie, a perfectly ordinary human, the exact type of person she tortures.

Like he can read my mind, Blake says, "I don't blame you for anything, but Callie will be harder to convince. She loves you, Laurel. But she doesn't understand the context. *Can't* understand the context. Do you have any idea what you're going to say to her?"

"Not yet." I'll have to plan for this. My one saving grace is that Callie doesn't know that I'm back yet, so I can take my time and come up with a strong plan.

But not too long. If I wait, then she'll just get more and more mad. I have to fix this sooner rather than later.

That reminds me. "I'm assuming the library fired me, didn't they?" I ask emptily. I don't blame them; there's only so many days you can no-call, no-show before they have to let you go. But I'm going to miss it. And I'm going to miss seeing Callie there.

"Yeah. Sorry." Blake does sound genuinely sorry, too.

"It's fine." I close my eyes, willing it to be fine. "I'll need a new job. Rent isn't going to pay itself."

The silence is so heavy I can taste it, so I open my eyes. "What?"

"If you think you're going back there with that *witch* on the loose, then you're out of your mind," Blaire bites out.

I raise an eyebrow, withdrawing my legs off her lap. She makes a noise in the back of her throat, chasing them, but she lets me go. "And what am I going to do? Cower in fear at your place?"

"Well, you're not required to cower," she mumbles. "That's a personal choice. But my place? Yeah. I'm pretty much always there. If you saw her, then she saw you. You didn't exactly sneak out of that party quietly, Laurel. And maybe all the time that passed meant she didn't recognize you, but I'm not willing to take that risk."

That's sweet. Overbearing, but sweet. "You want me with you?" I ask, because I wasn't sure if that would be true. She's forgiven me for running, that's obvious, but there's still something stilted and raw between us. I can't blame her.

She chases after my legs, pulling them back into her lap with a firm grip. "I want you with me," she says firmly, her thumb pushing up the cuffed sweatpants I'm still wearing and stroking across my ankle bone.

Blake turns down the road that leads to the cabin, and soon enough, we're home.

Home. My brain can't help but call it home already, and I don't know if that's a good thing or not.

Blake throws his sister the keys as soon as he steps out of the car, already walking toward his own. "I'll make phone calls on the way home. Let me know if you need help emptying out your apartment, Laurel. And make a plan to fix things with Callie. Soon, please. I can't tell her you're back without explaining why I know, and seeing her sad is killing me." He says it so matter-of-factly. He means it. I'm tearing him to pieces by making Callie cry.

"Come on," Blaire says as soon as Blake drives away in his own car. "Inside. I need you to eat again."

"Another protein bar?"

She stops, tilting her head. "I'll go grocery shopping."

"*I'll* go grocery shopping. I'm not sure I trust you around human food."

"*You* will go to sleep," Blaire says, nudging me inside. "I doubt you could tell me the last time you slept. And you've had a hell of a day."

I open my mouth to complain, but what can I say? She's not wrong.

"I'll make you a list," I mumble. Not because I particularly care about what I eat, but because I think human food actually overwhelms her a bit. A grocery store the size of a warehouse wouldn't have been something she experienced when she was alive, and she's had no reason to explore one before me. An entire aisle dedicated to brightly colored, sugary, artificial cereal might be a little shocking in that situation.

I keep it short and simple; it's not like I need much. Blaire reads it quickly, then nods. "I'll be back as quick as I can," she promises. "Don't—please don't go anywhere." I can see it in her eyes, the insecurity, the uncertainty.

"I won't," I promise.

"Sleep," she says, her eyes still uncertain even if she makes herself sound confident. "And I'll be back."

She looks back over her shoulder a half dozen times on the short walk to her car, and I bite my lip, seeing what I broke. I didn't mean to. I think I have a pretty decent excuse. But that doesn't change it.

Chapter Twenty-Two

S wearing and the smell of smoke wake me up.

Blaire's bed is cold, my body heat having not quite managed to warm it all the way up. I'd half-hoped that Blaire would have slipped into bed with me if she made it back before I woke up, but apparently, she decided to try to cook instead.

"What did you do?" I demand, rubbing sleep out of my eyes as I walk into the kitchen.

She gives me a look over her shoulder. "You slept fourteen hours, which is great, but I figured you'd need food again, so I tried, and, well—I tried," she repeats.

I look into the fry pan that she's now holding off the flame, suppressing a smirk. "So, eggs aren't supposed to be that color," I point out. "And you got shell in there."

"I fucking tried," she says, contrary now.

I walk up and take the pan from her, dumping the food into the trash before starting again. I can feel the hunger, and while I could go on ignoring it, there doesn't seem to be any real reason to.

"How was the grocery store?"

"Why do people push and shove for food?" she asks instead of answering. "It's not like it's in short supply. There's always like twenty boxes of the same thing. No one is worried about it running out anytime soon."

I snort, cracking the egg into the pan and watching the edges crisp up. "Thank you for suffering it for me," I tease.

"I would suffer a lot worse for you," she says, and there's no teasing in her tone. It's silent for a minute except the pop of the cooking egg, but then Blaire breaks the silence, voice raw. "If you need to run, take me with you. Don't go where I can't follow, Laurel. I won't ask any questions—just take me with you."

I swallow. "That's asking too much of you."

"It's *not*," she argues. "I'm telling you, begging you—please. Don't go without me. We'll figure it out. And I won't be mad if we have to run. Given everything, I'd get it. Just, don't go without me."

I picture the last couple of weeks if Blaire had been at my side. How different would it have been? How much faster would I have come back to myself and been able to think rationally?

I flip the egg out of the pan and onto a plate. I don't necessarily blame myself for what I did. I think I'm allowed to be a bit mistrustful when I see my torturer in her brother's home. But still, Blaire is Blaire. And I should trust her down to my bones.

"I'll talk to you," I promise her. "We'll make a decision together." If I thought that'd be hard to say, then I'd be sorely mistaken. It's one of the easier promises I've ever made.

She dips her head, acknowledging it, and sits down at the table opposite me. "Blake called the people he talks to regularly. I don't have anything else—no one has seen her. Or will admit to it, anyway, but I'd like to think they wouldn't do that. We've been pretty picky about who we talk to, and I'd like to believe none of them are monsters." A complicated, twisted look crosses her face. "Obviously, not picky enough."

"You couldn't have known who she was," I tell her, surprising even myself with my forgiveness.

"Maybe," she says darkly, then looks at my plate. "Eat your food. I don't want to know how badly you were starving yourself."

"It's nothing I—"

147

"—If you say *it's nothing I can't handle,* I think I might actually scream," she informs me matter-of-factly. "You slept outside. If you slept at all; you haven't told me that bit yet, but you slept fourteen hours straight, so I'm guessing you haven't slept much. You walked who-knows how far, came back to me muddy and wet and starving. That's not okay. That'll never be okay."

That's the reality of my life. Yes, I like towns and having my own apartment and cushy jobs that let me be inside in air conditioning. But I don't need any of it and I know it. When things are difficult, I'm perfectly capable of going to ground exactly like I did. I've done it before and I'll probably do it again.

But not alone. I somehow doubt I'll be doing it alone again, and I wonder how that will change things.

"I missed you when I was gone, you know," I tell her, both because it's true and it seems like she needs to hear it.

Yes, I'd worried she'd betrayed me. And yes, I'd worried that I'd been duped in a way I'd never come back from. But I'd also ached for her in a way I never have for another person. And being back here with her feels like being whole in a way I didn't understand before.

"It felt like you fucking ripped my heart straight out of my chest and took it with you," she tells me in response.

My breath catches in my chest at the raw ache of that. *Fuck.* I did this, and she might not hate me for it, but I can't let that thought go.

I eat another bite of my eggs, and Blaire watches me like the act of eating is suddenly fascinating to her. I take another bite.

"I promise," I tell her again, because I think she needs to hear it. "I won't run without you. We'll do this together."

"And you'll trust me to protect you?" she asks me. "I know we don't know where Madge is. For all we know, she's halfway across the world by now and we could go another nine hundred years before running into her again. But until we know for sure—I'll be here. At your side, watching."

Fuck, I hope she's gone. I hope Blaire's little scenario is real, but it seems too good to be true.

I finish my eggs, then get up and put my plate in the sink. I reach over to grab the pan, intent on getting the dishes clean, but Blaire grabs me from behind, arms firm around my middle as she molds her body to mine.

"Can I—" She swallows, and it's like a full-body movement that I can feel with her pressed against me. "Can I take you to bed?"

"Sending me back to sleep?" I tease. I know fourteen hours barely makes a dent in my sleep deficit, but I've never felt less tired in my life than right this moment.

"No. I mean, if that's what you want. I'm happy to hold you while you sleep. But I was thinking—"

"Relax," I tell her, resting one hand on top of hers, interlaced on my stomach. "I'd like that."

I didn't realize how lonely I'd been until she held me like this. I came home but I still felt alone, striking out against the world and trying to drag Blaire along behind me. But now, this is settled. This is soothing.

This is *safe*.

"Leave the dishes for tomorrow," she tells me softly, mouth right next to my ear.

A quick glance out the window tells me that it's way too early in the afternoon for that type of statement, so either Blaire has a high estimate of how long this will take, or else she's thinking she'll send me right back to sleep after. Either option is fine with me, although I know which one I'd prefer.

I step away from the sink. Blaire keeps pace with me, contorting her body around mine as we walk toward the bedroom. When we're inside, she kicks the door shut and practically throws me onto the bed, hovering over me and staring at me like she's drinking me in.

"I'm here," I tell her, because I think she needs to hear it. "I'm here, Blaire. I'm not going anywhere."

She nods, looking a little unsure still, regardless. And then her hands are on me, moving me this way and that until my clothes are gone. It's not that hard, considering how big they are on me, and I make a note that we need a plan to get my things. Then she touches me and I forget such practical things.

Her hands are on my ribs, feather light as she explores the skin there. She touches every inch, and eventually I start squirming.

She grins. "I didn't know you were ticklish."

I roll my eyes. "Unfortunately, being cursed with immortality didn't cure me of ticklishness. Seems like I'm stuck with that forever."

She keeps touching me like she has to test the theory, and I don't stop her, just squirming under her hands on the bed. I'm fully aware that I'm completely naked and she's still dressed, but I don't do anything about it yet. She can take her time. I'll let her set the pace today.

"Put your hands up here," Blaire murmurs, her mouth inches from my belly, her breath a warm puff of air against my skin. One of her hands takes my left wrist and guides it up by my head, so I follow suit with my right, interested to see where she's going with this.

Her mouth presses kisses over every inch of my stomach, warm and gentle and so soft. My belly contracts under her touch, but this time, it's not from being tickled.

"Blaire—" I mean it as a warning, but I'm positive it comes out like a plea. "Please, I need—"

"I know what you need." Then, like she has to prove it, she kisses my breast, flicking my nipple with her tongue and making me arch against her.

"Blaire." It comes out a little firmer this time. "Please."

"Oh, I like that." She keeps kissing around my breast, flicking the tip of her tongue against my skin. "Patience, Laurel."

I have no patience left in me. I waited for weeks now. I was alone, and now I'm not, but she won't be kind enough to give me this.

"At least take your clothes off."

She pulls back slightly, seeming to take that into consideration before she strips with an efficiency I didn't expect. Her clothes end up in a pile on the floor and she's back on top of me in barely a minute, the warm weight of her the most reassuring thing I've felt in a long time.

My hands are still by my head, but it's not like she restrained them, so I take that as permission to move them. My thighs find her hips and my hands her shoulders, pulling her closer to me, deeper into me. I need her. I need to be consumed by her and consume her in turn. The need is like a spark between us, like a live wire lighting both of us up.

"Laurel—" It's a warning and a plea, and I feel a sharp surge of pride that I brought it out of her already.

My hand snakes between us and finds her folds, wet and soft. She groans when I touch her, her head falling on my shoulder, and I tease her clit, feeling it harden and jump under my touch. She needs me as badly as I need her.

"I want you to come for me," I tell her. "Please, Blaire."

She groans again. "How the fuck could I say no to that?"

"Don't." I stroke her clit again, searching out the perfect pressure to make her see stars. I know I find it when she turns her head away from me, moaning out my name and biting her own lip.

She doesn't want to bite me. My heart grows at the sight, and I double my efforts, determined to see her fall over the edge for me.

"Baby—" It sounds wrecked, strangled, so I keep going, knowing she's close, chasing what we both need. She's so wet and hot under my fingertips, and it just makes me want to taste. Not yet, though. I need to see her come first.

A few more strokes is all it takes, and then Blaire is coming, pinning my hand to her while she rides out the orgasm, groaning my name as her body shudders with the pleasure of it. "That's it," I whisper, using my free hand to stroke the back of her neck. "Feel good, baby?"

"Gah." It seems to be all she can say, verbose, articulate Blaire gone entirely for the present moment. I keep stroking her neck while I slowly pull my hand away, bringing it to my lips for the taste I wanted so badly a few moments ago.

She tastes perfect, and she seems to come back to earth while I'm sucking her juices off my fingers, chasing each and every bit of it while her eyes lock onto me, hungry and desperate.

"My turn," she growls, voice a little raspy now. Before I can respond to that, she pounces, pinning my hands back over my head while she trails kisses down my torso. "Leave your damned arms there."

I nod, holding the pillow so I won't accidentally move. "What do you have planned?"

"Gonna taste you until you soak the bed," she promises me. "Think you can handle that?"

I have no idea. But I'm fucking excited to try.

Blaire makes good on her promise, her mouth on my cunt until I'm thrashing, begging. When she finally sends me over, when my come soaks her face and my thighs, she shows me no mercy, not moving her face an inch as her tongue continues to torment me.

"Blaire—"

"Shush," she murmurs against my thigh, giving me the briefest respite, and I can't tell if I love it or hate it. "Unless you actually need to stop. But otherwise, enjoy the ride. I'm going to remind you exactly why you should take me with you next time."

I wonder if she meant to say that last part out loud, but I don't get a chance to ask when she returns to my cunt with renewed enthusiasm, pushing me right to the edge again as I moan her name, arching my back, looking for more.

She makes me come four times, all in rapid succession, before I finally push her head away. "No more," I whimper, my whole body tingling and over-sensitive. I subtly flex my fingers and toes, almost surprised when they move. I'd lost feeling in my extremities there for a moment.

Blaire pulls back and licks her lips before wiping her face with the back of her hand, eyes still on me as I lay splayed out across our bed.

"Not soaked," she murmurs. I'd like to argue the point; we might not have soaked the bed through, but we certainly made a good effort, and I'm definitely lying in a wet spot. But Blaire continues before I can protest. "But I know you're tired, and I'm a considerate girlfriend, so I'll make sure you get sleep. We can try again in the morning."

It's a threat and a promise, and it sends a shiver right down my spine.

Chapter Twenty-Three

I n the morning, Blaire wakes me up with her tongue. I groan through an orgasm before she makes me eat breakfast. It's like she's trying to ensure I replace every calorie I missed.

And after breakfast, it's time to face something I've been putting off since I got home.

I don't say anything, but my continuous looking out the window must give it away. "Want me to come with you?" Blaire asks.

"Would it offend you if I said no?" Not because I don't want Blaire there or don't like having her around. But this is my mess, and I need to clean it up. And I don't think Callie would react well to me hiding behind her sister-in-law. She was my friend first, and I owe it to her to figure this out.

"Not at all. Your keys are by the door, by the way."

Right. My car's been sitting here since before I left, since Blaire drove us to that party. At least I don't have to hunt that down.

***

The drive into town doesn't take exceptionally long, but it does feel strange. Nothing changed while I was gone except everything fading further into winter, but it feels different nonetheless. I look around, trying to find what's causing the feeling, but I can't latch onto anything.

Maybe it's me. After all, if I don't live here anymore and I don't work here, what's the point of me even being here?

Going into my apartment is surreal, but I need my own clothes before I approach Callie. I have no desire to explain why I'm still wearing Blaire's clothes.

This place feels like a ghost is haunting it now, and my eyes continually dart to that window that I never nailed shut. Has someone been here while I've been gone?

Maybe Blaire and Blake are right. Maybe moving in with Blaire is the right thing to do. The trouble is, I don't see an end date to it; it's not like this thing with the witch—with *Madge*—will be over soon.

Then again, is it so bad to not have an end date? I was practically already living at the cabin even before all this.

Once I change, I hurry out of there and back to my car. I drive to Callie's house, the flower beds buried under snow, the stepping stones obscured. I crunch through the snow, making my way to the front door, and after taking a few calming deep breaths, I knock.

I wait an exceptionally long time, and I worry she's at work, that her hours have somehow changed, or else that she's gone out. But eventually, the door opens, and there she is.

Callie. Sweet, kind, human Callie, who has no idea what's happened. Who I can't tell about it, because knowing could kill her.

I didn't plan what to say. I didn't want to dream up a lie, so I thought I'd come over here and give her as much of the truth as I can.

She stops and stares at me. "Laurel?"

"Hi Callie." I swallow, my throat suddenly bone dry. "I—hi. I'm back."

She stares, and then the door starts to close. I wince. It's fair enough, but all I need is half a chance. "Callie, please." I slip my foot in the doorway, hoping for a few extra seconds.

"I don't know if I want to talk to you," Callie says, looking somewhere over my shoulder and pushing the door closed a little further.

I nod, stung, but I try not to show it. She's more than entitled to feel that way. "Understandable. Can you give me five minutes? Or I can leave."

Callie hesitates for a second, but then nods and steps aside. "Come in."

I don't wait, kicking my shoes off at the door and looking around. It looks the same as it has since I first started coming here. I'm sure she went all out decorating for that party, and part of me is sad I didn't get to see it.

Callie backs up a few paces and stands there with her arms crossed over her chest and a frown I don't think I've ever seen before.

Oh, Callie can get upset and be angry or mad or frustrated or whatever else anyone else might feel. But she's generally so cheerful and uplifting. The guilt inside me compounds, because I know that I did that to her.

"Where have you been?" she asks. Straight to the point, then.

"I'm sorry." It's not an answer, but I physically can't stop myself from saying it. She deserves to hear it. "I ran."

It's the simplest way to say what I did, but it's the truth. I got scared and I ran. It doesn't matter if my fears are huge, and that they're beyond what Callie would understand. I don't want to lie to her, so I tell it to her as truthfully as I can.

"Ran? Why on Earth—?"

"You asked me a few times why I came here. From Wyoming," I interrupt her, nearly not stumbling over *Wyoming*. "And I never answered."

Callie shrugs, a quick, jerky movement. "It seemed like a sore subject. Like you didn't want to talk about it."

"Yeah." I run a hand through my hair. This is where I have to be careful, where I need to embellish the truth with a few small lies. "I was running from something."

"We assumed."

"Her name was Madge." There. Not quite the truth, but not quite a lie. Callie will make plenty of assumptions that aren't true, but it's the best I can do.

"What does this have to do with anything?" Callie asks, eyes narrowed as she takes me in. She's defensive and withdrawn, but she's not actively trying to kick me out.

"She was at your party, remember? Blonde. Small."

Callie squints for a second, then nods. "Yeah, I remember. Blake knows her. How does he know her?" The disinterest covering anger is gone, a tension rising in her voice that I don't think is just anger at me anymore.

It's my turn to shrug; Blake can make up his own lies. He's good at it. "It's just, it was her and I didn't expect to see her ever again, never mind here, and there she was, and I ran."

"Ran straight out of our lives." Callie's voice is ice cold.

I flinch, even though I deserve it. "Yeah. It's a bad excuse, but it's what happened. And I thought you deserved to know."

Callie nods once, slowly. "Thank you for telling me. I wish you told me then. Called me or texted me if you couldn't stay. I had her here and I didn't even know it was hurting you, and I wish you trusted me to fix it."

"I trust you." Just not to fix Madge. I wish she was never anywhere near Madge. Blake put Callie on her radar long before I did, but even so, the idea that I left Madge near Callie makes something gross and wrong bloom in my gut.

"Not enough," she murmurs, and that cuts. She hesitates a second, seemingly struggling with herself, and I hold my breath. "I'm so sorry that happened. I'm pissed you just *ran* but I've never been where you were. I don't know how I feel right now, but I want you to leave now."

Tears prick at the back of my eyes, but I bury them. That's not Callie's problem to deal with, and she deserves time to process this. I ran away and took weeks when I got overwhelmed; I can't expect her to process her feelings in just a few minutes. "Alright." I hesitate one second by the door after I slip my shoes back on. "Can I see you again?" I hold my breath, waiting. If she tells me to leave her alone forever, then I'd understand. But I hope we can get past this.

For one brief moment, something on her face breaks. "Of course, Laurel. But not right now. Please—go."

"Bye, Callie. Thanks for listening." I know I've pushed enough. I know this is the best I'm going to get. So I leave, and I hope this isn't over.

***

Blaire is waiting for me when I get back to the cabin. "How'd it go?"

"Alright." I kick off my shoes and remove my jacket, then stand in front of the fire. Like she can read my mind, Blaire stands up from the couch, walking over to wrap me in her arms.

"Seriously." She squeezes me as she says it, and I lean into her.

"Seriously. She's mad. But I don't know. She didn't tell me to never come back." I close my eyes, letting her hold me up as the fire warms my front. "We'll try again when she's ready."

"Hey," she says softly, "in case you haven't heard it or you forgot it—you're a good friend to her."

"I ran out on her." I left her with Madge, with no explanation. I made her cry.

"You kept going back even when you were convinced she was surrounded by two dangerous vampires," she points out. "That's not nothing. Just because she doesn't know that's what happened doesn't make it not true. And you went there today."

"The least I could do," I dismiss.

She squeezes me tighter. "No. It's not. Everything will be okay; give her time."

I leave my eyes closed, letting her hold me and the fire and her belief in me warm me up.

Chapter Twenty-Four

I can't sit around Blaire's place forever. Well, she thinks I can, but I'm going to lose my mind if I do this any longer.

Packing up my possessions and canceling my lease took a few days, but since then I've had nothing to do but be bored. Blaire is always here, but she does work during the day, and it turns out watching her type isn't that interesting.

She does take me to the library a few miles from her house when she's done with work one day, and that's all well and good, but I can't read all day every day. I like feeling useful in some way. And this cabin is too small to really need a full-time caretaker. I'm the only one who eats, so I cook and wash my own dishes. Blaire and I share the rest of the chores, none of which take very long.

So I need a job. I doubt I'm going to find another library position around here—although I did check when I got my new library card—but I can still do something. I scroll through job postings while Blaire works a few feet away, make a list of possibilities, and reach out to a few of them.

A seafood restaurant in the next town responds to my application. It's been a while since I've been a waitress, but I'm sure it'll come back to me with a little bit of practice. And it's still the middle of winter; busy season for the restaurant won't start for a few months. I have plenty of time to figure it out.

The interview goes well enough, and I'm pretty confident that I'll get a call from them in the next few days. I'm sitting in my car afterward when my new phone buzzes with a text from Callie.

Hey, can we talk?

My heart jumps into my throat. I haven't heard a thing from her since that day at her house. Blake has told me through Blaire that she's doing as well as can be expected. She's talked about me, although Blake obviously won't disclose what she said. He's said to give it more time.

Apparently, it's now been the right amount of time.

When I'm debating if I should text her back or just call her, I see a flash of blonde hair out of the corner of my eye. That's not unusual. A lot of people are blonde.

But it catches my attention.

The woman is all the way across the parking lot, turning to go behind the building. It should be nothing. It *might* be nothing, but something about her posture, the way she holds herself as she walks—

It takes me a long minute to process who it is and decide what to do. Do I chase Madge down? Do I start the car and get as far away as possible? The indecision leaves me paralyzed, my heart beating double time and my limbs too heavy to work, until no doubt my indecision has made my mind up for me. There's no way she's still here.

If she ever was.

I don't think I'm hallucinating. But I wouldn't put it past myself to let my paranoia put Madge's face onto someone else.

I'm still clutching my phone, and it's with a leap in my heart that I realize it's ringing. I accidentally called Callie, and I have no idea what I want to say.

"Hello? Laurel?" She picked up fast; she must have been waiting for my call. "Hello?"

I unstick my throat. "Hi, Callie."

"Hey." I can hear her let out a heavy breath, and I think absently that she might be as nervous as I am. Or was, a few moments ago. Right now, I don't have it in me to be nervous about this call. I'm genuinely terrified for far bigger things. "Can we talk?"

"Yeah." My mouth is so dry right now that the word feels like it scrapes coming out.

"Are you alright?" Damn Callie. Pissed at me and still picking up that there's something very, very wrong with me. I press a hand to my heart; it still hasn't slowed down any.

"Fine. I'm fine," I lie through my teeth. "I want to talk. Should I come over, or...?"

"Yes," she says immediately. "Come here. Please."

I force myself to take a deep breath. "I'll be there as soon as I can," I say, then disconnect the call before I lose control entirely.

***

I bring a bottle of wine. It might be overly hopeful, but I do it anyway, and I carry it under one arm as I crunch through the snow and up to the front door. My free hand shakes the whole time, and I clench it into a fist to try to stop it. It doesn't help.

Callie opens the door before I even knock. She's still dressed for work—today's dress has dinosaurs on it—but her hair is down and loose, and she has something red smudged on her face. I peer closely, worried that something happened, but I think it's sauce.

"Oh good," she says. She doesn't smile, but her posture is loose enough for me to think she's at least not openly hostile anymore. "Dinner is almost ready."

It's too early for dinner, but I don't say anything. "Where's Blake tonight?"

Callie fidgets with her hands. "I asked him to go out for dinner. Give us some time to talk."

So he's probably sitting in his car somewhere. Or maybe he's at the cabin.

"It's just pasta for dinner, sorry. I started it when I got home—"

"Pasta is fine. Great, even." I'll take what I can get. Her wanting to feed me at all is a miracle. "How can I help?"

"Want to make a salad?"

"Can do." I dig through her fridge for everything I'll need, and then I start chopping, mixing ingredients in a big bowl. We work in silence, and it's companionable enough. I don't think there's any hostility in the air, but my whole body feels stiff with tension, waiting for the hammer to drop, waiting to hear whatever Callie wants to say.

Between maybe seeing Madge and this conversation, I'm a spring pulled tight, ready to snap.

We make it halfway through dinner before Callie decides to speak up. "I'm still pissed at you."

"That's fair." I never expected anything less.

"I don't want to be," Callie adds. "I'm not mad that you were scared, Laurel."

"Then what are you mad about?"

"That you never *called us*," she snaps, hands balling into fists on top of the table. "You're scared, you run, fine. No one could blame you. But you were scared and alone for *weeks*, Laurel. How could you never think about calling us? How could you just *ignore* us for that long? We're your family, Laurel. We would have helped."

Family? I haven't applied that word to anything in my life for a long time. But she's right, is the thing. They do feel like family. "I'm sorry," I murmur. "I'm not used to having a family."

Callie looks at me for a moment and then sighs, seeming to deflate a bit. "We're here for you," she says softly. "We would have helped you. Protected you."

"I'm good at running," I admit. An understatement really. "I don't have any practice at staying."

"Don't run again," Callie says. "Or if you do, find a phone and call me."

She's so fierce about it, but I do fully believe that this little human, not that much taller than me, would protect me from any danger she found. "I promise. I've already heard the same from Blaire, trust me."

"I bet you have. She was heartbroken."

Blaire has been so good at accepting me back, at acting like all that time was ultimately nothing, but I know deep down that it was a bigger deal than she acts like. Still, to hear that I broke her heart said so plainly hurts. "Yeah?"

"She tried to look for you."

Did she? What did that entail? Did she try to follow me? Did she lose my scent? I swallow, not sure if I want those answers or not.

"She was bad, Laurel. You make her happy and it was awful, to see her how she used to be, only somehow worse. Sadder, all the time." She looks at me sideways, not making direct eye contact. "Are you and her good?"

"Yeah, we're good. Really."

Callie manages a small smile. "I'm glad."

I'm struck by the urge to tell her about how wonderful Blaire has been. How she trusted me about Madge, even when I broke her heart and ran away, even when she had no reason to believe me. How Blaire has held me and loved me and made me feel safe after everything.

But I can't tell her anything. The world isn't fair and I have to keep her in the dark, so I keep my mouth shut.

"You can be sure that that bitch won't be here anymore," Callie says vehemently. I've never heard her swear like that before. "Blake was absolutely appalled when he found out. You know, that we invited her. That he was friendly with someone who hurts people."

"Not his fault," I manage to murmur. "She's good at that." She thinks Madge is my abusive ex; I led her to believe that, and there's really no other way to explain this to her. I don't know how I feel about this, adding one more lie to everything she believes.

The cut on my hand aches. It's not a truth, but maybe not the worst lie I've told.

"I'm sorry you went through that."

I shake myself out of my thoughts. "It's in the past now, though." Except it's not really, and I need Callie to know one thing. "If you see her, stay away from her. I'm not joking, and I'm not just, I don't know, over-invested or anything. She's dangerous. Don't let her in your house, don't go near her."

"Like I'd want to see her, anyway," Callie huffs, but she must see the seriousness in my eyes because her voice softens. "I promise. I won't go near her."

"Good," is all I can say. "Good. Thank you."

I think it's done; I warned Callie, we're done talking about it, and she might even forgive me.

And then a car engine revs up the street, and I jump so hard I nearly fall out of my chair.

"Jesus Christ," Callie murmurs, jumping to stand. I flinch. It's not because of her. I'm not scared of her. I just don't want anyone close to me right this second. "Are you okay?"

"I'm fine." Even I can tell that I don't sound fine.

It's a fucking car. Just a car, a perfectly ordinary sound. Yes, it was loud, and yes, my life has been quiet recently. But that doesn't explain this level of panic.

"You sounded freaked out earlier, too," Callie muses, eyes narrowed as she studies me. She doesn't try to get any closer again. "What happened?"

"Nothing happened."

She sits down again, but pulls her chair closer to me, and then gives me an unimpressed look. "You're really going to take this opportunity from me to start over and ruin it by lying to me?" The words are harsh, but her tone isn't. And the reminder is timely. I don't want to lie to her anymore. I weigh telling her against losing her, but I know which one I'm going to choose.

"It's probably nothing," I hedge.

"Laurel."

"Fine. I thought I saw her earlier. I was out and when I got in the car, right around when you texted me, I thought I saw her," I confess. I don't look at her as I say it, because it sounds ridiculous.

"Madge?"

It still feels weird for the witch to have a name at all. It almost makes her sound human, small and normal and far less formidable than the monster that's been built up in my mind.

"Yeah."

She sucks her teeth. "You need to file for a restraining order, Laurel."

I can picture that now. No last name, no proof of our history, a story too fantastical to be believable, and then the scrutiny that would put on my own forged documents. "I don't even know I saw her," I argue. "I could be—she's been on my mind, Callie. I could be imagining things."

"Laurel. You're scared of her." She must see that I'm not going to budge on this, so she nods. "Did you at least tell Blaire?"

"Not yet." Maybe not ever. I don't need to freak her out over nothing.

"Laurel." I'm getting real sick of her saying my name like that.

And the thing is, I know she's not wrong. If this were anyone else, someone who really is fleeing an abusive partner, I'd be first in line to tell them all the things that Callie is telling me. But this isn't a normal situation, and I can't explain that to her.

"I saw blonde hair and lost my shit," I tell her slowly, trying to sound more confident than I feel. "That's all this is. I can't make a big deal out of that."

She studies me for a long time. "Alright," she says slowly. "But don't shut us out. I don't care if it's real or not, Laurel. If you're scared, then tell us. If she's not there and you're just scared, that's fine. You've been traumatized, and you're allowed to be. We're not going to judge you for it or be mad at you even if it's not her. We'll be here for you."

That sounds too good to be true, but I appreciate it nonetheless.

"Do you want dessert?" she asks, giving me an out that I appreciate. "Blake bought me this pie I really like. It's basically chocolate pudding in a pie shell, but I had it once and I loved it, so he picked it up for me, and most of it is still left."

"I'd love some pie." I stand, ignoring how shaky my legs are. "And I'll pour us more wine."

***

I wake up, bleary-eyed and with the sense that something has gone wrong. "Where am I?" I mumble.

There's a chuckle from my left. "In my bed."

Fuck. I force myself to focus and look, and there's Blake, sitting in a chair strewn with some of Callie's dresses while he watches me.

"How...?" I ask, trying to sit up only to realize there's an arm across me. I turn. Callie, passed out next to me, mouth open, hair a mess.

"My best guess? You two ate an entire pie and drank two bottles of wine between you. When I came home, you two were passed out on the couch, so I put you here."

"Sorry." I work my way out from under Callie's arm, managing to sit upright. I don't drink more than a glass of alcohol very often, and to tell the truth,

I wasn't sure if alcohol could affect me like this. Maybe it didn't. Maybe it's stress. Yesterday was a lot.

"Don't be. I take it you two made up?"

"Think so." I comb my fingers through my hair, taking stock of myself. Still fully dressed, thankfully, and I'm functioning fine this morning, if a little tired. Nothing that's not par for the course, then.

"Great. So maybe you can explain why my wife woke up when I was carrying her, told me I needed to protect you from your ex because she's back, and then passed out again?"

I freeze. *Oh, shit.* "Callie thinks Madge is my ex," I explain slowly, then look down at her. "Should we be talking about this here?"

"I know she thinks Madge is your ex. *I'm* the one who told her that. And Callie could sleep through the fire alarm. We're fine. Don't change the damned subject."

Good to know. Still, I get out of bed, more comfortable moving this conversation away from her. "She's worried. It's nothing."

"It's not. Because you wouldn't be doing this little song-and-dance if it was." His eyes are sharp. "Not to be an ass, but whatever you do or don't tell us affects more than just you. It affects my wife, my sister—and me, too. So. Don't withhold shit from us."

This damn family and their guilt trips. The thing is, they're not wrong. But I'm definitely not used to having to take other people into account.

"I thought I saw her," I admit. "It was a trick of the light, probably. Paranoia, you know?"

He studies me like he can see right through me. I'm fighting not to squirm under his gaze when he says, "Alright. But keep us in the loop, okay?"

He and Callie apparently think exactly alike. "Yeah, I got it," I mutter. "Can I get a shower before I go?"

Chapter Twenty-Five

B laire is looking deeply unimpressed when I get home, and I know without asking that Blake called her and ratted me out.

"Sorry I wasn't home last night," I tell her, because it does feel important to say that.

"I'd have appreciated a call," she says from the couch, head tilted back as she takes me in.

Yeah, I bet. "Tell the truth, I don't remember much after we started drinking."

"Were you *drunk*?" she sounds incredulous, maybe even slightly amused by it.

I shake my hand back and forth in an *ehhh* gesture. "Maybe? For a few minutes, at least. I think I just passed out."

"Yeah, well. It sounds like you had a long day." And there it is. The judgment is back.

I sigh and sit down on the couch, hoping she'll follow me. She does, sitting on the other cushion, looking at me and waiting for answers.

"I did have that job interview," I agree.

"Laurel."

Alright, I get it. Having the same conversation three times in like twelve hours is annoying, though. "It probably wasn't real."

"You should have called me."

"And said what? There's a blonde lady in this parking lot, and I didn't get a good look at her face?" It sounds so *stupid*. It sounded stupid since I drove away. It's an overreaction, some primitive lizard-brain fear response that I can't shake.

"Did it feel real?"

The question throws me. I expected a lot of questions, possibly some accusations, but not that one. "I—of course it did. At the time. That doesn't mean it was real, though."

"And how do you feel about it now?"

"Like an idiot." It's out before I can stop myself. *Fuck*. "I mean, I know it's an overreaction, alright?"

Blaire scoots closer to me, and I'm in her arms before I can even process what's going on. "Oh, Laurel." She presses a kiss to the crown of my head. "She tortured you. She took your life away from you. She was more than willing to kill you. It's not a surprise that you're scared of her."

I squirm in her arms, but I'm not really trying to get away. "It's not a surprise when I really see her. When I really saw her in your brother's house, that was something different. But a random sighting?"

I can't freak out at every short blonde woman. For fuck's sake, Callie is blonde. I need to get this under control.

Blaire strokes my spine. "We don't know where she is," she reasons. "That's bound to mess with you a bit."

I haven't known where she is for nine hundred years and I've been fine. I open my mouth to say that, but Blaire isn't having it. "Laurel. If you think you saw her, then I want to hear about it. Whether or not it's real doesn't matter. You don't have to know that yet. Just tell me." She kisses the top of my head again. "This is what people do when they care about someone," she adds, putting a stop to anything I might have said back.

So I say the one thing I haven't let myself think about yet. "If it was somehow real," I whisper, "then I worry about all of you. She knows where Callie and Blake are. She knows who you are. And I just—I don't want her within a thousand miles of you all."

It's not real. But if it is—

Well. I don't know what would happen next.

"Thank you for being honest," Blaire murmurs. "Blake and I are on the lookout now, alright? She won't get to us."

I don't think anything is that simple, but I also need it to be. I need to let myself believe that I've found safety, that these people I love can protect me from every danger out there. I've run for so long; I'm going to latch onto the pipe dream that I'm safe now.

"If you want," Blaire continues, "we can go."

I turn my head. "Go?"

"Go. Run. I told you, I'll run with you if you need. Just take me with you. We could be gone in an hour or two, get as far away as you need."

We could. Neither of us have much. We could put everything we need in one of the cars and run, ditch the car somewhere, buy a new one, and keep moving until we start a completely new life, until there's no hope of anyone finding us. The idea is more than tempting.

But we can't. Blake and Callie won't come. We could never explain it to Callie, and her life is here. Blake won't leave his wife. Which means not only would my fear mean leaving them vulnerable to Madge, but it would mean making Blaire lose contact with her brother. And that's not possible.

"No," I decide. "We're staying. It's fine. It's all fine."

And I wonder if either of us believe that.

***

Two days later, I quietly turned down the waitressing job offer. I feel like a free loader, but the thought of going back to the restaurant makes me think I'll pass out. I can't handle wondering if Madge is around every corner.

I keep telling myself that I'll try again when things feel better, but I don't know when that will be. It's not like there's a deadline to the end of nine-century-old paranoia.

I'm making lunch in my new self-imposed isolation when Blaire comes and stands at the table, watching me cook. "I don't understand what that is."

I roll my eyes. "You can't keep pretending that the concept of food is too confusing for you to grasp. You *were* a human. You ate."

"Not that."

No, it would be weird if she had. "It's called a mozzarella stick. They're delicious." And they sell them frozen at the grocery store in boxes that could feed a family of fifty. It's fantastic.

She watches me set the piping-hot plate down, then get the little cup of marinara I made. "What makes them so good?" she asks, eyeing the little logs of breaded goodness dubiously.

"Cheese."

She watches me eat the first one with a perverse fascination, and then she sits down across from me. "So, Blake and I are talking about going to the club tonight."

"Oh." That's last minute. I nod, considering. "I'll see if Callie wants to hang out with me, then."

Blaire bites her lip, her little fang on display. "I was kind of hoping you'd come."

I frown, because I know it's been a while, but I thought we were pretty clear after last time that it wasn't ideal for me. I'm glad I went with her once, but the nightmares it gave me are not an experience that I need to repeat.

"Blaire, I—"

"Laurel, Madge might be out there," she interrupts. "And if she is, then I want you with me. Safe."

"I imagined her," I say with as much confidence as I can muster, which admittedly isn't very convincing. "You know it's probably nothing."

"*Probably* aren't odds I'm taking."

Blaire's taking this more seriously than I am. I don't think she truly believes I saw Madge anymore than I do. I think we think the same thing, that it's possible but highly unlikely. But she hasn't wavered in her support of this. She hasn't judged me or said one negative comment. She's continued to treat it like it's real and that my fears are justified.

"Alright," I tell her. "I'll go with you. But I'm bringing a book."

She snorts, squeezing my thigh. "Peak club behavior," she says mock-solemnly. "Hottest girl in the place." That part, at least, sounds more serious.

"Yeah, yeah. What time do you want to leave?"

She glances out the window. "Can you be ready by eight?"

***

After a light dinner and pulling on the exact same clothes I wore last time we did this, I'm ready to go. Blaire is also wearing the same clothes, so I'm thinking of these as our clubbing uniforms now. Or maybe costumes; it does feel like we're playing a part.

"You're really bringing the book, huh?" Blaire asks when she sees I have the beat up library copy of *Dracula* under one arm, which I mostly checked out to see how long it would take to get under Blaire's skin. She hasn't reacted yet, although there's no way she doesn't know what I'm reading. She's well-read enough, and even if she wasn't, sheer cultural osmosis would surely have taught her about this by now.

I'm checking out *Twilight* next week. Just to see what happens.

"I'm really bringing the book," I confirm, wishing I had a small bag to carry it in. "Ready to go?"

The club is as loud and crowded as I remember, but Blake and Blaire cut through the crowd easily, finding me a table to lean on while they go do what they need.

I make it a few dozen pages before Blaire is back, sliding to the opposite side of the table, then leaning closer to me, taking up my space.

"What's the prettiest girl in the bar doing reading?" she asks, voice pitched husky and tempting, and something low in my gut responds.

"Oh, you know," I play along, faking disinterest when I am *very much* interested in her. "Kind of bored here, to be honest."

Blaire is suddenly right in my space, and I know she moved faster than a human should be able to. I don't have it in me to say anything, my breath catching in my throat. "Is that right?" she murmurs, and one hand comes out to gently cup my elbow, the fingertips pressing into the skin there. "Well, we'll have to fix that, won't we?"

I swallow, searching for my voice. "What do you suggest we do?" I manage to ask.

"I think," Blaire begins, her voice coming out in a breathy whisper fanning against my face, "that I need to show you a proper good time."

She's close enough that I could kiss her now, and she's only pulling me closer, the grip on my elbow firming up until she can lead me where she wants. "Dance with me, book girl," she commands.

I couldn't dance like this if I had a manual and a map, but I nod anyway, unable to put anything into words. *Her.* I want her, want this moment with her.

It's not lost on me what she's doing, turning me on here to try to make a positive association with the place. And I appreciate it. I'm not sure it's going to work, but I'm not going to stop her. The turning me on portion of her plan is certainly working.

She pulls me through the throng of people, the hand on my arm firm. I chase after her like she's a siren and I'm more than happy to crash on the rocks.

"Dance we me, book girl," she murmurs again, pulling me in close and beginning to move to the beat. Her hands and hips keep me right on time, so I let myself go, letting my eyes slide closed as I enjoy the music and the game and *her.*

Alright. Coming to the club with Blaire might not be that bad. Not if she touches me like this.

"How far is this little charade going?" I murmur, trusting that her vampire senses will hear me over the pounding music. "Does it end with your teeth in my neck like all of them?"

She leans down and runs her nose along my jaw. "It ends when I get you so turned on that you drag me out of here."

Well. Mission fucking accomplished, then. I'm soaked, my panties sticking to my skin, and I'm practically rubbing my thighs together for friction on the very public dance floor.

"Blaire—"

She kisses my jaw this time. "Yeah, baby?"

"Get me out of here."

"No." Her hands tighten on my waist, moving me to the music and reminding me that we're supposed to be dancing. "I don't think you're there yet."

I am literally going to drag her out of here if she keeps going, but I let her hold me, let her tease me, let her drive us both higher.

When I can't take it any more, I tell her, "You need to decide. If you want to fuck at home, then we need to leave now. If you want to fuck in the alley, you can keep playing this game."

I'm pressed so close to her that her chuckle reverberates through my entire body. "Alright, alright," she agrees. "We'll leave."

Then, like a switch was flipped, she takes me by the wrist, fingers drumming over my pulse while she pushes our way out of the crowd. They part for her, letting us spill out of the club and into the outside chill.

"C'mere, you," she practically growls, pulling me into her while at the same time pushing us both into the wall. "You are a fucking temptress."

I lift my head, looking for her mouth. "And you're a fucking tease, so, we're both at fault, here."

"Happy to be at fault for this," she murmurs, one hand slipping between us to rub lightly at the crotch of these too-tight jeans, making a high-pitched, embarrassing moan spill out of me.

"Hey, c'mon. You can't do that here. Go home."

I start, pushing myself backward even though there's nowhere to go. "Huh?"

The bouncer is shining a flashlight in our faces. "Go home," he repeats.

I blink back into reality, pulling myself away from the fantasy world that is only Blaire and I and land back in this dank alley. "We're going," I promise, and Blaire wraps an arm around me as we walk away. Combined, we're well over a thousand years old, and here we are, properly scolded like horny teenagers. I can't find it in me to regret it.

Once we're in the car and Blaire's pulled onto the road, she half turns to me and says, "Be honest. Was tonight okay? Are *you* okay?"

I'm sure she still remembers the nightmare I had last time. And I'll probably never separate any blood from what happened to me. But I can separate Blaire from the witch. "This isn't like that," I tell her, and I know she understands what I'm talking about without me explaining. "I don't think you've ever hurt anyone more than you absolutely needed to."

Something dark crosses her face. "There was a time when I wasn't so good at this, you know."

I'm sure. I don't know what it's like to be a young vampire, a rare vampire not born and raised into the ability but rather one who had the ability thrust upon them suddenly, and one who didn't seem to have great help figuring it out, either. I don't know what that's like, but I do know Blaire. "You did the best you could," I tell her. "And when you were able to do better, you did. That's what matters." She doesn't look entirely convinced, so I add, "Love that you're asking if tonight was okay when I dragged you out of the club because I was horny."

She barks a short laugh. "I didn't ask if *I* was okay; I know perfectly well that I'm great."

"Big head."

"Worth it," she shoots back.

A thought occurs to me. "Blaire—I left my book."

She chuckles. "Well, we're not going back."

"It's a library book!"

"And I'll pay to replace it."

I study her through narrowed eyes. "You did that on purpose," I decide, although I don't really know if it's true or not.

She chuckles again. "Read better books, Laurel." And then she steps a little harder on the gas. "I want to be home already. I'm not going back for your book."

And I can't really argue that.

Chapter Twenty-Six

W e spill in through the front door, barely remembering to slam it behind us. Blaire's kissing me hard enough that my lips are already swollen, her constant attention meaning they can't heal between all the kisses. I groan, tilting my head and wrapping one hand around the back of her neck, wanting her to continue, needing her to give me more.

"Does drinking blood always make you horny?" I ask between kisses, curious about this one.

She snorts, breaking away from me. "*You* make me horny, Laurel. Nothing to do with anything else. Need me to prove it to you?" Then, before I can answer, her palm is on the crotch of my jeans, grinding expertly against my clit through the fabric, making me squirm.

I'm so wet I'm surprised she can't feel it through my jeans. I'm so wet that I could drown in it, and my whole body feels like one giant nerve ending, desperately begging for her to touch me.

She looks at me, those brown eyes glowing faintly in the darkened room. We didn't bother with lights, didn't need them to touch, and I know she can see better than me, but I don't care. I press myself further into her, needing there to be no distance between us.

Her hand continues to drive me wild, and I need these jeans gone. I reach down and undo the button, then work down the fly, but Blaire stops me.

"Think I can make you come like this?" she asks, grinding her palm into me a little harder to emphasize what she means.

Without a single doubt. I think she could breathe on me too hard right now and I'd spill over that edge, the orgasm coiled in my belly and a fraction of a hair out of reach. I'll be going over soon whether I like it or not, and she's the devil who's going to make it happen.

She must see the answer to her question on my face, because she kisses the corner of my mouth and murmurs, "I want to see that."

Bastard. Or angel. I haven't decided yet. Whatever she is, she's playing me like an expert, knowing how to drag every reaction she desires from my body with no guidance from me. I groan under her touch as she continues to push me further.

"So fucking wet for me, aren't you?" she rasps, her free hand going to my outer thigh. "I can smell you, Laurel. You've been wet for me since we danced, haven't you?"

I should have known that she could smell that. I don't know if that's exciting or disturbing. Maybe both. "Blaire—"

"I know, baby." Her hand teases me, rubbing the seam of my jeans right into my clit, and I know I'm past the point of no return, clutching at her as I come.

"Pretty girl," Blaire coos, holding me as I ride it out. "Fuck, that's exactly what I wanted tonight."

"Oh yeah?" I manage to ask, resting all my weight on her. "That's what this was all about?"

She uses two fingers to tilt my chin up, then pulls me into a kiss I can feel all the way down to my toes. "Well, that," she murmurs. "And making sure I get fed. But mostly you coming on my hand, yeah."

"So, you're done?" I ask rhetorically, working my fingers into her jeans, just the barest touch. "Don't need anything else?"

She growls at me, leaning into me while her hands push up my sorry excuse for a shirt. "Not quite."

***

I wake up to the early morning sun streaming through the curtains we forgot to close last night. It's hitting my eyes at the worst angle, and I groan, turning to hide my face in Blaire's side, but it's no use. It's so bright and I can't stop noticing it, and I'm never getting back to sleep now.

I reluctantly get out of bed, putting my bare feet on the freezing cold floor and shuffle over to the window, eyes half open.

Something moves.

I freeze, completely naked in front of the window, trying to process what I'm seeing. There's a flash of blonde hair, and then sharp, piercing blue eyes, and—

"Oh shit," I choke out, all the air I'm able to get, my brain spinning so fast I can't even think about it—

And then I scream. It's ripped out of me, some sort of hoarse shout. I'd like to say it's some sort of warrior's cry, something meant to make me feel stronger, but the truth is I'm so terrified that I'm paralyzed in place.

"What?" Blaire barks, already out of bed, ready to face the threat.

The face is gone. Did I fucking imagine it again? Am I losing it?

I point to the window with a shaking hand. "She was here," I whisper, unable to say anything more, but that's all Blaire needs.

Completely ignoring her nudity, she runs outside. I make myself follow her even when all I want to do is hide under the bed. But if Blaire is out there in the cold, then I should be with her.

I manage to pull my jacket off the hook on the way out, giving myself some insulation from the cold. Blaire is standing on the porch, looking around at the wide vista of nothing.

"Sorry," I murmur, shame-faced now. "I must have still been dreaming or something—"

But Blaire is shaking her head. "No," she says definitively. "She was here. I can fucking smell it. That blood and death scent clings to her. And I'm just figuring out where the fuck she went."

The blood drains out of my face. "She—it's real?"

"It's real," Blaire says grimly. "And I'd chase her down, but like hell am I leaving you alone." Then, without any more explanation, she walks back inside, corralling me back in with her. She grabs her phone from where we left her jeans last night.

When whoever she dials picks up, she says, "Get here right now," and hangs up again.

I swallow. "Blaire?"

She turns to look at me, her eyes full of a tender, desperate sort of terror. She was *here*, looking through our window. Did she watch us have sex? How long did she watch us sleep? We're both thinking it. We're both vibrating with an all-consuming terror, and we're both realizing how deep into this we are.

"Get dressed," she says after taking a long look at me. "Blake will be here any minute."

I swallow. She's still standing there naked, looking like she'd put herself between me and anything. She's strong, and I know there's a lethal side of her hidden underneath all the layers of civility and normalcy she's built since her early days as a vampire.

But I don't want her to think she has to defend me. I want her to defend herself, too.

"You too," I tell her.

Her eyes grow even more intense. "Yeah, something tells me you won't be doing anything alone for a while," she tells me. "So yeah, I'll be with you. Consider me your personal shadow."

I want to argue that, tell her I don't need a shadow, that I'm perfectly capable of taking care of myself. I don't say a word. I can't get my heart rate to settle down, and I know I'll feel better if she's with me.

Chapter Twenty-Seven

Blake shows up thirty minutes later, fast enough that I know he made up an excuse to his wife and broke every speed limit getting here. "What is it?" he asks, eyes frantically darting around between the two of us.

We're fully dressed now, so at least that's been taken care of, but Blaire is still standing half in front of me like she has to shield me from the world. I gently push around her, not wanting to upset her but needing to be a part of this conversation. This is my life, after all.

"She was here," I tell him. "Madge. At our window. And it's real this time—Blaire could smell her."

Blake blinks at me, then turns to his sister. "So why am I not looking at a dead witch?" he demands, so casually talking about death. It's like it never occurred to him to think that Blaire wouldn't murder someone.

"She ran," Blaire says shortly, also not objecting to the murderous intent. "And I couldn't leave Laurel."

He nods. "Got it. Go inside and stay there." And then he starts moving faster than should be possible.

"Alright, inside," Blaire says, watching after her brother for a second before ushering me in. She locks the door behind her, then jerks the curtains shut on every window in the little cabin. It's like we're in a bunker now, and I'm not sure I like the feeling.

We both collapse onto the couch. There doesn't seem to be much else to do. I can't even read my book, since I left it at the club last night.

"It's going to be okay," Blaire murmurs.

'I appreciate the attempt, but I'm too old to be placated by false promises.

The minutes pass by. It's not that I expected Blake to instantly have answers or anything, but I'm too keyed up to be any good at waiting right now. I wonder if him taking a while is a good sign or a bad one.

I pull out my phone to distract myself, needing something to do with my hands, so I scroll through a news app. I've been essentially isolated from the world since I first saw Madge, hiding away here except for a few careful, supervised trips. I need to reconnect with the world, see what's happening out there—

Suzanne Masters, 23, missing after a night out with friends.

My fingers go numb as I clutch my phone tighter, reading the news that makes my fear spike higher and higher with every sentence. "What's wrong?" Blaire asks immediately, trying to turn me so she can look me in the eyes, but I can't take my eyes off the phone.

She went missing from the club. The club where we were last night.

She's twenty-three. Maybe she found a partner and went to their place and forgot to tell her friends. But if they're already reporting her as *missing*, they probably have good reason to suspect that's not true.

I turn the phone toward Blaire. She has to take it from me, my hands are shaking so hard.

"I drank from her," Blaire whispers. "Last night. I recognize her."

Fuck. "Blaire, she—it's Madge." I technically can't say it for sure. But a young woman going missing is exactly the type of thing she does. Was the club a taunt to show she's following us, or was she there on her own and followed us after seeing us there? How much does Madge know about us?

The walls suddenly feel like they're closing in, like there are eyes everywhere. I know she ran away from Blaire, and that Blake is actively looking for her. I can't shake the feeling that, if I threw the curtains open again, she'd be right there, waiting. Watching.

"It's okay, Laurel," Blaire mutters, but she doesn't sound any less disturbed than I am.

I take the phone back and mindlessly type in the name of the restaurant I interviewed at. Nothing newsworthy comes up recently. I widen the search to the whole town, and there's a news story.

Missing father of two's cellphone found in park.

I suck in another breath. So that's three that I've found so far—the college student I blamed on Blake and Blaire, and these two. How many more are there?

I don't have the library and the archives anymore, but these are recent enough. I scan all the local news sites for missing persons reports, looking back since before I ran away.

I'd stopped looking after I realized Blaire and Blake didn't kill that college kid. It hadn't seemed necessary when I'd attributed it to a freak occurrence. But now, knowing what I know, knowing what kind of monster is lurking out there—

I find two more disappearances, one a hundred miles from here, and another in the state park. Madge is poaching off this land, taking what she needs from the local human population.

There's a knock at the door, sharp and sudden enough to make me jump. Blaire runs a hand up and down my arm. "It's okay," she murmurs. "It's just Blake."

Vampire senses have their uses. I relax into the couch as much as I can, which isn't much at all. Blaire gets up and opens the door, and I don't miss the defensive posture, the way her eyes dart around like a threat could emerge from any angle.

"Well?"

Blake sighs, stepping inside so Blaire can shut and lock the door again. It's probably overkill, but none of us protest it. "She's gone. I think she had a car not too far from here. I'm guessing you two were distracted, or else you would have heard the car pull up."

"Can you follow the car?" I ask.

Blake gives me a sympathetic look. "There are like three hundred million cars in this country, and they all essentially smell the same. I could track it to the end of this road, since she's one of the few cars that's been on it. After that, nothing. It's too intermingled with all the other car scents."

Right. That makes sense. I nod, accepting that we've lost her as dread weighs me down further.

"There're a lot of ways to destroy scent," Blaire says. "Cover yourself with another scent. Water can do it, if you stay in the water long enough. A car. She could have done any of it. But she's hiding from us."

And she has a twenty-three year old kid at her mercy now. Suzanne is going to have a short and miserable rest of her life. For her sake, I hope it ends quickly. That sounds callous and unfeeling, but it's true. Madge can make it last and make it miserable. It's better for Suzanne if she doesn't have to suffer that for too long.

"Alright," Blake says crisply, suddenly standing more upright. "What's the plan? Do we run?"

"What?"

"Run? Is that the next logical step?"

It throws me to hear him talk about running so casually, like he has a life so easy to pack up and move. Like he can just tell Callie they have to go on the run, and she'll lose her job, her house, her friends, and she can't ask him any questions about it. Yeah, right.

"We could go," Blaire muses, and somehow I feel like I'm the only one thinking logically here. "If we go far enough, she won't be able to find us."

Something in me doubts that. If Madge wants me, then she'll do what it takes. She's been taking people with no remorse for who knows how long. "We can't run," I tell them. "You can't take Callie, Blake." And leaving her isn't an option any of us would consider.

"I could work something out," he insists.

"And tell her what?"

"I'd tell her—" He can't think of an answer, exactly like I knew he wouldn't be able to. I nod.

Blaire sighs. "So, we're here. And we're vigilant. And we're drinking once a week to stay as strong as possible. And you'll call everyone we know again, and tell them the update?"

"Yeah," Blake agrees, nodding slowly.

"And tell them Laurel is pretty convinced she's kidnapped and killed at least five people."

"Oh, fuck," he breathes. "What does she want them for?"

"For her spell ingredients," I tell him, touching the scar on my hand. "She needs someone brewing the spell that keeps her alive constantly. And it always kills the brewer—except for me. Before me, the longest surviving person made it only a few months, she told me." I hate thinking back on that time. I've kept it behind a permanent, foggy haze, only inadvertently letting it out during nightmares that would shake me for days. I have a sinking suspicion that I'll be spending a lot more time looking back on those days now. I'm going to be asked too many questions about Madge not to be thinking about that time.

"So she chops them up?"

"When they're no longer useful to her." I'd seen it. I wish I didn't have to know, wish I didn't have to see and hear all the ways she could divide up a human body. She'd do it with cold precision, sorting and organizing her kill into piles, sometimes absently telling me what the pieces would be used for. I wish I never knew any of that. "But until then, they brew the spell. Someone has to monitor it essentially non stop. You can get a few hours of sleep at a time at certain points, but for some of it you're awake for days on end, bleeding into a cauldron over and over and over again. If I wasn't like this, I know I'd have bled out. And then pain is—" I shudder. I don't want to say it. I'm compelled to say it. "It should just be a cut, but it's not. Whatever the magic is, it's like lightning in your veins."

The silence in the room is palpable and heavy. They both stare at me like they can unwind my brain through watching me, and I make myself look back.

"You could stay with us," Blake suggests. "The three of us in the same place is better protection."

It's not a terrible idea, except for the human living in Blake's house. Madge knows full well where they live. She was even invited in once, but, as far as we know, she's never sniffed around their house. And I'm not going to give her a reason to start, not with Callie there.

"No," I say firmly. "I won't draw any more attention to Callie. She's human, Blake. And Madge already kidnapped and probably killed five of them in the last few months. We're not putting a neon sign up offering her another one."

He bares his teeth. "You're insane if you think I'd let her anywhere near my wife."

"Then let's not give her any reason to even look at your wife, right?" I push back.

The twins look at each other for a long moment. "Alright," Blake says after a long pause, turning to give me a nod. "We'll be on high alert." He looks at me with a shocking, sweet sincerity in his eyes. "We won't let her touch you, Laurel."

This is the second time in the last few hours that the twins are making promises that they can't keep. I appreciate that they're trying, but I know better than to believe them.

I'll stay here in the locked cabin with the window shades drawn. I'll hide behind my vampire lover. And I'll hope that's all enough.

Blake says something to Blaire that I'm not paying attention to, too trapped in my own thoughts. Then he's gone, and it's just Blaire and I hiding out in a cabin that I can't decide if it's a prison or a sanctuary.

Madge watched us. She watched us through the window, and who knows how much she saw? Either way, she invaded the careful safety we built. She invaded our privacy, Blaire's carefully isolated little world. She not only threatened our lives with her very presence; she's making me doubt every action, every step.

I've been torn apart for her too many times. I don't want to give her another piece of me.

"You didn't eat this morning," Blaire murmurs eventually. "You need food, baby."

I have absolutely no desire to eat. To tell the truth, I don't have a desire for anything outside of curling up into a little ball to hide away from it all. Unfortunately, that's not an option. Hiding doesn't make any of us any safer.

I need to keep my hands busy, because the second I let that go, then my mind will be busy, and it'll be busy turning over every horrific scenario that ends with Madge taking me back that I can possibly conjure up. I cook an early lunch, wash the dishes, and scrub the floor so I have something to do.

Chapter Twenty-Eight

We stay locked inside for almost a week, only leaving to go to the library a single time when Blaire decides I've been looking too morose without a book. She stands vigilantly behind me the entire time, and I'm in and out of the library in less than fifteen minutes. Anything more seems like pushing our luck.

Callie calls me on Thursday to complain that she hasn't heard from me. She says it differently, of course. She says she misses seeing me every day now that we don't work together anymore, and that we need to make sure we still see each other on a regular basis, and do I want to come over for dinner Saturday night? She tells me to bring Blaire, and I agree because I don't know what else to say. I can't exactly tell her we're in lock down over here; Callie knows Madge is a threat, but the scale we're dealing with is completely foreign to her. She'd just tell me to get a restraining order again.

Blaire doesn't react great. "Are you out of your mind?" she demands, eyes flicking to the window like she's going to see someone watching us through it. "Laurel, I get that you want to see your friend, but someone is trying to kill you, and—"

"No," I say firmly. "First of all, she's not trying to kill me. She wants me because she *can't* kill me."

"That's not better. You know that's not better, right?"

"You don't need to tell me what she'd do to me; I already lived it once," I tell her, which shuts her up real fast. "And two, she's older than me, Blaire. And I'm nine hundred years old. She's not going to disappear. We have to figure out how to live knowing she's out there. Otherwise, we're staying in this cabin forever, and I'll lose my mind."

Blaire doesn't have a counterargument to that. "We'll go," she concedes, shoulders slumping. "But if we sense anything off, if I even get a whiff of her—we're leaving."

I nod, because that's a fair concession, and then I turn away, trying to brace myself for going outside.

I want it. I need it. I'm terrified of it. All those thoughts swirl around in me at the same time. I try not to show it to Blaire—I don't want to give her another excuse to try to stay in—but I can't hide it completely.

We're going, though. I'm going to claw this much of my life back, at least.

***

Having three people as tense as if a war might break out any second and a fourth completely oblivious is a bit of a mind trip. Callie tells me about the library, teases Blaire for not helping set the table, and kisses her husband while the three of us keep looking out the window like we might see Madge lurking in the hedges.

Fuck, I should remind Blake that I once lurked in his hedges. They're great for lurking. He should do something to ensure that no one else tries that.

I help Callie with the food, feeling a prickling on the back of my neck the entire time. But every time I turn around, trying not to overreact but unable to help it, it's Blaire watching me.

Madge isn't here. And breaking into a house like this wouldn't be her style. I have to keep reminding myself of that. We're safe here.

Probably.

When dinner is on the table, when Blake is unenthusiastically eating a taco and Blaire is pushing hers around and dumping it on my plate whenever Callie isn't looking, when Callie is asking about my job search, things feel almost normal. Almost.

I keep my answers to Callie vague. It's not like I can say much; how would I explain why I'm no longer searching for a job? I turn the conversation back onto her as quickly as I can.

Blaire is getting twitchy right after dinner is done. I know our time is almost at its end, but I pretend I don't see anything, helping Callie wash the dishes while Blake wipes down the table.

"Everyone seems a little tense," Callie whispers to me, proving she's not as unobservant as we all pretend she is. I know the vampires in this house can hear her whisper without any effort, but I try to pretend this is a conversation for just us.

I shrug. "I didn't notice that." I feel terrible as soon as the lie is out of my mouth. I try to minimize how much I lie to Callie, but this might be the most outright lie I've ever told. Like anyone missed that tension.

But I can't tell her why we're so tense, so I deflect.

"Really?" she asks skeptically. I shrug, so she sighs, putting the plates away. "I don't know. Maybe it's just been too long. We have to make sure we have dinners regularly."

"That sounds nice." Another lie. Not that I don't like spending time with Callie, because of course I do. But if tonight taught me anything, it's that this return to normalcy isn't so normal. I don't know if anything will ever be normal again.

"Laurel," Blaire says from behind us, making me jump. She frowns when I look at her, eyes worried. I know I'm more jumpy than usual, but it's not like she doesn't know why. "It's getting late. We should go."

It's barely eight, but I know that I've already pushed this too far. Blaire is tense as a bowstring about to snap, and she deserves to go home where she can let go of at least some of that vigilance.

But when we're in the car, she surprises me by clutching the steering wheel and muttering, "I want to go to the club."

"What? Why?" It hasn't even been a full week yet.

"Because we're already out and I don't think I can handle doing it again tomorrow. Because the more blood I take, the stronger I am and the more able I am to protect you."

Blaire really does see herself as the last defense between me and Madge, and it makes my heart ache. I appreciate how she wants to take care of me. I love that she loves me like this. But the tension in her, the hypervigilance—that's no way to live.

I did this to her. I brought this to her door. And I know I said we shouldn't run, but if I ran alone, if I took this away from the people I care about—

No. Blaire made me promise not to run alone again, and the least I can do is honor that. She's made her choice, and I should respect that.

But it boggles my mind to think she'd choose *me* when it takes this much effort to love me.

"Alright," I tell her, trying to keep my voice neutral. "Should we go home and change?"

She looks conflicted for a minute, but shakes her head. "If I get you into that house, I won't let you out again," she says. "I won't be strong enough to do that. So, we go like this."

I look both of us over, noting the total lack of club readiness. It's a Saturday night; surely the club has standards.

But Blaire has that mesmer, so I have no doubt we'll get in.

"Maybe I'll get lucky and they'll still have my book somewhere," I muse.

She gives me a quick, strained smile. "Sure. You can read your vampire book instead of hanging out with your actual, real-life vampire. Whatever floats your boat."

***

Blaire kisses me inside the door of the club, the type of kiss that makes my knees go a little weak, my breath a little short. I lean in when she pulls away, half-tempted to follow her out onto the dance floor. "I'll hear you if you shout," she murmurs, a promise, and then disappears into the crowd.

My first stop is the bar, who actually have my book in an overflowing cardboard box beneath the counter. Satisfied with my prize, I make my way around the edge, looking for a table to hide out at.

The floor is crowded and the music cranked up loud enough to rattle my eardrums. Even through the crowd, I can see flashes of Blaire, moving sensually throughout the throngs of people, seeking out her prey. And I'm having trouble looking away from her.

Am I scared by the vampire blood-drinking thing, or am I turned on by it? My brain apparently doesn't know anymore, but I want Blaire something awful right now. If we can get through tonight without freaking out about the last time we left the club, then I plan to make her come until she passes out on me later.

My eyes dart around, but nothing seems out of place. There're plenty of young people living their best lives, the alcohol is flowing, and the dancing is bordering on indecent.

Blaire finds a partner, hands a gentle tease on her shoulders, sucking her right into her trap. Then the crowd shifts, and I lose sight of her.

"She should have left you with the brother."

My whole body goes cold, my blood replaced with ice. I turn my head slowly, not daring to breathe.

Madge sits opposite of me, like she's been there for hours. She smiles slightly, and I shudder at the sight.

"She doesn't know my voice," she says, almost conversationally. "And if you say a word I'll kill every single one of these humans I can get to." She sets a wicked looking knife on the table between us. I nod, eyes flicking between the knife and her face. They're both equally dangerous.

"I have a spell so potent it could probably kill every human here," she continues. "It's in my sleeve and if I drop it, it's over."

The thing about Madge is she doesn't bluff; she has no need. If she's making threats, it's because she means it. I keep my mouth shut as my heart pounds, knowing that this is it. This is the end.

"So now that we're on the same page, let's go. Or I swear I'll start killing them." Madge looks out at the dance floor but her hand tightens on the knife as she looks away. I don't twitch, refusing to react. "I'd wager you have about thirty seconds to make up your mind."

Blaire must be distracted, then. Thirty seconds...

Thirty seconds is no time at all, no time to make a plan, no time to alert Blaire without the witch knowing. Thirty seconds are the last free moments of my life.

The knife glints under the club lights. I close my eyes for a second, remembering my promise not to run, to take Blaire with me if I had to go.

Blaire will understand. I hope it's true, anyway. I can't stand the idea of her thinking I abandoned her.

My book. I'm still holding that stupid book, the *Dracula* book I checked out to taunt Blaire with. I lay it on the table, cover up. Blaire will understand.

"Leave your cellphone."

Moving slowly enough so she doesn't spook and drop that spell, I pull the phone from my pocket. If I could dial Blaire, could I tip her off? Would she pick up her phone from the dance floor?

Madge interrupts my thinking. "Now, pet. We need to go."

I feel like it's my last line of defense, like I'm naked without it, but I put my phone down next to the book. This is it, then.

I can feel my heart pounding, but my brain just feels calm, like this was entirely expected. I've been waiting for this, and it's finally arrived. I don't have to wait anymore.

Madge's smile grows. "Wonderful. Let's go." She stands and waits for me to join her. The worst part is she doesn't threaten me again, doesn't wave the knife around or say anything. She just waits, because she knows she's got me. She knows I'll follow, and, hating myself a bit, I do.

As soon as we get outside, I look for an opening. There are less people for Madge to hurt out here. Whatever deadly spell she apparently has likely won't work as well without the enclosed, tightly packed space of the club.

I could run. I could get away and meet up with Blaire again later, keep her safe by staying away for a while, but ultimately come back in the end.

Madge grips my upper arm so tight she's likely creating bruises. They'll fade in minutes, but the tight pressure makes me grit my teeth. "You always were a squirrelly one," she muses, and before I can retort, I feel a stabbing in my arm.

***

I wake up with a jolt as the car goes over a bump. When I try to move, I realize I'm cuffed hand and foot to some heavy bolts Madge must have added into this car. How prepared is she for this? Or is this how she took those other people too? Am I one more in a long series of people to be kept here?

Madge looks at me from the rearview mirror. "Huh," she says. "That wore off faster than anticipated."

"Yeah," I rasp, voice rough from whatever was in that drug. "I'm good at that." I try to force myself to sit upright so I'm not slouched over like a drunken party girl, but the cuffs don't give me a lot of room.

"I wonder what else won't work on you..." Madge muses, but it's clear my input isn't expected. Madge has already started viewing me like an object, and I bet she's dreaming up experiments for me.

I give one tug on the cuffs, already knowing it's useless. As expected, it doesn't move an inch. "You planning to keep me cuffed forever?" I demand.

"I thought a cell would work fine."

Another cell. Of course. What else did I expect? It's right back to where I started from.

"Blaire'll come for me."

Madge snorts. "How? How will she find you, hm? We walked out of the club. She was too busy to notice. We're forty miles away by car now. How is she going to find you, pet?"

All good questions, and I don't have an answer. And truthfully, I don't know if Blaire ever will find me. But I need to say it. I need to pretend I believe it. "She'll come."

Madge laughs at me, and then doesn't pay me any more attention for the rest of the ride.

Eventually, she stops the car. The sky is starting to lighten with dawn, and I try to get a look outside to figure out any clues about where we are, but I can't get a good view outside before Madge turns around. Fast as lightning, she stabs

190

me in the neck again. I make some sort of protest at the prick of the needle, and then I'm unconscious.

Chapter Twenty-Nine

I wake up in what is obviously a cell.

The bars are steel and the floor is concrete, but otherwise it's straight out of my nightmares. Sure, this isn't the earth-packed floor from nine hundred years ago. But there's the cauldron in the middle, a thin blanket in one corner, and a bucket in the other. Still the same set up. Still the same nightmares.

"I won't do it," I say, feeling suddenly, stupidly brave. But what else can Madge do to me? She's already taken everything, and I doubt I'll suddenly become able to die.

And even if Madge did figure out a way to make it happen, maybe it wouldn't be such a bad thing. Dying is infinitely better than being stuck here with her.

I've known happiness, now. I've known warm mornings in bed with Blaire, and family dinners with Callie and Blake, and how it lights up every nerve to kiss Blaire. I won't live in a cage after all that.

"I won't brew it for you." I raise my voice, knowing she can hear me even if I can't see her. "You can live without it." Or not, really. I'd prefer her not to live.

Madge's laugh echoes from the top of the stairs. My head spins, but I can't see her through the shadows. Everything in me recoils at knowing she's nearby and out of sight, but I force myself to hold firm. "You're a fool, pet, if you think

I'd ever let your choices get in my way. I have someone brewing it as we speak at my last residence. But she won't last forever."

Which of the people that she stole, then? I wonder, but I also know I'll never get my answer. Another human will die in a way their loved ones will never understand. They'll probably never find the body.

"I won't take over for her. I won't do it." I try to sound firm, but I'm not sure I succeed.

The basement is painfully, terrifyingly still for a moment. Then Madge's voice breaks the silence, like nails on the chalkboard down my spine. "You will."

***

Despite her threat, Madge doesn't seem eager to force the issue. I'm left in the basement alone, with no food or water. I have no idea how long I've been here, considering there are no windows, but it's probably been a few days.

Blaire will be frantic. She'll likely blame herself, considering all the talk about protecting me, and that's what hurts the most. I set her up to be hurt.

Maybe we should have run. There are plenty of places in the world to hide, and I've been to so many of them that I'd love to share with Blaire.

It's too late to think about that now that I'm stuck in this cell. I can't change the choices I made, but maybe, if I'm very smart, I'll find my way back to Blaire.

But probably not. I know how high the odds are stacked against me.

I can't bend the bars or punch through the wall. I'm not strong, so even if Madge did slip up and let me get too close to her, I'd probably lose in a fight. There's nothing I can do, not yet.

But if I did get away... I close my eyes, curling up underneath the thin blanket, and imagine it. I'd go back to Blaire. Apologize to Callie again, and in my mind Callie will accept it. We'll have dinners together. The cabin will be home again.

I shiver in the night, the warmth of the imaginary cabin not enough to sustain me.

***

I'm woken abruptly when the cell door opens and a body is thrown in.

I freeze, looking at the open door, but there really is no question. There's no way I could make it past Madge, and I'd hate myself forever if I left whoever this is here. I left people behind the last time I ran from Madge, and I still can't stop thinking about them; I won't do it again.

I scramble to the body as the cell door closes. She's breathing. She's human, I assume, with red hair and freckles. I flip her so she's on her side, facing me. "What did you do to her?" I demand.

Madge stands by the closed and locked cell door, a smug smile that twists up my insides on her face. She's so very beautiful, in an elfin, fairy-tale like way. It's a vicious contrast to the evil that lurks beneath. "If you won't do it, I'll find someone who will," she says simply.

I look down at the redhead's delicate little wrists, imagining the amount of blood that'll be needed spilling from them, and nausea rises to my throat.

She won't last long. A month, maybe two, three if she's extraordinary. And then she'll die like all the humans do. I can't. I can't have that on my conscience again. "Don't kill her."

"I wasn't planning on it," she says, pursing her lips as she looks us over, eyes dispassionate. I can feel the measurement in her eyes; this is a witch experienced with her evil spells, and using hundreds of years of practice to make estimates of how long we'll make it.

I force a deep breath, trying to maintain some amount of control. "You know what I mean. She'll die."

"They all die, pet. *You* all die. It's the way of the world."

"Witches are supposed to die too," I push, remembering what Blaire told me.

Madge's smile is laced with cruelty. "If humans could avoid death they would. Let's not pretend I'm so unusual. I just have the ability to do it."

"She could live longer." She's so young. She has a lifetime in front of her, decades of living left to do. But not if Madge gets to her.

Madge shrugs. "Maybe, maybe not. Not my problem."

I take a deep breath, trying to steady myself. I'm not crying, but I almost wish I was. I wish I could be surprised by what she's doing, but I already knew she had this type of cruel manipulation in her. "What do you want?"

"I want my spell. It doesn't matter to me whether you brew it or she does."

"And you'll, what, let me go if she does it?" I ask incredulously. There is no world where I can imagine her doing that, and I wonder if she thinks I'm stupid enough to fall for that promise.

Madge laughs, short and sharp. "No. You're too much of a *curiosity* to let go, pet. Plenty of people are interested in the blood of a human who can't die. You'll stay. But it's your choice: do you spare yourself a little bit of pain at her expense, or do you take the pain?"

"I could die too," I point out.

"I think we both know we wouldn't be having this conversation if that was true." Madge, already so close to the bars, steps closer, as if involuntarily. "*Twenty* lunar cycles. Imagine what could have happened if we weren't interrupted. Potentially indefinitely. You're the richest resource I've ever seen, pet."

I manage to snort, even if laughing is the last thing I feel like doing. "Doesn't sound like a great deal for me."

Madge makes a face and I think it's supposed to approximate sympathy. "Yes, well, that's the way of the world, pet. Someone rules and someone else is ruled. I have the power. I rule." She shakes off the sympathy and returns to business. "So, what's it going to be?"

It's really no choice at all. Dread pools in my gut, but I can't see a way out of this one. "How do I know you'll keep your word?"

"I thought you might ask." Her eyes light up, like she was planning this. She withdraws a vial from her dress pocket. "It's a blood pact," she says. "I made it myself. Whatever vow you make, if you seal it with blood, it's guaranteed under pain of death."

"I don't die," I remind her. "And neither do you."

Madge turns the small vial between her fingers. "This will kill you," she says, looking at the vial instead of me. Her eyes are perversely fascinated, like she enjoys holding something so deadly in her hands. "It'll kill anyone. Simply suck the life right out your body, break it down into tiny little pieces. I've seen it work." I look at it. It doesn't look that serious—it's a pale yellow color, seemingly benign and tiny to boot. But I believe her. Whatever else Madge is, she knows how her spells work.

"I promise to brew the spell, keep you alive, you promise not to make anyone else do it?"

"No," Madge says, eyes narrowed. "You promise to *obey* me. Can't have you running away again."

I don't functionally see the difference, but I won't give her what she wants so easily. "I'll obey you about the spell."

"You'll obey me in all things, pet. I have the power here."

I know she does. I'm the one behind bars, and she's the only person who even knows where I am. I've never felt smaller than I do right now. The words taste like ash coming up. "I promise to obey you."

"Say it with blood, or it doesn't count," Madge says. "Give me your hand."

I only hesitate a second, knowing I'm out of options. I walk to the bars and extend a hand through it. The old scar on my palm sits there between the two of us.

Madge cuts across my scar with a small knife, and then grabs my palm, twisting it so it can drip into the vial. "Say it," Madge hisses at me, watching the blood drip with wide, fascinated eyes.

It strings, and it stings more when Madge digs her fingers in so more blood drips out. I remind myself that I should start thinking of this as a minor pain. It only gets worse from here. "I promise to obey you."

Madge studies the spell and nods. After a few seconds, she releases my hand, and I step away as quickly as I can before she decides that she needs more.

Madge cuts her own hand, wincing as she does, and drips a few drops into the vial. As soon as Madge's blood hits it, it turns a deep, burnished gold.

"I promise that *only* you will brew it forevermore," Madge says, a light of triumph in her eyes as she corks the small bottle. "It's done." She tucks the bottle in her pocket, making it disappear from sight. "The new moon is on Tuesday. You start as soon as the lunar cycle does."

Bizarrely, I feel calm now, a deep, lethargic sort of feeling washing through my body. It's all out of my hands now. "Let her go."

"Why would I do that?" Madge asks, mouth curling into a slow smirk.

My stomach falls out, even though at this point, I don't know why I'm surprised. "Are you serious? You promised."

"I promised I wouldn't make anyone else brew the spell. And I won't. Why would I? I have you." She turns away and leaves, leaving me behind her in sickened, paralyzed shock.

***

The woman wakes up. She comes to slowly, and doesn't move at first. I wouldn't know she was alive if I weren't sitting right next to her, listening to her breathe.

I don't move when she wakes, not wanting to scare her any more. "Hello," I say softly.

The woman's body tenses, but she tries not to react.

"My name's Laurel," I continue, fighting to keep the same calm voice. "What's yours?"

She's silent for a moment. "Where am I?" she finally asks, voice so soft it might dissolve into nothing.

I hesitate. I should have prepared a better answer, but I don't have one. "We were both taken," I tell her evasively. "I don't know too much. Sorry."

The woman sits up, hugging her knees to herself. "How long have you been here?" She looks small, and I'm forced to think the word *breakable* about her again.

"It's hard to tell time down here." It's an evasive answer, but I don't really have a more precise one. Madge said the new moon is on Tuesday, but I couldn't tell you when Tuesday is if my life depended on it, nor how many days have passed since I was brought here.

"What does she want?"

Blood. Eternal life. Slaves. I keep my mouth shut and my face neutral. Is it better or worse to know, at this point?

The woman looks over at me, and must catch the dried blood on my hand. "Did she hurt you?"

I curl my fist up. "It's nothing bad," I tell her. "It's already healed."

"Must've been here a while then," the woman notes. Right. Because humans take a long time to heal. I make a mental note of that, but I have no idea

197

how I'm going to hide what my body does when I start cutting into myself for that damned spell.

The woman hesitantly uncurls herself. "When does she bring food?"

I have no idea, but Madge is going to have to if she wants this human to live. I haven't eaten since that dinner at Callie's.

"It's hard to track time down here," is what I tell her.

The woman looks over at me, and I can read the mistrust in her eyes, which is fair enough; I've told her so many lies already. But she's alone down here with me, and there's no one else for her to trust.

She uncurls more and turns herself to face Laurel. "My name's Polly."

I swallow. "Hi, Polly. Nice to meet you."

***

Tuesday is apparently not too far away. Polly is hungry but not starving when Madge shows up and opens the cell door long enough to deposit a lighter and a small knife. I eye the weapon, but it's little more than a pocketknife; it'll be useful for cutting myself open, but I won't be pulling off any daring escapes with it.

Which I can't do anyway, I remind myself. I'm bound to follow Madge's orders, and she's told me to stay here and brew the spell.

"I'll bring down everything else as you need it. Get started—you know what to do," she says, and then turns to leave.

Polly is clearly thrown by the odd assortment of items, but she doesn't let the opportunity get away from her. "Wait! Can we have some food? Water? Please?"

"I do need water to start this," I point out. It's true, but I want to get poor Polly some water.

Madge sighs. "Water it is, then. Don't waste it; I won't give you more than you need. And don't worry," she says, turning to Polly, a predatory smile in place. "I won't allow you to starve."

"This would be a lot easier with a window," I gamble. "Something to help me track where we are in the lunar cycle."

I can't leave. But perhaps Polly can escape. And it's a long-shot, but maybe I can teach her Blaire's phone number.

Blaire must be looking for me. It's like a fist squeezing at my heart. I want to make it out of here. I don't know if it's possible, but I want it with my whole being. But whatever happens, I can't leave Blaire to wonder. It'll eat her alive.

"You did fine before without a window," Madge dismisses. "I'm perfectly capable of telling you. Stop complaining and get to work, pet." She turns and walks away.

I bring the wood over to the still-standing cauldron and set it up, no other choice than to get started. One good thing is she gave me an actual lighter, which is definitely an improvement on how we lit fires nine centuries ago.

When it's all set up, I know I can't delay any longer. I hold the knife in my unscarred hand, psyching myself up to cut into myself and start the pain once more.

"What the fuck are you doing?" Polly shouts at me.

I take a deep breath through the pain, ignoring the lightning shooting through every one of my nerves. I keep the knife pressed into the cut so my hand doesn't heal. The first day always takes a lot of blood, and the less times I have to re-cut myself, the better. "Trust me," I grit out through clenched teeth, "You don't want to know."

***

I keep the knife in my skin until the bottom of the cauldron is properly coated, and it feels like it takes hours. Madge returns toward at the end, giving us a few gallon jugs of water. I'm still standing over the cauldron, watching her with more hate than I think I've ever felt in my entire life.

"Two for you, pet, and one for drinking." She looks me over. "You'd go faster if you cut something more major."

"I'm not worried about speed."

"What, you want her to bleed out?" Polly demands.

199

Madge chuckles, which sounds even more grating than usual with the amount of pain I'm in. "I'm sure she'd be fine. Pet here is very, hm, *resilient*, isn't she?"

I sigh, exhaustion weighing on me as I study the bottom of the cauldron in the dim light. "Let her go."

"She seems useful for keeping you in line," Madge says, shaking her head.

"You already saw to that!"

"Call it extra insurance. Now get to work; moon is about to set." She turns to leave again, and I watch, loathing building in my gut. I want her to die. I want to kill her. I've lived a long time, but Madge is the only person I've ever wanted to watch the life leave their eyes.

"What is going on?"

I don't know how long I can put Polly off. "I'm going to teach you a phone number," I say softly. I promised to obey Madge, and I am; I'm brewing her spell. It's her fault she didn't think to forbid me from doing this. "When you get out of here, I need you to call it. Tell the woman who answers everything you know."

"What? What's that going to do?"

I shrug. "Might save my life. Will you help me move these?"

***

Madge brings me more ingredients as time passes, as well as a lunar calendar and an old fashioned clock, but after two days I don't really need them. Even with nine hundred years between then and now, I slip right back into the brewing of the spell, like it's second nature. There are some things you evidently never forget.

Polly gets more and more listless without food, and the water Madge sets aside for her to drink runs out quickly. I try to get more, but Madge ignores my request.

Madge said she wouldn't let Polly starve, but I can't see another way this ends.

Until Madge appears at the cell door one day, a wicked looking knife at her hand and a jar in the other. "It's time," she says, and with a sickening lurch, I suddenly know exactly what's going to happen.

It's like a car wreck; I can see it but not stop it. I should say something, but what could Polly do? I still try to get something out, but my voice feels like it's caught in my chest, squashed under the weight of what's coming. I can't breathe. I want to run, to stand in front of Polly, but my feet are glued to the floor, horror making my whole body heavy.

Madge unlocks the cell door, holding her knife pointed at me. "I haven't forgotten what happened last time," she warns. "Just remember mine's bigger. And you betray me, you try to leave, you'll die. It's written in blood, now."

My eyes dart from Polly to the cell door, back and forth, back and forth. There's only one last chance. I open my mouth, testing it. I don't know if the spell will let me talk, but I have to try. "Run."

Polly tries, bolting for the door, but she hasn't eaten in a while now, and Madge catches her easily, one deceptively strong hand wrapping around Polly's bicep, holding her while Polly flails.

Then Madge uses that wickedly long knife to stab Polly in the throat.

A jagged scream rips out of me, sharp and angry and so, so hurt. It didn't have to end this way. It never should have ended this way.

Madge watches Polly die dispassionately, then drops the body onto the cold concrete floor. "Clever, pet," she says, turning away and looking over at me. "But not clever enough."

"Why would you do that?" I want to shout it at her, but it comes out weak, shaky, barely above a whisper.

"Why wouldn't I? What use is she to me otherwise?" Madge asks. "Now, hurry. I need the organs before they cool."

I blanch, fighting down vomit at the thought. "You're disgusting!"

"I'm a survivor," Madge corrects. "I can't help if your kind are prey animals. Or, not your kind anymore, perhaps. If they ever were. Now, quickly. You'll help me with this."

I try to cross my arms, try to refuse her, but we both know the blood pact means I have to obey her. I wonder with a sickening sort of clarity if this is exactly the type of situation she had in mind when she made me swear that.

Slowly, reluctantly, as if my feet are encased in lead, I stumble forward. "What do you need me to do?" I ask hoarsely.

"I'll cut. You hold," Madge orders and furiously, reluctantly, I do.

Chapter Thirty

Madge makes the process as long and grueling as possible, carrying each individual jarred organ upstairs before she brings down a fresh jar. I swear she's doing it to torment me, just to leave me longer with this body.

Polly was a person a few hours ago, and now I can barely recognize her as such. Does Madge do this to all her victims?

"Pity I can't use you for this dirty work," she muses when she finally moves the desecrated corpse. Even Madge, who always looks above the filth and squalor of this basement, is covered in blood now. "But I don't trust you out of this cell. And you have a spell to look after." She drops Polly's corpse outside the cell, then locks it again before carrying the body upstairs.

I can't move, watching the blood puddle on the floor while I'm rooted in place.

Madge has killed people in front of me before. Many actually, the side effect of being with her for so long. I've seen countless others paraded in and known they would die sooner rather than later.

I don't know why this one was so shocking. I guess I got complacent, or else I forgot how bad it can be.

There's a horrific, gory mess on the cell floor that will stain. I don't have any way to wash it away, and the cell already smelled of blood, anyway. I just hate looking at it. Whether or not Madge intended it that way, the blood stain is one more thing keeping me away from the cell door.

I think of the basement Blaire, Blake, and I found. It was covered in blood and viscera, stained beyond any person's imagination. It reeked of blood even long after it was emptied, and the grime of the place seemed to stick to my skin. I know exactly how this place is going to end up.

The door to the house slams somewhere above me, shaking me out of my thoughts.

There's nothing else to do but live with it. I turn back to the spell and start working out when it'll demand more blood, feeling like Polly's ghost is staring reproachfully over my shoulder the whole time. I don't blame her.

***

When the new moon comes, I stir until my arms ache and then push beyond that, not stopping until I'm half worried I'll fall into the cauldron from exhaustion and drown.

The basement grows colder without the fire to keep me warm, and I involuntarily remember the way Blaire's hands would hold me in the night. She was always so warm.

Then I force myself to keep stirring. It doesn't do me any good to remember. It just makes me more desperate for things I probably can't ever have again.

At last, it's done. The spell is deep and red and has stopped bubbling, and I start to fill the vials Madge brought down a few hours ago. I struggle to place the cork in, my muscles exhausted and less coordinated than usual, but I'm careful not to spill a drop. I don't want to know what the blood oath would do to me if I waste any of the spell.

The minute the spell is done, Madge comes downstairs with a fresh, empty cauldron. "Let's see if you're still any good at this," she says, depositing the new cauldron and immediately turning to the just-finished spell, only half of it already bottled.

As much as I hate it, I know I'm still good at this. There are some things you can never forget, and Madge wouldn't have let me mess it up.

Madge takes an already filled vial, then drinks deeply from it, both hands cupping the tiny vial and holding it to her face. Her eyes slip closed, and some of the tension in her shoulders eases.

The red liquid stains Madge's lips and teeth, and her cruel smile takes on a truly frightening edge. "I think I'll keep you," she announces, as if either of us were ever under the impression that she wouldn't. "Now, start again."

"I need food," I tell her, trying to sound as defiant as I possibly can. There's a tugging inside my chest, and I know without asking it's some sort of compulsion, the blood oath pulling at me for not immediately obeying her order. I grit my teeth and fight it. "And water. Maybe something fresh to wear. A shower wouldn't go amiss."

Madge's lip curls, still stained red. "You must misunderstand our relationship here, *pet*."

"The food and water aren't optional," I press. Maybe the shower was too much to hope for, but I'm going to get something out of this, dammit.

Madge raises an eyebrow and looks me up and down. "Clearly they are," she points out. "You seem to be doing fine."

"I'm weak," I argue. "Your spell takes a lot out of me, alright? I haven't eaten in, what, a month and a half? Just because I *can* survive doesn't make it easy."

Madge tilts her head, curls bouncing with the move. "Alright," she says after a moment. "You'll get dinner. We'll talk about the shower later. I'll bottle up the rest. Start the new one."

"Food first."

Madge laughs cruelly. "Take the win you got, pet. Don't push for more."

***

The thing about this spell is that once I finish, I'm starting all over again practically immediately, and giving my blood until I feel like death. When Madge comes to bring me food—bread and water, by the looks of things—I'm covered in fresh blood once more, using my truly gross shirt to mop up the fresh wound.

"Any thoughts about the shower?" I ask. "I'm sure I'm pretty unpleasant to be around."

Madge chuckles, sliding the food under the bars and then standing back upright. "If you get too bad I'll throw a bucket of water on you, like in the old days. Don't worry, pet. There's no one here to look pretty for. Your precious vampire isn't here to see you."

"Don't talk about her." I wish my voice came out stronger. I wish I sounded angry instead of scared. But I don't like the idea that Blaire is on Madge's mind.

Madge chuckles again, edged with cruelty. "Don't like hearing about her? I'll tell you, she is a pain. Been asking around about me and you. But don't worry, pet. She'll never take you away from me. I've been doing this for a long time."

"She'll come for me." I wish I sounded more sure.

"How? The world is big, pet. And she's one vampire."

She'll come for me. I don't say it again, but I try to make myself believe it as Madge walks away.

***

When I sleep, I dream of Blaire.

Sleep comes rarely, considering the level of tending the spell requires, but without fail, every time I slip under, Blaire is there.

It's funny, because when I was with Blaire, I couldn't stop dreaming of Madge. But now that I'm here, the sweet dreams finally come.

They're always the quiet moments. When she'd tell me to eat, when she'd hold me, when I'd curl up with her with my book. Every time I wake up, they slip away and it's bittersweet and painful.

I'd give anything for those days back. I'm pretty sure I'm never going to get them again.

The spell takes more and more out of me every day. I don't know how I made it twenty months last time; it hasn't even been two yet, and I'm ready to give up. I could do it. I could stop. Refuse to brew the spell, and let Madge's ominous blood oath take me.

It'd be easy, but I don't do it. Death is so final.

It's not that I'm scared of it. I'm nine hundred years old, and while it's intimidating to think of death as the one thing I've never been able to know, I'm not scared. I'm confident that this is worse than any death.

But I don't do it. I'm pretty sure I'll never see Blaire again, but *pretty sure* isn't absolute. And on the off chance I somehow win this, if there's a miracle and I survive—

I'll hold on. I want to see Blaire one more time.

Chapter Thirty-One

When I bottle the next batch for Madge, my arms still shooting with pain from where the spell drew my blood from me, Madge watches the whole process dispassionately. I'm soaked in blood to the elbow, and she stands there in her pristine flowy dress, looking like she's on an afternoon stroll. If it wouldn't kill me, I'd throw a vial at her.

"You could help," I snap, because surely expecting me to cork all these little bottles isn't realistic.

She *tuts*. "Now, now, pet. And you were so close to a reward. Don't ruin it now."

I stop, considering. "What kind of reward?"

"I bought a steak dinner for myself tonight. I'll let you choose: you can have half of it, or you can have a shower."

"Shower," I tell her immediately. My clothes are crusted with two and a half months worth of dirt. My blood and Polly's blood has made the cloth stiff. My skin feels like it might fall off with how bad it itches. I'd give a lot more than I'm comfortable admitting for a shower right now.

"Alright then," she says briskly. She steps toward the door, then freezes. "Don't try to hurt me, pet. You'll regret it if you do."

I nod, and I swear I can feel the spell that binds me to her tightening around my chest like some sort of choking vine.

She lets me out, then leads the way back upstairs. I blink in the brighter light, shocked to see daylight for the first time in so long.

This is a perfectly ordinary house, with a kitchen out of a storybook. I could picture someone's grandmother cooking there, and that table could sit a family of six. I try to catch any clues I can out the windows, but between the blinding sunlight and Madge hurrying me along, I get nothing. We're probably in suburbia somewhere, with a large yard and some distance between neighbors. Madge's ability to blend in in plain sight is truly terrifying.

"Upstairs," she commands briskly, so I walk up the stairs with her at my back, an uncomfortable prickling sensation on the back of my neck as she stares at me. "Second door to the left."

I push it open to reveal a tiny bathroom, and I'm left wondering who Madge stole this house from. I somehow doubt that she put the little duck stickers on the wall herself.

"Can I get a change of clothes?" I ask her. When she doesn't respond right away, I say, "C'mon. You have to admit that showering and putting this back on defeats the point."

She looks me over with a pursed lip, and I know I have her; even she has to acknowledge how appallingly gross I look. I know Madge doesn't mind getting her hands dirty, but she's usually so clean, so pristine in the ugly world she's made for herself. Surely my condition must offend her somewhat. "I'll get you something. Come on."

I follow behind her as she crosses the hall to a bedroom, and I crane to look over her shoulder, hopefully not being too obvious about it. I know I'm getting locked back in my cell at the end of this, but maybe this little excursion will convince her to give me more. I haven't forgotten the thing Blaire did with tracking Madge's number. If she's left out a cellphone, or maybe a computer—

"Don't get any ideas, pet," Madge says, shoving a bundle of fabric into my hands. I shake it out, looking it over. It's the same type of flowy, patterned dress she seems to favor, with poofy sleeves and an ankle-length skirt. This one is yellow, with off-white flowers. It'll be too big on me, but beggars can't be choosers. It's clean, and that's enough right now.

"I'm giving you ten minutes exactly," she says. "Consider it a reward for good behavior. If you're not out in ten minutes, then I'll come drag you out."

I swallow, nodding. Ten minutes. Ten minutes with an actual wall between me and anyone else.

Ten minutes isn't enough time to get myself clean from this blood, but something is better than nothing.

When the door clicks shut behind me, I almost collapse in relief. A flimsy door isn't nearly enough of a barrier between Madge and me, but even it feels amazing right now. But I can't waste a second.

I turn the water on, relieved that it heats up quickly, then shed my gross clothes, sincerely hoping Madge burns them. I'm sure this dress will be as bad within days, considering I'll be starting the spell all over again, but I'll take what I can get.

And as soon as the water is running, and hopefully drowning out the sound of me moving, I quietly creep around and look for anything that might be useful to me.

I'm once again stuck wondering who lived here before, because I doubt Madge bought all these products. What does she need with medicine and anti-wrinkle cream? I check the date on them, and I don't know if it's better or worse that they're more than five years old.

And then, underneath the sink, I find something actually interesting. It's one of those bleach mixtures you use to clean a toilet, the kind you squirt into the toilet bowl. I look it over, scanning down the ingredients, and see it's real bleach.

One of those medicine bottles contains liquid. I take it into the shower with me, dumping the contents down the drain while my whole body practically collapses under the hot water, melting as the dirt and blood sluices off my skin.

I don't have enough time to scrub myself properly. I wish I did, but I know Madge wasn't kidding about pulling me out of here, so I cursorily wash my hair. It's fine. I'll keep it tied up and I almost won't notice how filthy and disgusting it is. I'm practically immune to my own stench at this point, anyway.

I scrub over my skin, taking blood and dirt off, and then wish I had a way to know exactly how long it's been. The last thing I need is Madge bursting in while I'm doing this.

Not bothering with a towel, I leave the shower running to cover up any sounds I make, then squirt some of the bleach into the medicine bottle before setting everything back so it hopefully looks like nothing was disturbed.

The last step is the dress. I shut the water off, pull the dress over my still-wet skin, then shove the little bottle into the puffy sleeve.

It'll be obvious it's there if Madge looks too close. If she searches me, it's over. But why would she? She didn't even think to empty this bathroom. She mustn't think any of this stuff is dangerous.

Maybe it's not. Maybe nothing can hurt her and I'm wasting my time, but I need something.

I'll keep my arms still as I walk. That should hide the weird shape.

The door bursts open, Madge standing there like she's almost hoping she has to drag me out. She's probably disappointed that I'm already ready to go.

"Thank you," I tell her, because she likes it when I fake being broken by her. And hopefully if I fake it well enough, we can get back to my cell as quickly as possible.

***

I hide the bottle of bleach under the flimsy blanket. It's not a great hiding place, but she hasn't searched the cell yet, so I doubt she's about to start now.

I know full well I can't just dump it into the spell, since she's ordered me to not hurt her and to brew it correctly. But I think about that little bottle all the time, and holding onto that thought is the only bright light I have.

My victory is short-lived, though; I need to restart the spell after my shower, which requires me to slice open my hand for hours. The dress is ruined before the night is out.

When the moon sets and I collapse with the temporary blood loss, Madge shows up with a crust of bread and the water for the spell. I take it greedily, biting off a hunk of bread more like an animal than a person.

"You could thank me, pet," Madge says, watching me distastefully.

"For giving me the energy to suffer for you?" I ask, another bite of bread already in my mouth.

Madge sighs. "Petulant child."

I manage to smile around my mouthful of food. "That's me." I take a drink once I swallow the bread, gulping down water.

I think involuntarily of all the times Blaire bugged me to eat, even though she hated food. And all the times I told her flippantly that I didn't actually need food. I mentally promise I'll never give her shit again if I just get to hear her bothering me about it one more time.

When I finish my meal, I reluctantly stand and add the water to the cauldron, keeping an eye on the spell as the blood changes the water to a bubbling, sickening red hue. "How'd you even learn to make this, anyway?" I ask, since Madge still hasn't left. "Neither Blaire nor Blake nor anyone they knew had ever heard of it. They're all convinced witches can't live forever."

"Oh, it's ancient," Madge says flippantly. "Older than you and your little friends several times over. And I had time to experiment, get it right. The resources, too."

"You mean humans," I say, trying to keep my voice neutral even when all I want to do is recoil in disgust.

"Naturally. We conquered many places. The one thing we never had a short supply of was humans."

"Who *are* you?" I ask, something I've never wanted to know before. Knowing anything about Madge would make her almost human, and she's always been the bogeyman in my mind instead.

But now I need to know.

Madge hesitates for a moment, tilting her head. "Four thousand years ago, I was born into a powerful coven, where power actually meant something and the strong dominated," she says slowly, like she hasn't thought the words in a long while. "I stood at the king's right hand, and we seized endless land. Conquered the humans, and anyone else who crossed our path."

"What happened?" I ask. "Clearly your empire didn't last forever."

"Our king brought back a pet of his own. A seer." She says it with a violent sneer. "She told him many things he wanted to hear, almost all of which came to pass. And then, when he was eating out of her hand, she killed him. Poisoned his drink and watched him die."

I wonder what it says about me that I feel some sort of grim satisfaction hearing that. Good. People like that deserve to die.

Madge's smile is stony. "I took his throne, and I sentenced her to die. She got one last prediction in before I chopped off her head." Her face doesn't change even the slightest, but I think I know her well enough by now to see something in her eyes.

"What did she predict?" I dare to ask.

Madge's eyes go a little distant, as if she's been transported back to that very moment. How do memories look after all that time? I've forgotten the finer points of a million things, and I'm less than a quarter of Madge's age. "That I would die drowning in my own blood, and the souls of those I killed would be waiting to torment me."

Fuck, but I do hope she dies that way. And I hope I get to see it. "I didn't know your kind believe in the afterlife."

Madge seems to stir herself out of her reverie. "It's the one thing we don't know any better than any human," she says. She looks at me like she's processing that I'm here. "Enough about me. Don't you have work to do?"

I might point out all the work I've done today, but I hold my tongue. I got all I'm going to out of her, and if I keep her here, I risk her getting upset. And an upset Madge is a dangerous one.

I watch her retreat up the stairs and I hear what she said again. *Die drowning in my own blood.*

I try not to look over at where I hid the bleach, just in case she turns around. But I can't stop thinking about it.

I can't pour it, not as things stand right now. But that doesn't mean that there's no way.

Chapter Thirty-Two

I'm stealing a few hours of sleep curled up by the fire when the cell door swings open. I scramble upright, instinctively making sure the blanket doesn't move and hides everything I need it to. If Madge has suddenly decided to inspect the cell—

A body collapses by the door before it's slammed shut again. Another one.

"Why?" I croak. She brought poor Polly in to show me that she controlled everything, to remind me of my place. What did I do to deserve another one? I've done everything she asked.

Does she know about the bleach? I can't even use it.

"I don't need a reason to do anything, pet," she says airily, turning away. "I'm sure you'll help her settle in." And with that, she turns to walk upstairs.

I crawl over to the form on the ground, taking it in as I go. Blonde hair, a dress with constellations on it—

Wait.

Heart in my throat, I crawl faster, then turn the face toward me.

Callie.

"No," I whisper. But it is. Callie is here.

"Madge!" I shout, loud enough for my voice to penetrate between the floors. "Come down here!"

Nothing happens. There's not as much as a twitch from the stairs, and I grit my teeth.

Callie doesn't look injured. There's no blood or obvious bruising, so Madge probably drugged her like she did me. I find her pulse, and it feels normal enough.

What did I do to deserve this? Why does Madge feel the need to do this *now*?

"Callie?" I ask. "Callie? Can you wake up for me?"

It takes the better part of an hour, and she stirs slowly, her body lethargic as she wakes. "Callie, it's me," I tell her, voice low. "You're alright." *Alright* is putting it strongly, but she's not actively dying, and I don't want to panic her right away. "Can you open your eyes?"

"Laurel?"

"Yeah, it's me." Her eyes are still closed, but her voice is steady.

"What happened?"

That's what I want to know. "What do you remember?" I ask.

"I was leaving work and..." Her brow crinkles. "Someone grabbed me?"

Probably. "Can you open your eyes?"

She does, albeit slowly, but I watch her pupils and they seem normal at least. I'm no expert on human first aid, but I think Callie is in as good of shape as she can possibly be.

"You didn't run," she says, reaching out to touch my arm. "You didn't."

"I didn't," I agree. "I was—I've been here. I'm sorry, Callie. I never wanted you to think I ran again."

"Blaire didn't think you ran either," she murmurs, and hearing Blaire's name sends a jolt through me. It's a longing, deep sort of pang for something I can probably never have again.

No. I can't think like that. I can't give up hope, because Callie needs me to find a way out of here for both of us.

"Where is *here*?" Callie asks.

Fuck. I have no idea what to tell her, how to manipulate this so I don't have to tell her the whole truth. Blaire and Blake both said the truth could kill her, but I'm not going to let that happen. Callie is going to survive this. Callie is going to return home and be with her husband and make kids happy at the library. She's going to get to be an old lady someday. And all that depends on not telling her.

But she is going to see who took her hostage. "Madge's basement," I tell her, hoping she's suddenly decided not to be inquisitive.

No such luck. "You've been in this basement the whole time?" she demands. "She's just kept you here?"

"Yeah."

"That's so fucked up." Her eyes dart around, taking in the cell that's become essentially my whole world recently. Her eyes linger on the giant cauldron, but they also linger on the bucket in the corner, so I'm hoping she's not going to ask too many questions yet. "Your ex is fucked up, Laurel."

I hide my wince. Right. My ex. Because she thinks Madge is my ex, and I have to keep that illusion up while we're here. Gross.

"How is everyone?" I ask her, desperate for news of the outside world. It's not fair to ask, but I do anyway.

"Before I was kidnapped? Blaire was frantic and Blake wasn't much better. Now? I bet they're both a mess."

Frantic. I feel bad that Blaire's distressed, but there's a part of me that's secretly glad that she isn't over me already. I know I'm more trouble than I'm worth. "I'm sorry, Callie."

She moves to sit up and I help her, watching closely. She seems steady enough, so the drug must be leaving her system. "Why? It's not your fault."

Except it probably is. I don't know what I did to make Madge think this was necessary, but she went to a lot of trouble to get Callie. It can only be my fault.

"You shouldn't be anywhere near any of this."

"Neither should you." She takes the tiny cell in again, and this time, her eyes stick to the cauldron. "What's that?"

"C'mon, let's sit over there. It's warm," I offer, evading the question.

She raises an eyebrow. "Weird source of heat. What is it?"

"A pot."

"What, does she have you cooking your own food or something?"

If only. "Yeah, don't eat that," I tell her. "Trust me."

She doesn't move. "Laurel. What the fuck is going on here?"

Right. I swallow, buying a few seconds to come up with a plan. "Listen. Madge is someone you don't want to piss off. Don't ask questions. Don't react if you can avoid it. And maybe, she won't notice you too much."

Hopefully. Madge has probably already parceled Callie out though, aware what every inch of her body can be used for as spell ingredients.

No. I won't let that happen.

"What does that *mean*?" Callie presses, but I hear the door at the top of the stairs open, and we both freeze.

Callie takes Madge in. I know she met her at that party, but it's like this is the first time she truly sees her.

Madge doesn't look like anyone's idea of a monster. No too-sharp teeth, no horns, no glowing red eyes. She's just a small woman watching us both.

"Good," she says, and even puts on an obviously fake smile. "You're awake. And in one piece." She looks over at me, eyes boring into my soul. "I'm sure your friend here will help make sure you cooperate."

What have I been doing if not cooperating?

"I want some of your blood," Madge tells me.

I blink. "What do you call all that?" I demand, gesturing to the bubbling cauldron behind me. Callie starts, and I fervently hope that she keeps her mouth shut.

"Separate blood," she clarifies, like that's even a remotely normal thing to be asking for.

"And if I don't want to?"

She raises an eyebrow. "Then I order it, and you can choose between dying or complying. And I kill your friend. That, too."

Well. When she puts it like that.

"My knife or yours?" I ask heavily.

"Give me your wrist," she says, and I suppose that's an answer. Reluctantly, I extend my arm through the bars, offering it to her palm up.

"Hold still."

Like I don't have significant practice slicing myself open right now. And this has the advantage of not coming with the shooting electrical pain of the spell.

It would be easier if I could do it myself, though. Anticipating her cutting into me is worse than the actual cut.

Callie makes a noise, seemingly unable to help it, but she doesn't say anything at least. Even so, Madge's eyes leave me to lock onto her, lip curling in a cruel smirk. "I look forward to how you explain this," she murmurs to me, and then digs the knife deeper, turning my wrist so the blood drips into a small vial.

"What do you want with it?" I half expected her to extort another binding vow from me, but there's nothing else in the vial.

"Not your business, pet," she says, removing the knife from my skin. She drops my wrist, and I pull it back through the bars, shaking out the pain.

She looks us over and smirks. "Behave, you two," she says, and then she disappears up the stairs.

"Laurel, what the fuck—"

"Sh." I listen, but I think Madge truly is gone, so I turn to Callie and face my fate.

Her face is an interesting mix of terror and fury. The reminder of her very human feelings is a bit of a shock, because I've been so distant from them for so long. The terror and the fury are far behind me.

"I need you not to ask too many questions," I tell her heavily, knowing it's an impossible ask.

"Why the fuck would I—"

"Because I am going to get you out of here," I interrupt, doing math in my head. There're two more weeks until the lunar cycle ends. I need to keep her alive for two more weeks. Two weeks. I can do that. "And I might not be able to if you know too much."

Is Callie ever going to forget this? No. But Blake seems far better at lying to her than I am, and in two weeks, it'll be his problem. I won't be there to mess it up.

Chapter Thirty-Three

C allie, naturally, doesn't stop asking questions, and she's getting more and more angry that I don't answer them. I cut my hand open and get bombarded with questions. I stir the cauldron and she has fifty things to say. I try to curl up and sleep and she has more to ask.

I spend so much time not answering her that she actually circles all the way around to petulant silence, which is both gratifying and guilt-inducing. Every minute she's not asking me questions is a minute she's not endangering her own life, but I hate that I made her feel like this. I hate that Callie's last memories of me are going to be someone who ignored her and scared her.

Madge delivers food every moonrise, and I make Callie eat most of it. I can't take none; if I don't eat, then she'll have more questions. But she needs it far more than I do.

"She really left you here for two and a half months?" Callie asks me.

I mentally count lunar cycles in my head. "Past three now, actually."

"Laurel."

"Yeah. I was here the whole time."

"Cutting yourself open?"

"Mhm."

"Is she—what's wrong with her?"

Well, she's immortal, terrified of death, and unfortunately privy to ancient and horrifying magic. Not that I can say any of that to Callie. "I don't know."

"How do we get out of here?"

There's the question. We're almost at the end of another lunar cycle. At that point, it'll be do or die; I doubt Madge will keep Callie around forever.

***

There's a week left to go on the spell when Madge delivers food and doesn't immediately retreat. She stands at the bars, watching me like an animal in a zoo. "What?" I snap.

"Manners, pet."

I don't have any manners to give, so I keep silent. After watching me, she asks, "What do you remember of your childhood?"

Is this a joke? Some weird psychological profile? Does she regret ripping me away from it all those years ago? "Not much," I say truthfully, because the memories are distant now. I had a mother and sisters, but I don't remember their faces anymore. And none of that is information that Madge deserves.

"No, I imagine you wouldn't. It was a long time ago," she muses. "Your mother?"

"What do you want?" I snap. "I haven't seen her in nine hundred years, alright? I don't have anything for you."

I hear the sharp inhalation from behind me and wince. *Fuck.*

Madge steps closer to the bars. "Where did you come from, pet?"

"I don't know what you're talking about." I doubt she's looking for directions to where my family home once stood.

"You're not human," she says, a cruel smirk to her lips, and I know she means for her words to hit, but I barely feel anything. *No shit.* Humans don't live as long as I have, they don't survive what I have. I don't know what to call myself if not human, but I understand that I'm not one of them anymore, not really.

"I tested your blood," she continues.

I blink. "What, like a DNA test? A 23-and-me kit?"

"No, idiot. A spell. I got curious. You're a little marvel, and I like knowing what I'm getting myself into. It's better for business. I should have done this sooner, honestly."

Trepidation builds in my throat. "What does that mean?" What does she know about me that I don't?

Am I finally about to learn why I am this way?

"You, pet, are a changeling," she says precisely. "A fae child, and one of the last ones I've ever heard of."

"Fae?" I repeat, voice suddenly far away from my thoughts. My mind spins, trying to remember everything I've ever read about the fae and their changeling children, every myth I ever found. There's so much information, and most of it is a contradictory, fantastical mess.

I'm not even my mother's child. I was replaced as an infant, probably, left in this human world because they preferred the human child instead. I feel a pang of pity for my mother's human baby—no fae story I've ever heard ends happily for the humans—and then wonder who my real parents are.

"Fae," Madge confirms. "They didn't want you, pet. They traded you away for some human to abuse. Guess your life hasn't changed much, has it?"

"What the fuck are you talking about?" Callie demands from behind me.

Shit. I don't think there's a good way to walk this all back. Not now that she asked in front of Madge, who's already turning to look at her, cruel smirk on her face.

"Your friend here isn't even human, girl," she says. "She's older than even your husband over there, and she's been lying to you this whole time. How do you feel about that?"

I want to curse at her, but I bite my tongue. That'll only make it worse.

"You've lost it," Callie decides, looking between the two of us. I know she expects some reassurance from me, but I don't know how to provide it.

Madge smirks. "Ask her." She turns back to me. "Now we both know. And you, pet, you have so much untapped potential. I always thought the spell tasted sweeter with your blood. Think of all the things your body can do for me."

"Haven't I given you enough?" Fear shoots down my spine. She's talking about carving me up like she did Polly, like I saw her do to so many others in the past. Will I survive it? Probably. Will surviving be worse than dying? Undoubtedly.

"I own you, pet. You haven't given enough until I've bled you dry." Like she has to so many other humans before me. No, not *other* humans—just humans, because I don't qualify as one. I wonder for half a second if she even knows how many people she's killed.

She can see that I'm thinking about it. "I'll leave you to discuss it, pet. I have some spellbooks to research."

I watch her walk away, feet stuck to the floor, brain spinning with what I was just told.

Me not being human isn't a new thought to me, even though I've always called myself human for lack of a better term. But to think I have a whole people, a species that I come from—

It's not like they wanted me, though. They abandoned me nine hundred years ago and never looked back. Can I really call them my people?

"Laurel," Callie says slowly, stepping up beside me, "what the fuck was that?"

***

"So, you've all been lying to me," Callie says when I finish my stumbling explanation.

This is only the second time in my entire life that I've had to explain this, and I've never had to explain it to a human with no prior knowledge outside of monster movies. This is infinitely worse than when I had to tell Blaire.

I tried for a second to tell her the story without giving up Blaire and Blake's secret, but there's no way to talk about what I am without explaining what they are. I give up the whole truth, deciding that a little is the same danger as a lot, and tell her everything.

"We've been trying to protect you," I tell her.

"I've been married to a man who I apparently don't know. My best friend is a *fae*. I feel real safe," she scoffs.

We're sitting on the floor by the fire, and we were sitting close until now. She pulls her legs closer to herself, withdrawing, and an ache fills me.

I can't help but to resent Blake for a moment. He should be the one telling her all this.

"Callie, Blake and Blaire made it clear to me that just knowing puts you in danger." Fuck. I didn't want her to know that either. I don't need her constantly looking over her shoulder, looking for whatever will end her life. "But don't worry. I'm going to keep you safe."

"You can't even keep yourself safe. You heard her. She's going to cut you up."

She's not wrong, but if Madge comes at me with a knife, then I'll have to accept that. I'll survive. I'm almost positive of it.

No, I am positive. Even if Madge finds a way to kill me now that she knows what I am, she won't take it. I'm too valuable to her alive.

"So you've been doing what for her, exactly?" Callie asks. "This time, tell me the truth."

"She has me brew a spell," I admit. "It takes constant tending, and she needs it every day. It's her version of immortality."

"Is she as old as you?"

"Older."

Callie turns her head into her knees, hiding away from it all for a moment, and I debate what to do. I want to comfort her, but I'm not sure if she wants any from me right now.

"Callie... I'm sorry," I tell her. "This is too much. You were better off not knowing."

She looks up, her eyes almost as bright as a vampire's now, only hers are from blinding, furious anger. "Fuck you." I flinch slightly. "You don't get to decide what I do and don't get to know, Laurel."

"I do if it keeps you alive."

"Fuck you," she says again, succinct and clearly done with me. She turns away again, and I'm left sitting there by the fire.

I have my closest friend in my cell with me, but this is the loneliest I've felt since Madge first took me.

Chapter Thirty-Four

I count the days in my head as Callie refuses to talk to me more than she absolutely has to. *Five days left. Four. Two.*

And then... it's here.

I look at the spell, critically studying the bubbling surface as I stir and stir and stir. My arms are exhausted, cramping up around my biceps, but I don't dare to stop. If it's not perfect, then I won't have time for anything else.

"Callie," I murmur, the first time we've spoken all day, and her name sounds like a gunshot in this basement. She gives me her attention but doesn't say anything. "I need you to go in the corner, under that blanket—there's a bottle. Bring it to me."

There's a tugging in my ribs, the pain from the blood oath. I ignore it. It's not killing me yet.

Technically, I'm still doing exactly as she told me. I'm still brewing the spell, and I haven't messed it up. I haven't harmed her.

Not yet.

Callie brings me the little bottle. For such an innocuous thing, I look at it like it's the holy grail. This is our lifeline. This is what will save Callie.

"What're you planning?" she asks me suspiciously.

"Nothing yet." I consider the timing carefully, watching the spell turn from its muddy color to a dark, crisp burgundy. "Alright. It's done." And Madge will be down any second; she knows the lunar cycle better than I do. I don't have long.

"Drink some," I tell her, hoping I accurately convey the urgency of this.

She balks. "What? No. That's not—your *blood* is in there, Laurel."

"Believe me, I'm aware." Acutely so, in fact. My arm still tingles with it, and I wonder if I could ever get the pain to go away fully. Not that it matters anymore. "Drink it, Callie. Just a few mouthfuls."

"Why the fuck would I do that?"

Because knowing the truth about the supernatural kills people, and being close to Madge does even more damage. I want Callie to have every protection I can give her before I do something stupid.

"It'll protect you."

Her nose wrinkles. "You said she has to drink it every day or she dies."

Sure, but that's because she's long ago outlived her lifespan. Or at least, I hope it is. I don't need Callie to live forever. She's human, and she deserves the beauty of growing old. I just need her to live through today.

"Callie, we don't have time for this. Drink it. *Now*."

Something in my tone must finally get through to her, and Callie hesitantly dips her hand in, cupping it to bring out a mouthful of the spell. Her fingers and lips are stained red, a grotesque parody of the vampire she's married to.

"That's disgusting," she rasps.

"Madge says it's sweeter with my blood," I tell her, trying to ignore the tugging inside of me. Only it's not really a tugging anymore; it's more like a tearing, and I fight to focus. It's getting harder to breathe. "Alright. Dump in the bottle."

"What's in it?" she asks, holding up the little bottle again.

"Bleach. Do it; I can't. And it has to be right now."

She dumps the bottle in quickly, and I watch the spell start to bubble again, turning a lighter shade of red. I have to hope Madge doesn't notice that.

"Will that kill her?" Callie whispers.

Maybe. Maybe not. "It'll ruin the spell, which is the same thing," I say. I should be on top of the world, having finally bested Madge, but it's short-lived. It's like my blood is somehow poisonous to me now, like it hurts as it moves through my veins.

As the spell at last settles and the bubbles die down, the tearing becomes too painful to ignore. It feels like something stabbed me in the chest, and I look down to see actual fresh blood seeping into the dress.

"Hide your hands. Don't face her," I tell Callie, and that's the last thing I get to say before Madge walks down.

There are too many suspicious things down here. My dress, Callie's hands and mouth, the slightly off color of the spell—this has to go perfectly.

Madge walks down the stairs holding the collection of little vials, ready for me to fill them.

"Callie needs better food," I tell her as soon as she hits the bottom step. "And this is the third time I've done this for you. I want that as my reward." If she's angry at me, she won't look at Callie.

Her eyes flash, just as I hoped. "Rewards are *given*, pet, not demanded. And you get nothing; you do what I tell you, or you die. And I can kill your little friend here, too." She opens the cell door and steps in, sliding the vials toward me. "Bottle it."

I bottle one and then hand it over, preparing the next one like nothing is wrong, waiting for something to happen.

She starts choking the second the spell touches her mouth, and I feel my throat start to close, my own blood filling it. I fight to keep my expression neutral.

There's no recourse for either of us now. I broke my oath. And I'm taking her down with me.

Madge eyes the cauldron suspiciously, bringing the empty vial back to her face, taking a deep sniff. Her whole face contorts, and then she rounds on me.

"You little rat," she hisses, lunging forward but stumbling. "You pathetic little rat." Her face twists with rage, but her body bends over, and she clutches her stomach.

"Callie, run!" I tell her, wanting to scream but barely getting out a choked moan around all the blood pooling in my mouth.

"What about you?" she whimpers, stepping closer, which is exactly where I don't want her.

"No," I tell her as firmly as I can. "Go. Tell Blaire where we are." Blaire won't make it in time, but she won't rest until she has answers, either. It's not in her nature. Finding my body might give her some peace. As last gifts go, it's a shitty one, but it's the best I have to give her. "Go."

She brushes past me, and I want to turn to her, to get one last look at my friend, the last friendly face I'll ever see, but I resist, keeping a careful eye on Madge.

I smile, stepping forward so I'll be the last thing Madge sees as she dies. Blood drips out of my mouth, but I force myself to ignore it. I can't give in and die until this is over. "That seer who told you the souls you killed would torment you for eternity? I'll be first in line."

Then I use all the strength left in me to stab the little pocketknife into her throat. I collapse forward, my legs no longer properly supporting me, but I use the force of me falling to push the knife deeper before my fingers stop working properly and I'm forced to let go, falling to my knees.

Madge looks at me, wide-eyed, and her hands go to her throat, scrambling for the knife. She pulls it out, dropping it to the floor, and with seeming herculean effort, withdraws her own knife. I want to laugh even as I don't have the energy. What's one more knife blow now? I'm already bleeding to death.

But the knife isn't meant for me. With a strength I didn't expect her to have left, Madge turns around and throws the knife, and with unerring accuracy, it lands in Callie's back. I hear her cry out, the sound nearly drowning out my own shout, but then I watch her continue to stumble up the stairs, swaying side to side and barely in control of her own body.

No. All of this—if Callie dies, none of it will be worth it.

Madge grins, bloody and ugly. "You lose," she rasps, the words sounding like broken glass. The strength seems to go out of her then, and she brings her hand to her throat, gasping and clearly not getting any air. She falls to her knees, the two of us across from each other on this filthy floor, our blood pooling around us. Blood bubbles up at the corner of her mouth, choking her, and I watch with calm detachment as the life leaves her eyes, her body collapsing onto the ground, a broken puppet abandoned at last.

I want to get up and go after Callie. I want to make sure she's okay, to get her help.

I want to see Blaire again.

But I'm not going to get any of that. I'm not even going to get to know if Callie gets away. My body pitches sideways, leaving me on the floor, staring into Madge's unseeing eyes.

I can feel the wet, sticky blood coating my face, and I think for a second about Madge's seer, who predicted she'd die drowning in her own blood. She was right, all these years later, and now here we are, the two of us. Dying. Dead.

The world goes fuzzy around the edges, then entirely white. I think for a moment I hear footsteps upstairs, have half a second to hope beyond hope that it's Blaire, somehow—and then there's nothing.

Chapter Thirty-Five

I 've spent a long time wondering what it's like to die.

I've tried not to; it didn't seem like the healthiest thing to fixate on. But like Madge said, it was the one thing I couldn't know. It stuck with me.

I didn't imagine it'd be anything like this.

I went back and forth wondering if death simply means ceasing to exist, or if there is some sort of afterlife like all those people thought. But I never expected *neither.*

The pain doesn't end. I don't get the relief of nothingness. But neither do I get some eternal paradise. Maybe this is hell.

It's so cold. I still can't see anything, but I can hear flashes of voices from time to time. That's Blaire, I think. Is hearing her voice again the grand cosmic reward everyone talks about?

At first her voice was frantic, desperate, and while I'll take any of Blaire over none of her, her panic makes me panic, even though I can't show it in my current state. But then she calms down, and the moments I can hear her are gentler, her crooning my name and calling me to her.

Is this a reward or a punishment? I honestly can't tell. It's torture to be so close and unable to have her again.

And then, after who knows how long, I open my eyes.

There's bright sunlight spilling across my face, illuminating the bed I'm in. It's the cabin. My body goes soft and warm. I could be away from here for a thousand years and I'd still recognize this place immediately.

"Laurel? Laurel?"

Is this a dream? I turn my head with great effort, and there's Blaire, sitting in a chair she's pulled up to the bed, staring at me. Both of her hands are clutching one of mine. I study her face. Unchanged, of course. Blaire is exactly how I remember her, but I think the crease of worry she had when we were evading Madge is more pronounced now.

"Blaire?"

She collapses forward, shoulders bowed as she clutches my hand even tighter. "Oh *fuck*. You're alive. Laurel. Hi. You're okay."

I have no idea if any of that is true, but I subtly flex each joint, and they all move, so maybe she is correct. "What happened?"

My body doesn't hurt anymore, I realize. There's still a distant ache, but that's all that's left. I lift my head to look down at my chest, only to see clean, warm blankets. With my free hand I push them aside. I'm clean, wearing clean clothes, and there's not a drop of blood anywhere.

I practically forgot what it was to be clean.

"Do you want the long story, or the short story?" Blaire asks me.

"How much time we got?"

She squeezes my hand again. "As much as we need, Laurel. There's no rush to anything."

"Then tell me the whole thing." My eyes drift halfway closed, but I force them open again. I don't want to miss a moment of Blaire.

"Callie called us."

My eyes shoot open. "Callie made it?" It's better than I feared. I knew she kept running, but she looked so injured...

Blaire's hesitation makes my heart freeze. "Kind of. She's fine now," she hastens to explain. "She found Madge's cellphone and called Blake. And we hauled ass to get there—we'd been looking for so long, Laurel, you have to believe me on that—"

"I know," I assure her. I never doubted it.

"When we got there Callie was—it was bad, Laurel. She wasn't going to make it. Maybe if we got there a half hour earlier, maybe if she could get to a hospital, but that didn't happen. We had to make a choice."

My heart is pounding now. "And?"

"And Blake made the call. He turned her into one of us. I thought it was prolonging the inevitable, that she'd die anyway, but she's up and walking around now. Pissed as hell at all of us, too."

"She's fine?" I check, staring at her to detect any sense of her lying to me. There's none. "She's a vampire?"

"She's fine. And yeah, she's a vampire now."

They were right then. No human can survive learning about the supernatural, and Callie's not an exception. It just happened differently than I feared.

"She said you made her drink something," Blaire continues. "A spell?"

Right. The spell. "Is that why the transformation actually took?"

"It might be," she shrugs. "Not like we'll ever know for sure, not unless we're going to run experiments, which we're obviously not going to do."

No. If I'm lucky, that spell will never be brewed again. Madge and I might genuinely have been the last two to know how to, and now she's dead. And I'll let this fucking awful spell die with me.

If I can even die. Madge told me about who I am and where I'm from, and I still haven't wrapped my head around it. How fae am I? Are there things about myself that I don't know? Can I ever die?

"Callie is fine?" I check again, needing to hear it one more time.

"She's fine," Blaire assures me. "Pissed as hell at her husband. I'm not sure she's spoken to him in two days."

I bite my lip. I always knew Callie would be pissed at all of us for keeping things from her.

"And she's a vampire now?"

"She's a vampire. Adjusting just fine."

I nod, taking that all in. I did it. Madge is dead. Callie lived, even if not in the way I initially wanted. The spell will die forever. It's done.

"How am I alive?" I ask, because that's really the only remaining piece of the puzzle.

Blaire is quiet for a long moment, and I'm about to ask again when she admits, "I changed you."

It takes me a minute to process that. "You... changed me?" I'm sure I heard wrong.

"It was working for Blake, and we didn't know about the spell yet, so I thought, maybe I could change you, too. You looked fucking dead, Laurel, lying there in a pool of your own blood. I couldn't even tell you were breathing at all at first. I thought maybe I could save you, and maybe the four of us could walk away. Could win this."

I take inventory of my body all over again. "So... I'm a vampire now?" I ask. I don't feel any different to how I did before, not really.

"Not exactly? You took to it, obviously. You didn't die. And you even started getting better, stopped coughing up your own blood, started breathing steadier. But nothing vampiric happened to you. Callie was going through all the changes, but you were just—I don't know. Fighting, I guess. Your body was fighting death or the vampirism or both. And we tried giving you blood when you were unconscious so long. Just in case you really are a vampire. But believe me, you did not like it. You spit it on me."

"I'm sorry?" I'm not, not really.

"I'll take anything if you're still alive, Laurel." She sounds so sincere. "Do you feel any different? I guess that's the real test."

I take further stock of my body. I don't feel any stronger, and I certainly don't crave blood. But when I look beyond the little world of me and Blaire, and I realize something has changed. There're footsteps, but they're not in the main room of the cabin. They're in the woods, muffled under leaves and dirt. How far away are they? I definitely wouldn't have been able to hear those before.

I take a deep, deep breath. It doesn't hurt to breathe like it did in the cell at the end, I'm relieved to note, but even more importantly, I can smell a thousand different things. It's overwhelming, and I bury my head in my hands to help close it out.

"Laurel?" Blaire's hand is on my back, tentative and unsure, but I appreciate how present it is nonetheless.

"Vampire senses," I mutter, my voice no doubt muffled, but if her senses are anything like mine, she can hear me just fine.

She rubs between my shoulder blades. "Oh, baby. It's okay. It'll take some getting used to."

That's *great*, but I'm losing my shit right now. But I force myself to turn, burying my face in Blaire's chest instead of my own hands. Between the sound of her heartbeat and the clean, minty smell of her skin, my body returns to something approximating calm.

"You okay?" she murmurs.

I have no idea, but I think I will be. I take another deep breath of her. "I don't think I can be full vampire," I tell her. "Because vampires are either born or made from humans, right?"

"Mhm."

"And I'm apparently fae, so... half vampire, half fae, weird results?" I shrug. "If it lets me bounce back to stay here a while longer, then I'll take it."

"Half... fae?" Blaire sounds it out like the language is entirely foreign to her. "Callie didn't tell you?"

"Callie doesn't want to tell us more than to go fuck ourselves."

"Madge figured it out. I'm a changeling baby. That's why I'm like this. Why I lived." I've been acquiring extra layers of magical protection since birth. Fae blood, whatever Madge's spell did to me, and now this off-brand vampirism. I don't know how I feel about all that.

Ah, fuck. If it brought me here, if it gives me this—Blaire, Callie, Blake, my future—then I don't hate it. And I'd probably do it all again.

"What does that mean?" Blaire asks, her hand still rubbing my back.

"Beats me. I've never met a fae. Judging by how Madge reacted, I don't think she knows them too well, either. And I don't really want to get to know them." Just because not all supernatural creatures are evil doesn't mean I want to expand my social circle. I'm still leery of most things out there, and the fae kidnapped a human and left me behind.

"I mean for you, baby."

Oh, that. "I have no idea. Guess I made it this long like this—now I just have to figure out this vampire thing."

"I can help with that. It gets easier," she promises me.

It better. I'm worried that if I move my face out of Blaire's chest, I'll get overwhelmed all over again.

I'm seconds away from asking if this is real again—I can't quite make my brain accept how good everything is—when there's a commotion outside the door.

"Oh, are you going to stop me from seeing my friends, too?" Callie says, her voice much louder than I'd usually expect it to be.

"Have they been here this whole time?" I whisper, entirely ineffective considering apparently everyone in this house has enhanced hearing.

"Uh, yeah. Seemed like the best place to be."

"What, have they been sleeping on your couch?" Blaire's cabin might be my idea of heaven, but it's certainly not meant for guests.

"Basically."

"—Callie, I really have no desire to stop you from doing anything, but maybe we should check first?"

The only sound on the other side of the door is breathing and what I sickeningly realize is *heartbeats*, and I remember what Blaire said; Callie's been giving Blake the silent treatment. That must gut him.

"Come in," I call. I think we all need to see each other.

The door pushes open with more force than necessary, banging off the back wall. Callie winces. "Whoops."

Them entering the room upsets my carefully maintained bubble, bringing in fresh scents and the sounds of hearts beating and lungs breathing and every step and shift of weight. This is maddening. Blaire keeps stroking my back, grounding me here.

"Callie is still adjusting to being a vampire," Blaire tells me, like it wasn't immediately obvious. Callie glares at her.

"You're alive," she whispers.

"Back at you." I raise the arm not tucked into Blaire's side and Callie takes it as the invitation it is, swooping in for a hug. We both squeeze each other, and I soak her in—warm, and alive, and *here*.

And then her mouth is on my neck, and I have a split second to panic before Blake yanks her away from me.

"Sorry," he mutters, looking at Callie but talking to me. "We're working on control."

Callie ignores him and turns to me with big, sorrowful eyes, and now I can see the vampirism in them, the almost-glowing irises as she watches me. "Fuck, I'm sorry Laurel. It's like a voice in my head and I'm not even paying attention to it, so my body just does without my conscious input and—I should leave."

"No, stay. It's only fair that we put up with the aches and pains of your supernatural transformation; it's kind of our fault, isn't it?" I ask.

She huffs. "You're not wrong." But she sits on the edge of the bed, so we might be okay. Not perfect yet, and I can already feel the frosty distance, but nearly dying on her probably won me some goodwill.

"Although I have to say, last time you drank my blood you acted like it was torture. And now you're all for it?" I tease, just to see how she'll react.

She huffs. "I know you saved my life, Laurel, but believe me when I say that it's too soon to joke about that."

Noted. I nod, conceding. All four of us had our lives turned upside down these past few months, but Callie had her whole worldview upended. We'll take things at her pace.

Blake sits a foot away from his wife, staring at her like she hung the moon. He opens his mouth to say something, then closes it. He looks like a kicked puppy, and I know Callie ignoring him is killing him. But I know him; he'll hold steady for her. He'll be there when she's ready.

They love each other. I know they do. I have confidence that they'll be okay.

Eventually. Callie doesn't so much as twitch in the direction of her husband, and I know he'll be in the doghouse for a while longer.

"What do you need?" Callie asks me. "Anything. You've been unconscious for almost a week, so let us know."

Has it been that long?

"I really am okay," I promise her. "I'm going to be fine." Once I figure out how to shut out all this extra sensory information, anyway.

Callie purses her lips, clearly not believing me, and I can't say I blame her. "Well, then I'll step out," she decides. "Since I clearly need some more practice with this whole blood drinking thing."

I catch her hand before she moves. "Come back soon," I tell her. "Blood drinking or not. You're my best friend."

Her face softens. "You're mine, too," she says, and then she leaves, Blake trailing after her like he hopes this time, she'll acknowledge him.

"He looks like he wants to cry," I murmur to Blaire.

She chuckles, her face pressed into my shoulder. "He does. She'll make him work for it. But he has forever to earn her forgiveness."

Let's hope it doesn't take that long. Blake's sad puppy eyes will kill me long before that.

Blaire presses a kiss to my shoulder, then another, and then another. "You're going to be okay?" she checks between kisses.

"I will be," I promise her. "If you stay here with me."

Epilogue

I nearly trip over another box as I make my way to the front door.

You'd think being part fae would give me some sort of preternatural grace, but sadly, I'm the least coordinated one in this house by a mile. All I got were stupid senses. Blake, Blaire, and Callie have the grace of professional ballerinas, and I feel like an elephant by comparison.

In my defense, this box wasn't here the last time I walked through.

Moving has been a mess, but it became clear pretty quickly that Callie isn't ready to live in town and work with the public. They assure me she'll gain her control quickly, but it won't be instantaneous. And honestly, while I was happy enough in the cabin, the thought of going into town while I still don't have the greatest control over these senses is nauseating.

So we all move on, the four of us packing up everything we own, saying goodbye to the yellow house and the cabin, and finding a new, remote place to start over.

Blaire's thrilled that Callie's current eccentricities mean being in the middle of the woods is the best course of action. She found a multi-bedroom cabin, one for each couple and two more to turn into offices as we all learn about work from home jobs, and we all moved in together.

It's bigger than the cabin Blaire and I shared, but sometimes I think it's not big enough to hold all we have going on between the four of us. Callie is thawing, slowly, but she's still frosty, especially when she gets pissed off by the way her life has changed. Poor Blake seems to be taking the worst of it, but I did see her fall asleep on his shoulder the other day, so. Progress.

As for Blaire and I, we took the bedroom with the big window, because I can't stand being trapped in the dark anymore. She holds me when I sleep, because very few nights are peaceful for me. I don't think any of us exactly sleep well anymore.

But today is a gorgeous day, and the workday is over, and I know without asking where my girlfriend is. Sure enough, after I make it around the last of the boxes we haven't unpacked yet, I find her sitting on the rocking bench Callie wanted for the porch.

Callie might have insisted, but Blaire and I use it way more than she does. Without even turning her head, she opens her arm, and I slide into her side, nuzzling my face into her neck.

The sun still sets pretty early this far north, but summer will be here soon enough. For now, we sit together and watch the last of the dying sunset, not moving or saying anything until Blaire tilts my head and kisses me, thumb and forefinger holding my chin.

She's taken to doing this whenever she needs to confirm for herself that it's all over, that I'm back and I survived. I just kiss her back, offering all the reassurance I know how.

I move my hand from her hip to higher up her back, pushing up her leather jacket, needing to get close to her. Needing the both of us to know that we're still here.

"Easy," she chuckles, her breath fanning against my lips.

Easy? When she started it?

She must see my indignant look, because she outright laughs, low and teasing, making goosebumps break across my skin. "I know, I know," she croons in fake sympathy. "But we have forever now, Laurel. We don't need to rush and fuck outside where we'll literally get caught."

"Yes, not again," Callie mutters inside.

It was one time. I don't say that back. It *was* one time, but since Callie and Blake's most risqué act has been touching hands, I don't think it's a good time to tell her to be less of a prude and lay off.

Well, we'll see who gets the last word in. At some point, she and Blake are going to fix this thing between them, and then we'll see who's the bigger nuisance.

"Forever?" I ask Blaire instead of stirring the pot with Callie. It's not an idle question, either. Sometimes, I need the reminder.

I am nine hundred years old, give or take a few years. I've survived floods, falls, disease, and evil witches bleeding me dry. I've had *forever* open before me for a long, long time now, but it never felt like this.

Forever used to be a life sentence. Now, it's a reward.

"Forever," Blaire echoes, a vow wrapped in her words, so I kiss her again, this time soft and sweet, and I like to think she hears my vow in that kiss.

Looking for more?

Want to know if Callie forgives Blake? Sign up for my newsletter to get an exclusive bonus epilogue to see how Callie handles her new life as a vampire. Visit www.addyjameswriter.com for more information.

Also by

The Crae Romance Series

Callum
Bryce
Heath
Celia
Silas
Estrid

The Supernatural Christmas Series

A Werewolf for Christmas
A Recipe for Love
Snowed In With A Werewolf

Standalones

Dragon's Treasure
The Heat Cure

About the author

Addison James is a romance book author from New England. They are obsessed with all things mythical, mystical, and magical. A lifelong fantasy reader, that evolved to fantasy romance as they grew up. Addison always has a story to tell and is excited to introduce you to their world of fantasy romance.

www.ingramcontent.com/pod-product-compliance
Lightning Source LLC
Chambersburg PA
CBHW050200120726
47903CB00002B/703